PRAISE FOR

QUICKSAND

"[*Quicksand*] provides a razor-sharp view of modern Sweden and its criminal justice system, yet is a tonic for readers who have had enough of the brooding, often-bloody 'Scandi-crime' that has been so popular in recent years."

—NPR

"Astonishing . . . a dark exploration of the crumbling European social order and the psyche of rich Swedish teens . . . the incisive language that's on display here surely involves translation precision that's second to none."

—*Booklist* (starred review)

"[*Quicksand*] is structured as a courtroom procedural, yet it clearly has ambitions beyond that, addressing Sweden's underlying economic and racial tensions."

—*New York Times Book Review*

"Brilliantly conceived and executed, this extraordinary legal thriller is not to be missed."

—*Library Journal* (starred review)

"Haunting and immersive." —*Publishers Weekly*

“Expert dialogue and irresistible momentum make an all-too-realistic story come breathing off the page . . . Part courtroom thriller, part introspection, *Quicksand* is pulled tight throughout by the suspense, not only of Maja’s verdict, but of the elusive ‘truth’ of what really happened in the classroom that day.” —*Shelf Awareness*

“Thrilling.” —*TIME*

“Sharp social commentary through the tragic story of a young woman’s trial for mass murder . . . The rhythm, tone, and language are just right . . . a splendid work of fiction.” —*Kirkus Reviews*

“Persson Giolito’s craft takes us on a psychological ride.” —*Huffington Post*

“A compelling, multilayered study of a terrible school shooting.” —*Boston Herald*

PRAISE FOR
BEYOND ALL REASONABLE DOUBT

“Absorbing . . . [*Beyond All Reasonable Doubt*] imitates life, in all its messiness and obfuscation . . . you want to meet Sophia Weber again.” —*New York Times Book Review*

“Giolito has come up with another knockout legal thriller . . . Weber is a wonderfully textured creation, a poignant mix of determined braininess and nagging doubts.” —*Washington Post*

"Gripping . . . Persson Giolito addresses the question of guilt in provocative ways." —BBC

"Calling all fans of courtroom dramas and Netflix's shockingly tense show *Quicksand*: This is the page-turner for you . . . [a] courtroom drama that will make you question every testimony."

—*Refinery29*, The Best Beach Reads of Summer 2019

"Since the whole Millennium trilogy, we've been inundated with Scandinavian thrillers of various qualities. This one stands out as something up to par with Larsson. *Beyond All Reasonable Doubt* is more than a legal thriller, with a search for truth that often can bring disturbing answers."

—*Strand Magazine*, Top Twelve Mystery Novels of 2019

"[A] searing legal thriller . . . meticulously crafted . . . Fans of Nordic noir won't want to miss this one."

—*Publishers Weekly* (starred review)

"Intriguing . . . keep[s] the reader guessing right up to the two very different twists that make for a gut-punching finale . . . [an] insightful look at the subtle variations of guilt . . . [a] smart, well-written legal and procedural drama."

—*Kirkus Reviews* (starred review)

"Giolito excels at portraying those accused of horrible crimes . . . an intricate examination of the psyches of criminals and those who work with them, accompanied by pointed questions about who is served by the justice system . . . [a] great read." —*Booklist*

"Chilling and complex. The truth in this story is a cracked mirror, changing at every angle. Giolito masterfully plumbs the nature of guilt or innocence until no character, nor even the reader, is left unscathed."

—Joanna Schaffhausen, author of *The Vanishing Season*

"Another breathtaking novel from Malin Persson Giolito! *Beyond All Reasonable Doubt* masterfully questions the role media and public opinion play in court. A deeply moving suspense novel that zeroes in on humanity's deepest flaws."

—Viveca Sten, author of *In the Heat of the Moment*

PRAISE FOR
DELIVER ME

"Giolito . . . deftly blends social commentary with exacting psychological insight, pathos, and a good deal of empathy for her characters . . . a beautifully written and gutting work of suspense."

—*Shelf Awareness*

"An ambitious tale of adolescent violence and the forces that enable it . . . Giolito dedicates significant space to the social problems—including restrictive immigration policies, corrupt law enforcement, and economic inequality—that surround gangs in contemporary Sweden. The sociological perspective joins with a strong emotional current to effectively convey the magnitude of the novel's central tragedy. This will strike a chord with genre fans who are just as interested in the 'why' as the 'who.'"

—*Publishers Weekly*

"A brutal and beautiful read, enthralling from start to finish, *Deliver Me* paints an enduring portrait of two boys caught in an intractable landslide of violence. Malin Persson Giolito writes with unflinching precision and also great compassion for her characters' humanity. A stunning crime novel that grapples with impossible questions about justice and responsibility, and reaches an unforgettable crescendo. You'll read with your heart in your throat."

—Katie Gutierrez, bestselling author of *More Than You'll Ever Know*

"*Deliver Me* succeeds with something very few crime novels do: Already on the first page, we know who the murderer is. And yet, we keep turning the pages, faster and faster until we reach the harrowing end. Sometimes fiction is needed to understand the reality we live in. *Deliver Me* is a masterful crime novel that hits like a well-aimed punch to the gut."

—Christoffer Carlsson, author of *Under the Storm* and *Blaze Me a Sun*

"Like the Baltimore of *The Wire*, the Stockholm of Malin Persson Giolito's *Deliver Me* is revealed to be more than just a hostile concrete backdrop for the age-old crusade of 'good' against 'evil': instead, it's a vast and complex network of familial care and interdependence, of best intentions stymied by judicial bureaucracy, of fear-based panopticons and manufactured scarcity, of the various limitations and empowerments conferred by race, class, and gender. Most importantly, *Deliver Me* is the story of kids who never got to be kids, to whom love and support is rarely extended on the societal level. Combining the legal savvy of a Grisham thriller with the big-hearted social realism of a Dickens novel, this book is a passionate call for change that ought to be heeded."

—Rafael Frumkin, author of
Confidence and *Bugsy & Other Stories*

"Stunningly crafted and taut with tension, *Deliver Me* deftly exposes the dark underbelly of suburban Stockholm, where the reverberations of familial trauma and gang violence ensnare communities and hold for ransom the fate and friendship of two young boys. With this page-turning crime procedural, Giolito compels us to consider what justice means when morality is compromised by intolerance and prejudice."

—Tania Malik, author of
Hope You Are Satisfied and *Three Bargains*

"As this gritty, tightly paced procedural unfolds, deftly weaving past and present, it's clear that *Deliver Me* is more than a page-turner: it's a poignant examination of place, family, and social class that asks how we become the people we are. It's a character study of two very different boys and how their environments—and their friendship—shaped their fates. Intensely compelling, a true heartbreaker of a novel, *Deliver Me* is crime fiction at its finest."

—Samantha Jayne Allen, author of
Pay Dirt Road and *Hard Rain*

STILL LIFE

ALSO BY MALIN PERSSON GIOLITO

Quicksand

Beyond All Reasonable Doubt

Deliver Me

STILL LIFE

TEN CRIME STORIES

MALIN PERSSON GIOLITO

Translated from the Swedish
by Rachel Willson-Broyles

OTHER PRESS
NEW YORK

Originally published in Swedish as *Motiv: 10 berättelser om brott* by
Wahlström & Widstrand
Published by agreement with Paloma Agency

The cost of this translation was supported by a subsidy from
the Swedish Arts Council, gratefully acknowledged.

SWEDISH
ARTSCOUNCIL

Production editor: Yvonne E. Cárdenas
Text designer: Patrice Sheridan
This book was set in Times New Roman by
Alpha Design & Composition of Pittsfield, NH

1 3 5 7 9 10 8 6 4 2

 Printed in the United States of America on acid-free paper. For information write to Other Press LLC, 267 Fifth Avenue, 6th Floor, New York, NY 10016. Or visit our Web site: www.otherpress.com

Library of Congress Cataloging-in-Publication Data
Names: Persson Giolito, Malin, 1969- author |
Willson-Broyles, Rachel translator
Title: Still life : ten crime stories / Malin Persson Giolito ; translated from
the Swedish by Rachel Willson-Broyles.
Other titles: Motiv. English
Description: New York : Other Press, 2026.
Identifiers: LCCN 2025037274 (print) | LCCN 2025037275 (ebook) |
ISBN 9781635425567 paperback | ISBN 9781635425574 ebook
Subjects: LCGFT: Detective and mystery fiction | Short stories
Classification: LCC PT9877.26.E79 M6813 2026 (print) |
LCC PT9877.26.E79 (ebook)
LC record available at https://lccn.loc.gov/2025037274
LC ebook record available at https://lccn.loc.gov/2025037275

Publisher's Note: This is a work of fiction. Names, characters, places, and incidents either are the product of the author's imagination or are used fictitiously, and any resemblance to actual persons, living or dead, events, or locales is entirely coincidental.

And nothing 'gainst Time's scythe can make defense
Save breed, to brave him when he takes thee hence.

WILLIAM SHAKESPEARE, SONNET 12

CONTENTS

ANDERS

CRIMINAL CODE 3:7

Anders should have been off duty the day after the murder. It was a Saturday, and he usually spent Saturdays working out and hanging with friends, but not this time. Instead he was going to return to the scene of the crime.

Just months ago, he had still been a cadet at the police academy, and now he was about to work on his first homicide case. It felt meaningful in a way he couldn't quite put into words, and it was, at least to some extent, an opportunity of his own making. When he'd turned in his report late the night before, he'd asked the head of the preliminary investigation if he could lend a hand. Chief Inspector Henriksson had looked him straight in the eye in a very particular sort of way. As if to assess whether he could handle the pressure. Anders had gazed steadily back at him. And his boss nodded, as though he liked what he saw.

Anders understood, of course, that the reason he was put on the investigation probably had more to do with the staff shortage than with Henriksson thinking he was special. Everyone was aware of the situation. You couldn't walk into the station without hearing the complaints; you couldn't turn on the news without being bombarded with the laments of clueless politicians. Working overtime was never a problem; any and all hours would be approved. But his report on the incident had been meticulous; he'd done exactly what he was meant to and had not panicked. Perhaps his boss even appreciated his asking to be included. It had seemed so.

Anders was supposed to start his shift at five p.m., but he arrived at the station two hours early. He wanted to attend the investigation team's meeting, and when that was over, he got to help go through security camera footage. There was no footage from the scene of the crime; those cameras had been out of order. Nor had the weapon been recovered. During the meeting, Henriksson had looked at Anders when stating that the wounds on the body indicated the victim had been shot with a submachine gun.

"We need to put eyes on the scene," Henriksson had declared. He sent Anders.

The plan was to let the sports complex reopen as scheduled on Monday morning, that the forensic investigation would be finished before then. Accordingly, the complex would remain closed for at least one more day, but someone needed to be on-site to keep people out of the cordoned-off area.

"As long as you're there, you can keep an eye on the rubberneckers. Try to eavesdrop on them, if you can. You never know with these idiots. They might bring their girlfriends over to brag, say they know exactly how it all went down."

Or they'll come because they're the ones who did it, Anders thought. *The killer returning to the scene of the crime? Happens all the time, according to Dad at least.*

"Make sure no one disturbs the area," Henriksson continued. "Might be helpful in case we have to go back... for nothing to have changed."

Anders left the station to drive to the scene of the crime at four minutes past four. It was already dark out. It took him just over twenty minutes to reach his destination. He drove the last stretch slowly, the better to fully absorb everything he saw. Everything looked different than it had the night before, when he and his partner were the first to arrive on the scene. Now blue-and-white police tape was strung all around the parking lot. Two white tents stood in the most critical areas: the spot where the car and body had been found, and the mark where the techs had determined the shooter had stood. Someone had fixed the lighting on-site. In addition, relentlessly bright spotlights had been erected in each corner of the parking lot. It had been pitch black here less than twenty-four hours before. Now the scene was lit up like a stage. It even looked like the streetlights all the way down to the commuter rail station had been repaired. If anyone turned up, he should have no trouble seeing them, even if he had no idea how he was supposed to eavesdrop. Especially not if he was sitting in his patrol car, wearing his uniform.

When the call came over the radio, Anders and his partner had been less than a mile from the scene. Just half an hour earlier, they had driven past the sports complex where the shooting took place. But since it wasn't one of the red zones designated by Operation Night Owl—the massive effort to combat gang-related crime in the area, launched by the national police commissioner just a few weeks earlier—they had left the neighborhood and headed up to the city center, then down to the commuter rail station, then back to the city center.

"Jesus goddamn fucking Christ," his partner had muttered, mostly to himself, while Anders turned the car around to drive back.

The call had reported one individual with gunshot wounds. But it was impossible to know what to expect; they'd been instructed to leave the car just outside the parking lot and secure the area on foot. It could have been a false alarm; each week, dispatch got about a dozen prank calls describing made-up incidents in the area. Or it might be a real emergency, with armed suspects still on the scene.

His partner went first, with Anders behind and slightly to the side; they proceeded as Anders had been taught to do during practical maneuvers at the academy. They needed to maintain a clear view of their surroundings, cover one another, their weapons raised, their eyes sharp. There was no need to remind each other to be cautious, to approach the car and its open door slowly; they did it automatically. This was no false alarm.

The parking lot seemed enormous, as if it would never end. The sports complex had been closed for a few hours by this time, and the parking lot was empty aside from a single car parked diagonally across two spaces, with one of its doors wide open. Anders had time to consider that they should have driven closer before they set out on foot, that they had been safer in the patrol car than they were outside.

But there was no ambush awaiting them, only a body. The victim was a large man; they could tell even before they reached him. He was lying on his side below the open car door. Anders's partner stood with his weapon raised and his gaze anxiously sweeping the parking lot as Anders bent down to see if the man was dead or alive. He had been shot in the leg and the head. He was bleeding heavily from the wound in his leg, more than from the one in his head, even though the head wound was more serious. Anders had never seen a gunshot victim before. When he felt the man's pulse, he wondered at first if he was imagining it. How could this man's heart still be beating when his face was split in two? But it looked like the man was blinking the one eye he had left, so Anders took his tin of snus, placed it over the leg wound, and fastened it there with the help of the belt his partner removed from around the man's waist and handed to him. Next Anders began to do chest compressions. This was what they were supposed to do, according to the handbook. But he couldn't do the other part of CPR.

We didn't practice that, Anders thought. *No one explained how to do mouth-to-mouth resuscitation when the victim's chin is gone.*

His partner had called for backup and an ambulance. The officers who arrived on the scene after them took as many photographs as they could on their phones; one of them got ten pictures of what might have been footprints leading away from the parking lot, down to the station and the road. The footprints appeared to have been left by at least two people. Anders had been asked to take a look at those pictures when he returned to the station to debrief. They wondered if he had seen any tire tracks as well, anything to indicate another vehicle had been at the scene. But he didn't know, and when they showed him the pictures his colleague had taken, he couldn't even say where they had come from, they were too blurry. He pointed out that it was awfully dark by the time he and his partner arrived.

"So you can't say whether our suspect was on foot or in a car?"

And Anders had no choice but to say he had been too focused on trying to see if there was anyone else still on the scene, someone who might be armed, someone who might be lingering around the edges of the parking lot. There had only been the one car in the parking lot, and it looked abandoned.

The truth was, he hadn't been thinking about evidence, hadn't looked for any at all. But he didn't say so, exactly.

"I would have noticed if there were any tire tracks," he said instead. He said this in a voice that sounded much more confident than he really was. But that was because he felt ashamed—of course he knew that it was important to take note of evidence, that he should have been more attentive, that he had made a mistake.

I just kept counting: thirty, two. Thirty, two, he could have said. *I counted the breaths I couldn't give and the chest compressions I did.*

But he didn't try to explain himself or blame his partner. He didn't point out that his partner could have checked on all that stuff while Anders was trying to save a life. He didn't want to seem insecure or cowardly. He hated cowardly, insecure police officers; they were the worst.

His partner had let him do the chest compressions all by himself, even though all the instruction manuals said that it was a good idea to take turns if there were two of you. The man had died in the ambulance on the way to the hospital. Anders's counting had been pointless and now they had no idea who had killed the man; they had no idea whether it had been several people who left the scene on foot or by vehicle together or just a lone shooter in the night.

He hadn't even thought to look for evidence as he made his way back to the patrol car once he handed lifesaving measures over to the paramedics, because he had to devote all his attention to trying to walk back exactly the same way he'd come. That was what he had been taught to do. But this wasn't just a practice drill, and it was terribly difficult to concentrate on anything but the image of the man's head, which kept popping into Anders's mind each time he blinked. He had never seen anything like that, not even in a photograph. At last, he gave up and simply followed his partner instead. By then it was even darker out. It wasn't just the security cameras in the parking lot and by the entrance to the sports complex that were broken; the lot lights weren't working either.

Back in their patrol car, he spread a plastic bag over his seat before he got in. His partner wasn't as cautious.

Anders saw him through the window, scooting around the cordons and talking to people, and that was when it began to snow. Just a few minutes later, the flakes were so thick in the air that when his partner got more than a dozen yards away, he was no longer visible. Anders stayed in the car and waited for the technicians to come take a DNA sample from him. But it took a long time. Meanwhile, the snow formed an ever-thicker blanket over the car, and he figured they would have to shovel it out if they stayed much longer. But in the end, it wasn't necessary. When he finally got the okay to go back to the station and debrief, he was offered a ride with another colleague, who was parked even farther away, on the main road where the traffic kept the snow from accumulating. At the station, he left his bloody clothes at the reception desk and was immediately provided with a fresh set. They even had clean underwear and socks in his size. But he had kept his own.

Today, he'd had to drive to the scene of the crime by himself. This was his first assignment without a more experienced colleague by his side. Henriksson had instructed him to sign out a car and explained that he was still hoping more staff would become available, but for now there would just be two officers stationed around the area, and they each needed to have their own car.

"So you don't freeze to death and make me even more short-staffed."

Anders had not pointed out that the rules forbade working solo when there was a reasonable risk of violence. *I'm only going to be watching a crime scene*, he thought. *I don't need a babysitter.* Nor did he mention that he was still a trainee and had never gone on assignment alone.

In the car, he muttered to himself.

"Henriksson is the commanding officer, and in his view I can handle this, so obviously I can handle this."

It was seventeen minutes past four when he pulled into the parking lot and up to the patrol car that was parked just outside the cordon tape. He stepped out of his vehicle.

"Hey," said the colleague who had arrived first. He offered his hand in greeting. "I'm Martin. You were here yesterday, right?"

Anders nodded.

"Anders. That's right."

"You're here earlier than I expected. Did you miss it? Probably less of a party today, I'm afraid. But, welcome."

Anders mumbled something he hoped would suffice as a response. It felt too strange to say thanks.

"You can head over that way," Martin said, waving his right hand in the direction of the commuter rail station. "Park alongside the lot, as far away as you can get while you can still see me. Keep the radio open, and I'll call if you need to move. If anything comes up, you can call me or flash your brights."

Anders went back to the car. Once he'd parked where he thought Martin wanted him to, he gazed around the area. No one could approach or leave without his noticing. At least not as long as the person in question was walking along the now-illuminated footpath between the sports complex and the rail station. It was much darker on the other side, but that shouldn't matter too much. The important thing was to have a good view from the car, and he did.

He reclined the seat and stretched out his legs. It wasn't just the lighting that made it easier to see today than it had been yesterday. The snow had stuck, making everything brighter. They'd said at the station that it was supposed to snow again this evening, but for the moment conditions were ideal for a stakeout. *Like a perfect hunting trip*, he thought.

Next weekend, if he didn't have to work, he would head up to visit Dad and go moose-hunting. That would give him a chance to clear his head. Talk to Dad, maybe—Dad would understand, even if he didn't go into detail. Anders's father was a police officer too, retired now, and he had seen everything imaginable. He had found a dead baby in a microwave in a junkie den, had hauled any number of battered addicts out from under bridges where not even the rats wanted to live. He had fished corpses out of water and comforted survivors of rape. Dad would understand why he hadn't been able to give the victim mouth-to-mouth.

A submachine gun, he thought. *The guy was shot with a fucking submachine gun. There was nothing I could do, it wasn't my fault.* Then he thought of his partner's behavior the day before. He had broken all the rules—maybe it was just sloppiness, or maybe not. It was always hard to tell, Anders thought. When other officers did the opposite of what he'd been taught at the police academy, did it mean they were making mistakes, or was it because they'd learned more than just the theoretical stuff and he should emulate them? Maybe he would ask Dad about that, if he got the chance.

Oftentimes he simply followed the lead of his more experienced colleagues. It felt more important to blend in and do as they did rather than act like some sort of hall monitor. But not yesterday. Yesterday he had stayed in the patrol car until the technicians came over and sent him back to the station. This was partly because his knees felt weak, and he was afraid that his hands would start to shake as if his blood sugar had dropped following a tough workout. But no one had complained. One of the techs had even thanked him for waiting and following protocol. They wanted to take a sample from him, just as Anders knew they should.

"You wouldn't believe how often folks forget to follow the most basic guidelines," the technician had said as he handed Anders a cotton swab to stick in his mouth.

That had made him feel better, but it was a little embarrassing at the same time—he felt like a kid getting a prize from the dentist for being such a good brusher. Anders had always performed very well in the practical exercises, and one thing they'd learned during training was that if you had to go anywhere near a murder victim you should do your best not to do anything else afterward.

What the techs had said to his partner, he didn't know. But in any case, Henriksson hadn't brought him in. Only Anders would get to participate in the investigation.

He'd been staring out the car window for over an hour now, and it was almost six o'clock. He rubbed his eyes and opened the window a crack to get some air. It was cold outside, but inside the car it was way too hot. The heat whooshed from the vents. He started to get sleepy.

Another hour passed, and his back began to hurt. He was sick of listening to the monotonous static of the radio. Now it was almost seven. Was he supposed to sit here with the car idling all night? Or even longer? He would run out of gas. He'd turned the engine off a few times, but he quickly became too cold. As soon as the heat came back on, though, he felt tired again. He hadn't gotten much sleep last night before heading back to the station, and he wasn't sure how night-shift hours worked in cases like these. If there had been another officer with him, they could have taken turns napping. But he could hardly ask Martin to keep an eye on his spot while he took a little snooze.

Henriksson hadn't mentioned anything about when Anders would be relieved. "I'm short-staffed as hell," was all he had said. But whatever happened, Anders intended to stay put until someone else arrived. If resources were strained, you had to pitch in however you could. Not complain about safe working conditions and the handbook. But maybe he could get out and breathe some fresh air. It wouldn't make any difference if he stood next to the car for a bit, would it?

While Henriksson hadn't said a word about how long Anders would be on shift, he had asked him to come by the station before clocking out for the day. Even if Henriksson himself wasn't there, Anders needed to get an update on the investigation and receive his instructions for the next day, Henriksson had explained. This made Anders feel as though he really was part of the team. That he counted, just as his more senior colleagues did. And the first few hours after a homicide were the most crucial period, as Anders's father always said. Maybe he would have to work around the clock for a few days. That was just what you had to do, during important investigations, and he wasn't about to complain.

He got out of the car. He needed to stretch his legs and breathe some fresh air. He left the engine on and leaned against the hood. He could make out the main entrance of the sports complex, about a hundred yards away. The spotlights on the snow-covered running track emitted a flickering light that was visible even from Anders's location. Martin's car seemed to be turned off, or at least the headlights weren't on. Maybe he was making the rounds of the parking lot. When Anders was up there, he had found it apparently deserted. No more technicians searching for evidence. Maybe they were finished. Anders didn't know whether they'd found anything besides the backpack that had been recovered three yards from the main entrance of the complex. Henriksson had told him what was in it.

"Who knows," he'd said. "Maybe they'll think we missed it, and maybe they'll be stupid enough to come back for their shit."

Henriksson had spoken of the perpetrators in the plural. Indicating there were a few of them. At least two. Anders glanced up at Martin's car again; the engine still seemed to be off.

Up at the station, there were photographs of the victim. Anders had found out whose life he had failed to save. His colleagues in Major Crimes had tried to talk to the man after a shooting a few weeks ago, but they hadn't gotten anywhere, and ever since then, they had been doing their utmost to find a reason to lock him up. They would have thrown him in jail if he'd so much as slowed down in front of an ATM or taken too long to get out his debit card in the checkout line at the grocery store. But they hadn't even managed to keep an eye on him, and now he was dead. "Obviously we should have had a couple guys glued to him around the clock, but please tell me where I'm supposed to dig up the resources for that," Henriksson had said.

"Previously known to law enforcement," blared the morning news, even before it was made public that the man was deceased. Everyone knew what "known to law enforcement" meant. That he hadn't been killed by mistake, wasn't an innocent bystander. The victim was no choirboy, no Scout leader. It also meant that the prospects for solving the murder were dim. To be sure, the police already knew who they wanted to talk to. They always did. But those who knew what the police wanted to know were never chatty or compliant.

"Known to law enforcement" was also a euphemism for what everyone was thinking but hardly anyone said out loud: *He got what he deserved.*

Anders had called his father when he learned he would be allowed to take part in the investigation. He had told him that the victim had died in the ambulance on the way to the hospital.

"So there is justice in the world," his father had said. "Mourned by no one that matters. Congrats to us, one less idiot to keep an eye on."

Anders had added that there was a rumor the victim had been involved in another shooting. The police had been keeping an eye on him, but with no results.

"Exactly," his father said. "At *least* one less problem. No one will miss a fat gangster whose only future accomplishment would be becoming an even fatter gangster. With a little luck, and at this rate, maybe they'll all manage to kill each other before Christmas, and you can come home for a few days. Your ma would like that."

Anders took out his phone to check the time. Ten past seven. He could hear his father's voice. *Time flies when you're having fun.* Two more hours, and he would have been working for six hours, just today. Yesterday he had worked eleven hours. And in between he had gotten maybe three hours of sleep. Thus far, he hadn't spotted so much as an unleashed dog to report around this damn place. What's more, he had to pee. Not a soul in sight, and it was starting to snow besides. Soon it would be like trying to do a stakeout from inside a gunnysack. Where was everybody? They couldn't all be sleeping at this hour. Were they eating dinner? He'd only brought a plastic-wrapped sandwich and a protein bar, but maybe he would feel more alert if he ate. Were they watching TV? Lying on their sofas and staring at their phones? He would scarf down his sandwich when it got to be eight o'clock. But he had to wait until then. Otherwise, he would just get hungry again before it was really nighttime.

Anders stomped his feet a few times to ease the worst of the pressure on his bladder. The sharp snowflakes made his cheeks sting. The harder the wind blew, the more his excitement at being included on the investigation ebbed away. Right now, he couldn't even remember why he'd asked to help. What was he *doing* here? Henriksson couldn't seriously believe that a murderer would come back to look for a stupid bag, could he? It hadn't been hidden, just sitting there in plain sight on the steps up to the complex—presumably the victim had dropped it there; maybe he thought it would be enough for them to leave him alone. Why had it still been there when Anders and his partner arrived? How should he know? But the murderer must have guessed it had been discovered, known that it was pointless to return for it now.

He tried to wiggle his finger beneath his waistband. He undid his holster and loosened his belt. He couldn't hold out much longer; he had to pee. He opened the car door, bent in over the driver's seat, and flashed the brights a few times. Martin's car was still dark and silent. He didn't seem to be sitting inside it.

Anders leaned toward the radio and tuned to his colleague's frequency. But it was busy; he could hear Martin talking to someone. So he was somewhere nearby, at least. Before he turned the radio off, Anders heard him say he was out of snus. It would be a bad idea to ask Martin for help. If he asked him to come down to his location, there wouldn't be anyone up by the schoolyard. He straightened up, closed the car door, and swept his gaze across the area once more. Still quiet and deserted. It wouldn't take him long to pee, less than a minute. Maybe a few more seconds to get all his equipment back in place. He crossed to the other side of the car and pulled off one glove, unbuckling his belt and unzipping his fly as he went. When he reached the ditch, he stopped. No one could see him here. The commuter rail tracks were directly below. He relaxed and let out a long sigh of pleasure as the pressure was finally relieved.

He heard them before he saw them. They were five yards away, on the other side of the tracks, half hidden by the bushes. The whirling snow was thicker now, and the lighting was worse there, but as they stepped out, he saw that there were two of them. *Or three? No, two. Definitely just two.* They were wearing dark clothes, one with a hood covering their head. They laughed, saying something he couldn't catch, and then he couldn't see them anymore. *Where did they go?* The next time he spotted them, they had crossed the tracks and one of them was jogging toward the patrol car. There was something slung over his shoulder, thumping against his back. *Narrow on top, wider on the bottom. Could it be…? Was it a submachine gun?*

Anders blinked; he dropped his glove on the ground, fumbled with his fly, brought a hand up to get the snow out of his eyes, to see better. *Why didn't I take off both my gloves?* The cold burned his throat as he inhaled. His airways seemed to have shrunk. *The man who was murdered was shot with a submachine gun.*

Then he saw the other man. He was oddly short and slender, almost gangly. His hand was in his coat pocket, and he was no more than six feet away now, laughing loudly, shrilly; the man by the car was standing by the open door, and he leaned in and began to speak, loud and clear. His voice was strangely high-pitched. *Does he sound like that because he's high? Hyper?*

"The key's in the ignition. The car is on. What a fucking…"

The wind caught their voices, whipped up a whirlwind of snow. Now both of them were laughing. *Why are they laughing?* Anders tried to blink to get a better look. What were they doing? *They're going to steal the car.*

"Get the hell—" he shouted. But then he saw the gangly man take his hand from his pocket. A gleam. *Is that a Glock? Ruger? Colt? Is he going to shoot me? Are they going to steal the car and shoot me?*

The man had stepped another foot closer. He was waving his hand now, but Anders still couldn't tell what he was holding. But it was shiny. *Metal. What was that sound? Was that the safety? He's talking again.*

"He's taking a leak. The cop is taking a leak."

Anders raised his hands an inch or two, no more than that, but away from his fly. Yet the short man was still pointing the object at him. *Is he aiming at me?* Another gleam, almost a flash. Anders had heard of firearms that were equipped with white lasers for use in low light, but he had never seen one before. Now the man was laughing even louder. It appeared that he had turned his head to look at his friend; his gaze moved away from Anders and his hand lowered slightly. That was enough. Anders didn't need to see more. He had trained for this, the movements becoming muscle memory after all the times he had messed up and tried again, dozens, hundreds, maybe thousands of times, to learn exactly how to pass every test, get top scores in every drill. He knew precisely what to do. It was in his bones now, and that was why it happened so fast. It took him less than a second to draw his service weapon. Afterward he would say he had aimed for the shoulder, but the truth was he couldn't see clearly enough to aim at anything in particular. The shot fired, no louder than a firecracker. Brief, dull, irrevocable. It hit the short, skinny man in the throat. He fell. A beam of light swept over the snow, through the darkness, as the object in his hand hit the ground. *Is that what a white laser looks like?* Anders turned around and aimed his weapon at the man who had been about to steal his car. The light coming from the car was bright enough for him to see what he was aiming at. It was a boy. *A child? Yes, this is Sweden today, children with guns.* It's easier to get your hands on a gun than it is to get a doctor's appointment, as his father liked to say. Anders shouted and took two steps away from the ditch.

"Drop the weapon, you bastard!"

But the boy simply fell to his knees, as though all his muscles had stopped working at once. Anders saw the oblong object behind him. It was no submachine gun, no rifle, no weapon at all. It was a racket cover of some sort. Anders did up his pants as fast as he could with one hand as he held his gun trained on the other figure. He wanted to be fully covered up by the time his colleague arrived. Would he be forced to admit he had been taking a piss when they caught him by surprise? Presumably. Even if it were to come out, even if it caused him trouble, he had learned it was always best to answer any question honestly. He wouldn't think about what nicknames this might earn him. How they would laugh at him.

The idiot who almost got his patrol car stolen on his first solo assignment. The rookie who drew his weapon and fired with his balls out.

That couldn't happen, it wouldn't happen. He had been defending himself, they had threatened him with a firearm; he'd had no other choice. Maybe these were the boys who had shot the gang member they had run into the night before. It was very likely them. He had been doing his duty, the murderers had returned to the scene of the crime to kill a cop. Everyone knew they sent young boys to do jobs like that. Young enough that they couldn't end up in prison, because they were below the age of criminal responsibility. He knew of two cases in just the past year where the shooter had been thirteen. He had been under threat, he had been forced to defend himself, everyone would understand.

The boy he had shot made a gurgling sound. With his pants hastily buttoned and his belt still unbuckled, Anders grabbed the comm radio. He shouted into it: "Ambulance, backup, there were guns, there were two of them, they were armed," the words tripping over each other, "*They were going to shoot me and take the fucking car*," he couldn't stop the blood pumping from the boy's throat until he had explained what had happened. But he wasn't giving a very good explanation. The boy's face, the man from yesterday, they all seemed to merge, Anders touched the boy's chin, it wasn't injured. While the radio was still on he screamed at the other boy, who was on the ground now, *stay put, don't-you-move-you-bastard*, the curses just came out, he said words he shouldn't have, he called him things that were not allowed, but the boy wasn't moving, in any case, and here came Martin, Anders could see him running toward the scene, he was shouting questions, Anders couldn't make sense of them, he pulled the wounded boy into his lap, he didn't know how to stop the blood, it was flowing more sluggishly now, but he didn't know how to hold the radio at the same time, because that hadn't been covered in training. In the end he pressed the radio to the boy's neck, the blood stopped, he looked down at his hands. Bloody, just like yesterday. Would his hands always be bloody? How many times would he have to ask for a fresh, clean uniform at the station? How many times would he have to stand in the shower and watch rusty brown water trickle into the floor drain?

He saw Martin approach the other boy and pull him up off the ground; he saw Martin frisk him. Then he opened the door to the back seat and let the boy sit down inside. Then he left him and dashed over to Anders.

"Lay him down," he said breathlessly. Anders did as he was told. He wanted to say that they couldn't leave the other little fucker unmonitored, but his voice wouldn't work, and he let Martin crouch down beside the boy he'd shot. Martin would do what Anders had done the day before. *Count: thirty, two. As many times as it takes.*

One, two; one-two-three-four-five-six-seven. Today there would be two of them, and they could take turns.

But they didn't even have time to start. The ambulance must have been very close by already. It took no more than a few seconds for the paramedics to load the boy onto a stretcher and sweep him away. Anders and Martin found themselves sitting on the ground where the boy had been. They watched one of their colleagues take the other boy by the hand and help him out of Anders's car. It looked like the boy was crying. He had pulled his gym bag close and was hugging it like a teddy bear, the kind you could win at a carnival.

"Where's the gun?" Martin asked. "You said they threatened to shoot you, so where's the gun?"

Anders nodded toward the area where he'd seen the boy drop it. He wanted to ask Martin to explain to their colleagues what had happened, but Martin disappeared. He was gone for a long time. Instead of Martin, a forensic technician came to get Anders, the same one he'd met the night before. *He must have been working inside the tent, that's why I didn't notice him before.*

Today, the tech hardly acknowledged him. When Anders explained what had happened, there was no response. Not so much as a look—the tech simply held out a bag for Anders to drop his weapon into, and then he covered each of Anders's hands in a paper bag. He got to keep the single glove he was wearing. Then another colleague came and asked Anders to get into the back seat of a different car.

"More of our guys here today than there were yesterday," he mumbled. There was no reply.

"They were going to shoot me and steal the car," he said again, in a louder voice.

"We'll deal with that when we get to the station," his colleague said. He sounded grim.

"Sure," Anders said. "I get it. I know the protocol. But I can show you where he dropped his gun, if you want, I know right where it is, and I can show you so you don't miss it."

"We have people searching," his colleague said curtly. "If there's a gun, we'll find it."

"I saw where he dropped it. I can show you. I know it... he threatened me. I saw how he was threatening me, he pointed it straight at me. I saw—"

The tech interrupted him.

"It's best if we talk about this at the station. You'll be assigned an ombud, we'll take care of it..."

Anders's patience ran out.

"He was threatening me. What the fuck would you have done, he was standing two yards away and aiming a goddamn pistol in my face. And the other one, he must have had..." He had been about to say that the other guy had carried a submachine gun over his shoulder, probably the murder weapon, when he remembered that it had been a racket cover, maybe a tennis bag? "You would have done the same thing...," he said instead.

"It was a phone." His colleague took a breath. He seemed angry, as though he too had run out of patience. "He didn't have a gun, only a phone. He was filming you. Those two kids were on their way to play squash, they hadn't heard that the complex was still closed. They saw you with your pants down and wanted to post a funny video to TikTok…"

Anders shook his head.

"No, he had…he threatened me…"

"They're thirteen years old, and they're thinking, this cop is such a loser. You had left the engine running and the door unlocked. And you were taking a leak…a pig in uniform with his pants down, they thought it would make a hilarious video."

Anders shook his head again. "I saw—"

His colleague cut him off.

"Stop talking. I'm taking you to the station. You need to talk to your lawyer. Don't say another word until you've spoken to him." He placed a hand on Anders's shoulder. "The station is in total panic mode right now. I don't have a goddamn clue how you're going to get out of this, but one thing's for sure: You never should have been here in the first place, but you were, so believe me when I say that you need to shut up and speak only to your lawyer because no one is going to want to take the blame for this. Don't say another word."

Anders nodded. He gazed down at his lap and realized that his belt was still unbuckled and his holster open. But there was nothing he could do about it now; his hands were covered in the paper bags, and he couldn't exactly ask his colleague to help. So he didn't bring it up.

"Sure. I get it. We have to follow the protocol," he whispered instead. "It's best to follow the protocol. Of course we should follow the protocol. That's always the best option."

IDA

CRIMINAL CODE 12:1

Forever and ever. Ida loved Katti ever since the first time they'd met. When Ida switched schools mid-semester, she'd been late to her first class because she couldn't find the right room, and because she refused to let her mother come to school with her and ask humiliating questions of people they didn't know. Katti had been late too, and they'd struck up a conversation. She'd shown Ida where her classroom was, but instead of going inside they went out to the schoolyard to keep talking. No one would find it strange if Ida didn't show up before second period, Katti had explained. After all, it was her first day, and she probably had tons of stuff to take care of. And it was so common for Katti to be tardy that no one cared. Ever since that day, they were best friends forever and ever, and now it was Katti's birthday.

Ida's mother, Petra, seemed to think it was just an ordinary morning. An ordinary morning meant, besides cereal and milk, that Ida's mother roused her out of bed. Ida usually forgot to set an alarm on her phone, and if she did, she would typically fall asleep again after it went off.

But today she was awake before her mother came in. Ida wanted to be the first one to wish Katti happy birthday. So she had already prepared a post, a short video she'd edited together, photos and videos of the two of them, laughing, dancing, making funny faces. And some were of Katti by herself, when she was acting serious, or had just woken up, or was a little bit tipsy, but not drunk enough that her parents would notice if they could see the post.

When Ida walked into the kitchen, Mom told her they were out of milk. You couldn't have cereal without milk.

"That's okay," Ida replied, sitting down at her spot at the table. "I'm not hungry."

"You need to eat," Mom said. "You know what happens when—"

"It's Katti's birthday today," Ida said.

"Hmm," said Petra, glancing at Ida's father. But then she got a handle on her voice and her face and added, quickly, in a tone that was almost normal: "Wish her a happy birthday from us."

"For sure," Ida said. She didn't say anything about the face her mom was making, or the party Katti was going to throw. She could worry about that after school. Mom wouldn't say no. It was Friday, and she was allowed to go out on Fridays, at least most of the time.

Starting at a new school had been nerve-racking. But Katti had transformed Ida's nervousness to anticipation. It was clear that she was one of the most popular girls, the one everyone wanted to hang out with. Everything about Katti was so confident. The way she looked, the way she talked, the things she said and did. With Katti, Ida had the chance to forget, to start over, to become a new person.

Ida wasn't ugly, she wasn't, but you had to look very closely, really make an effort, to see that she was cute. Sometimes she said funny things, but only when she knew that someone was genuinely paying attention. She wasn't the type of person who could make others listen to her; the interest had to come from their side.

No one had made the effort at her old school; they were nothing but jerks who hated her, but Katti got Ida from day one. And since Katti was who she was, she made everyone else make an effort too. Katti was never afraid of anything, she was always the center of attention, at the front of the room, she was the girl everyone saw and heard.

Thanks to Katti, Ida had even gotten a boyfriend. His name was Fredrik, and he was Katti's ex's friend. Ida fell for him right away, and now she loved him, basically. Not that she'd told him so, obviously, but if they were together for just another month maybe she would, even if he didn't say it first. Sure, it was kind of too bad that Katti and Fredrik's friend had broken up just two weeks after Fredrik and Ida got together, but it didn't turn awkward. Things went on just like before, they could hang out as much as usual, and with the same group of friends.

But Ida's parents were still worried. They looked at her as though she were still the person she'd been at her old school. And Mom "felt sorry" for Katti; Ida had overheard her saying so to Dad more than once. What a typical grown-up thing to say. Grown-ups said they felt sorry for kids they actually didn't like, because they knew they were supposed to like all kids. Dad said, "Ida and Katti aren't good for each other," when what he really meant was that there was something wrong with Katti. Which was probably a little bit because of how she smelled like smoke and had three piercings in one ear. But mostly it was because she wasn't a suck-up. Katti never made a show of acting deferential around adults, never gave the impression that she thought they sounded so smart when they were droning on about crap no one cared about. Nothing was more alarming to people like Ida's parents than children who didn't play along and instead made them feel as dorky as they were. Also, Dad was always staring at Katti with his cop look, as though she had done something wrong. Ida had asked him to stop, but he pretended not to know what she was talking about.

While Ida checked her phone, Mom made her a cheese sandwich; she put it on a pink plate and placed it on the table next to her. Ida pulled up the happy birthday video she'd made. There were quite a few reactions already, but none was from Katti. Her profile showed she was logged in. And she had made a post of her own less than half an hour ago, a dark selfie in which she was wearing a sailor's cap and had her chin thrust out. #birthdaygrrl was all the caption said. It already had almost 200 likes and 120 comments, mostly hearts and little flames. Ida wanted to write something that was real, but she couldn't think of what. "You are my sunshine," she tried, but she knew what Katti would respond. "Mom on insta or sthg? Haha" or a cheese emoji, or something along those lines. Katti was the only one who was never cringe, only funny. So Ida deleted it just seconds later and went with a heart and a flame instead. At least it was a *black* heart, not a plain old red one. Then she checked again to see if Katti had commented on her post, but she hadn't.

"Can you put that down for a minute and focus on breakfast?"

Dad turned up the volume on the news, caught Mom's eye, and nodded at the radio.

"You don't get it, Petra. I don't know how this is going to end. He was shot in the back of the head. At close range. A goddamn execution. We couldn't do anything, he was already dead. We waited for the techs to arrive, but that was all."

Mom shook her head. Dad turned to Ida again.

"What the hell, Ida, didn't you hear what I said? Put down that goddamn phone for once."

"Shh... leave her alone, Hans," Mom whispered softly, stroking Dad's cheek. The way she often touched her children, to comfort them. But Dad picked up his coffee cup and walked out of the kitchen. A few seconds later, they heard the bathroom door slam. Ida had taken a bite of her sandwich. It expanded in her mouth. She felt a band of pressure over her chest. No reaction from Katti. She couldn't delete the post now, there were too many comments from other friends, and Katti must have seen it, so deleting it would be too weird.

"Take your sandwich with you," Mom said as she stood up and headed for the front hall. Ida did as she was told. She had to jog to catch the bus. When she sat down, she shoved the sandwich into the gap between the seat and the window. She wasn't hungry.

"Babe!" Katti shouted as Ida was pulling her math book out of her locker. She was walking arm-in-arm with Ida's boyfriend Fredrik and putting an extra swing in her hips. She never called Ida "babe" when it was just the two of them. When she reached Ida, she dropped Fredrik's arm and gave her a hug.

"I love you, you know that, right?" she said, her voice still a little too loud. "Tonight we're gonna party!" she declared, even louder this time. "Hell yeah we are," said Ida. She was so relieved that she almost burst out laughing. She stopped herself just in time. Katti didn't mention Ida's post, but it didn't seem like she was mad, anyway. "It's gonna be so fucking awesome," she added. But by then Katti had already taken off down the corridor, her stance exaggeratedly wide and her arms reaching out. She was heading for Helena, who was in their same grade but a different class.

"Babe!"

Helena let out a shriek and galloped over to meet her halfway.

Ida looked at Fredrik, who gazed back and shrugged.

"You have math now?" she asked, even though she knew he did.

He didn't respond, but they walked to the classroom together just like usual. The tube of silver peel-off face mask that had cost 700 kronor and could only be purchased online was still in her school bag, wrapped in bright pink paper. Ida hadn't had time to take it out before Katti ran off, and now she and Helena were gone.

I'll give it to her later, she thought. *It's not the end of the world, she'll get it later.*

"Where have you been?"

It was a reasonable question; Katti hadn't turned up to math class or their double-period geography class after that. But her tone sounded angry, and Ida immediately regretted asking. At least Katti was here now, along with Helena.

"Sorry, *Mom*," Katti said. "I didn't know I was grounded."

Helena laughed. Katti smiled and sat down across from Ida. Helena took the seat next to Fredrik's. But they hadn't gotten any food. Katti leaned over Ida's tray and inspected the contents as if she were going to grab a taste of something, but then she seemed to change her mind; she shook her head and made a face. Ida tried again. It *wasn't* a strange question; Katti had been gone all morning.

"I thought you went home or something."

Ida wished she could make her voice less whiny. Less doom-and-gloom, less dorky. But Katti didn't seem to care. She didn't answer the question, but she didn't seem annoyed either.

Suddenly she leaned into Helena, rested her head in her lap, and let her hair fall toward the floor. She looked hot, almost sweaty.

"I see the party started early," Fredrik observed. But Katti didn't seem to hear him. She closed her eyes for a moment, like she was totally exhausted. But then she flew up again and leaned across the table toward Ida once more.

"See you at my place," she whispered. Her forehead was shiny and there was alcohol on her musty breath, only slightly disguised by the scent of bubblegum. "We're leaving now. Because there's a couple things we have to do." She laughed and took Helena's hand. "Stop by your old school to see..."

Katti mouthed his name; everyone knew who that was and what he sold. Helena laughed too.

Ida wanted to ask if she could help. After all, it was *her* old school. She was the one who had told Katti about the guy who could get you everything you needed for a party, not just wine and vodka. Who dealt old-school, not over Snapchat. But she didn't say anything. It felt like Katti might refuse. One time she had asked to come along, but Katti had laughed and gone without her. She didn't want that to happen again.

Katti and Helena were out of the cafeteria before Ida remembered the present. It was still in her backpack. But she didn't get up and run to catch them. She would bring it to Katti's house tonight.

Last week Katti had said they would get ready together, shower and do their makeup and mix drinks and watch some TikToks. They had planned on it. But now it seemed like the plan had changed. Or did she mean Ida should come earlier? Maybe that's what she meant. But what time? Should she come right after school, or just an hour before the party? She didn't want to ask. Katti tended to get annoyed when she asked a lot of questions. It would have been best if Ida had skipped out with them now. The only class she had after lunch was P.E., and skipping P.E. was no problem, all you had to do was go to the school nurse and say you had horrific cramps, and you would get an excused slip. You could even get one two days later if you realized the P.E. teacher had marked you absent. The school nurse was called Jörgen and he was terrified of anything to do with periods. But now it was definitely too late to run after Katti and Helena.

The odors of tobacco and perfume lingered around the table. Helena smoked a pack a day, while at the same time using mint-flavored white snus to make the cigarettes taste like menthols. But the perfume came from Katti; Ida recognized it. She always smelled really good. Then Fredrik got up too. Ida dropped her fork and pushed her tray away. But before she could stand up, Fredrik shook his head.

"Oh, stay here. I'm just going to the bathroom. See you in P.E."

It wasn't the biggest house on the street, but it was on the best lot. That's what Ida's dad had said the first time he drove her there. Having the last house on a cul-de-sac, that was the kind of thing grown-ups lived for. And it was even on a rise—from Katti's house, you could see almost all the way to Ida's, and not just when the weather was good.

She had decided to arrive an hour and a half before Katti said the party would start. That way maybe they would have time to do face masks together. The tube would be enough for all three of them, Helena too, and Katti would still have plenty left over for herself.

But when Ida arrived, it was already hopping. Fredrik was there too. He was smoking in the driveway; Katti was standing by the open garage door, and her father's bright blue Porsche 911 Carrera Cabriolet was inside. It looked brand new. Katti was holding an open bottle of bubbly. Ida realized she must have taken it from the wine fridge in the garage. She had already changed clothes and put on makeup; her hair looked straight out of an ad. Ida hadn't gotten ready at all yet, expecting they would do it together.

"Are your parents home?"

Katti laughed and shook her head, then bent close to kiss Ida's cheek. Fredrik lifted his chin and blew out smoke but made no move to hug her.

"Are you nuts? Obviously not. They went to Copenhagen so I could celebrate my birthday with my friends," Katti replied. "But they hid the car keys," she said. "Or we could have gone into the city."

"Want me to hotwire it for you?" A guy from a school in the city, a friend of Helena's, waved his hand in the air. Katti took a sip from her bottle.

"Are you nuts?" she said again. "Don't you dare touch the car. Drink whatever you want, do whatever you want, but do not even think about the car or my dad will fucking kill me."

Ida took a step closer to Fredrik. But then he dropped his half-smoked cigarette on the ground and stamped it out.

"I'm freezing my dick off."

Ida followed him into the kitchen. She would sneak up to Katti's room and change clothes there, she didn't need to ask, Katti would understand.

It wasn't exactly the party of the year. The first time the cops showed up, it was only eight-thirty and Katti herself had called them. Ida didn't recognize any of the officers, but they drove off a gang of four guys who'd crashed the party. At that point Katti was still pretty sober; they hadn't started dancing yet.

At eleven o'clock, the cops came back. By then, everyone was drunk. One of the speakers had blown and was making a dull noise like a sad toad. A uniformed female officer yanked the plugs from the outlet to turn off the music. Also, Katti's dad had called from their hotel in Copenhagen. He'd gotten an alert from his private security company and when Katti didn't answer the phone he called the police, who passed his call along to an officer who was already at the home. When the officer handed the phone to Katti, everyone in the room could hear her dad shouting. Less than ten minutes later, everyone cleared out.

Even Helena went home, but only after vomiting blood-red liquid in Katti's yard. Ida and Fredrik stuck around, though. Ida had said she would sleep over at Katti's and that still seemed to be okay. They settled in the living room, all three of them on the same sofa. It was crowded. Fredrik was lying on one end, with Ida sitting on the other. Katti was in the middle. First they watched a movie, one Ida had already seen. Ten minutes in, Katti lay down next to Fredrik, with her head on his chest.

When Ida looked at them, she noticed that Fredrik's eyes were closed, and it looked like they were going to sleep.

It looks like she's *Fredrik's girlfriend*, Ida thought, but she didn't say anything, because what was there to say? All Fredrik had done was put his hand on Katti's shoulder and let her rest one leg between his own. What was Ida supposed to do about that? Try to squeeze in between them? That would make her seem crazy.

It's not cheating, she tried to think, *they're not kissing or anything. They're drunk, maybe they're going to fall asleep like that. As friends, super good friends, they've known each other forever. My best friend and my boyfriend, it's so great that they get along. Kinda cute.* No one was watching the movie anymore. Ida took out her phone. She watched one clip after the next, swiping faster and faster, flipping to a new one every other second. Now and then she glanced at Katti and Fredrik to see if they were asleep. But they weren't. After a few minutes, Katti got up and straddled Fredrik. She leaned over him; Ida couldn't see if his eyes were still closed. She was just inches away from them, and if she reached out, she could have shoved Katti off of him, stopped her from pulling off her top, unclasping her bra, and if she had done that then Fredrik wouldn't have kissed Katti, he wouldn't have started moaning softly, the way he always did when he was turned on. But she didn't.

Maybe he doesn't know what he's doing, she thought. *Maybe he's super drunk and thinks it's me, not Katti.* But he should have noticed that those weren't Ida's breasts, Katti was skinnier than Ida, but she still had bigger boobs. Ida knew she should leave. That she had to go, that she had to say something. But she was frozen, it was like her spine had disappeared and she was paralyzed. She was still holding on to her phone when Fredrik put both hands over Katti's breasts and took one nipple in his mouth. Now Katti was moaning. Ida had never heard her make a sound like that, not even as a joke, and now Ida managed to make a fist with the hand that wasn't holding her phone and bring it to her lips, press it hard against her teeth to keep from screaming.

She began to wriggle her way off the sofa. It was hard to get loose because her legs were trapped under Fredrik's, but she had to get out of there before she started to cry, and seriously, they had to know, feel, see that she was there, right?

Why don't they care? Do they want *me to see this? Why can't they wait?*

She tumbled to the floor with a crash and in her fall, she knocked over a glass, which shattered into a thousand pieces on the gleaming stone tile of the living room. But Katti and Fredrik didn't stop, didn't even react, it was like she didn't exist, like she had never even existed. She got up, gulping over and over and trying to swallow back down everything that was welling up, but it was too late, and now she was crying.

She backed up, hit her heel on the threshold, it hurt, and as she left the room she turned around and at first she went the wrong direction and ended up in the kitchen. When she reached the front hall, she shoved her feet into her shoes and slung her backpack over her shoulder. Then she realized she had left her jacket in Katti's room upstairs and didn't know what to do. She couldn't go back in, no way. She could hear them all the way from here, like they were being louder now that she was farther away. Katti called out, it sounded like a plea, Ida couldn't hear what she wanted, didn't want to know.

I'm gonna puke, she thought, swallowing again. *I have to get out of here.*

Katti's bright blue, waist-length down jacket was hanging under the hat rack; it was cold out, so Ida picked it up, but she dropped it like a hot potato when she smelled the perfume. The jacket fell onto Katti's dad's golf bag, which was leaning against the wall. The sounds from the living room were more frantic now.

They know I'm here. They know what they're doing, and they're doing it anyway.

The front door was locked from the inside. It could only be opened with a key, and she didn't know where Katti had put it. She couldn't get out that way. But the door that led into the garage would work. As Ida opened it, she grabbed one of the golf clubs. It was heavy. She closed her hand around its fat iron head, then grabbed the shaft with her other hand and took the club with her to the garage.

She could have run all the way home without stopping, but when she got to the end of Katti's street she turned the other way instead. She didn't know why, but that was where she wanted to go. It was only a mile or two, yet it was another world. She was cold at first, but gradually she got warm. After twenty minutes, she was so out of breath that her throat burned, and she walked the last stretch up to the square. She sat down on one of the benches outside the library.

The square was deserted. Now that she was sitting still, she began to freeze. She should have gone back in to get her jacket. It was way too cold to be without it. Yesterday's snow had melted, but now it was freezing over again. Ida shivered, her clothes wet with sweat, and she had to clench her jaw to keep her teeth from chattering. Suddenly she was exhausted. So terribly exhausted.

She had to call Dad, ask him to pick her up. But what would she say? She couldn't tell him about Fredrik and Katti, she couldn't tell her parents. And she definitely couldn't tell them what she had done. Mom and Dad would hate her if they knew, they would never forgive her.

Then she saw the car. It was approaching so slowly that you could hardly tell it was moving at all. It was on a pedestrian mall where vehicles weren't allowed to go, but there it was anyway. She stared at it as if paralyzed as it crept toward her, pulled up alongside her, and stopped.

"Ida," said one of the two police officers who climbed out. It wasn't a question, and she didn't respond. But one of them had circled around behind her so she couldn't run away. The officer sighed, sounding almost bored.

"Hop in the back and we'll drive you home."

They explained in the car. Katti had called the police. She had told them what Ida had done. She had been "extremely upset."

"It wasn't me," Ida tried, but the police hadn't specifically mentioned the trashed car yet, and the officer in the driver's seat caught her eye in the rearview mirror, looking at her as though he wondered if she was stupid.

The car alarm had gotten stuck on, one of them explained, and the neighbors were almost as upset as Katti, he said. They had seen her running off, had seen which way she was going, and it wasn't as if there were all that many young ladies out and about at this time of night. They hadn't had to search for long.

But first they had taken pictures of the car and confiscated the golf club. Katti and her boyfriend had also said they thought the police should "test Ida" because they thought she must have gone on a "bad trip."

"Do we need to take a blood sample?" one of the officers wondered, but at that Ida burst into tears. She tried to explain how angry she had been at Katti. She tried to explain that Fredrik was *her* boyfriend, not Katti's, and she hadn't taken a thing, she didn't do that stuff, but she could tell they thought she was lying again.

They didn't say anything after that. Ida tucked her hands under her butt. It wasn't cold in the car, but her whole body was trembling, and she felt like she might never get warm.

"I want to go home," she whispered at last.

"Your dad . . . ," one of the officers said. "He's spoken with Katti's dad."

She changed her mind. She didn't want to go home. She would go anywhere else, but not home.

Mom had been crying, she could tell. Ida's older brother, Justus, was sitting next to her on the sofa, his face pale, and her little sister had fallen asleep with her thumb in her mouth. Dad wasn't home.

"Thank you," Mom said when the officers stepped in, Ida between them.

"Hans is in the interrogation room," one of the officers said. "He wanted us to let you know that he's spoken with the owner of the car and will call you as soon as he can." He took a breath. When he spoke about Ida's father, he looked like he was talking about a rock star or some mega-celeb. "Hans will be here when he's done with his interrogation. You know he . . . he can't . . . he's the only one . . . anyway, he'll be here as soon as he can."

"Thank you," Mom said once more. And went back to crying.

She waited for the officers to leave before she turned to Ida. Ida had expected her to be angry, angrier than ever before. She had expected her mother to shout at her, maybe even handle her roughly, shake her, hurt her. But she didn't do any of those things. Mom looked frightened, terrified. Ida wanted her mom to hold her, tell her everything would be fine, tell her not to cry, that she understood, that it wasn't Ida's fault. Or else shout at her, chew her out. But she did none of that, and Ida couldn't cry, because if she did she would have to tell them everything, and even if they thought they already knew what had happened she couldn't tell them about what Fredrik and Katti had done.

As it turned out, she had to be the first to speak. Her voice sounded angry.

"What do you want me to say?"

Hardly any reaction from Mom. But Justus stood up and started yelling.

"You are crazy! You are totally insane."

There was a bang as he slammed his bedroom door. Ida knew why he was upset. Everyone at school would find out what had happened. Justus would suddenly be crazy Ida's poor big brother. If their lives were a movie, she could have told him the whole story, and he would have understood and maybe he would pick a fight with Fredrik, even throw a punch, to show that *no one treats my sister that way.* And he would have said something to Katti to make her feel ashamed and then Ida could have sat with Justus and his guy friends in the cafeteria, and everyone in the whole school would have taken Ida's side, and Katti and Fredrik would have become the outcasts.

But Ida's life was no movie.

Justus wouldn't ask her why. He wouldn't fight Fredrik. Justus was in math club and on student council, and his friends weren't the kind of people anyone wanted to sit with in the cafeteria. Katti had even said so one time, that it was so weird how her dad, the big, buff cop who was, like, all tough, had such wimpy kids. "Are you sure he's your real dad? Maybe your mom slept with some nerd because your dad was working too much." And then she laughed super loud to show that Ida wasn't supposed to be offended: "Can't you take a joke?"

Ida sat down on the sofa. Suddenly she realized there was blood on her hand. *Must be from the broken car windows*, she thought. But Mom didn't tell her to go wash up. She didn't get out the antiseptic and bandages from the medicine cabinet. She just scooped up Ida's little sister and left the room too. Ida was alone. She scraped at the blood with her fingernail and discovered that it hurt.

She went to the bathroom, took off her clothes, and showered. She brushed her teeth so hard that she was spitting blood. As she was standing naked in front of the mirror, her phone screen blinked. Katti had commented on her birthday post. She opened the app.

"You fucking cunt. You are dead to me."

The hours got all tangled up. How long had she been lying in bed with her hand on her phone, letting her mind race? She was waiting for Dad. Even so, she didn't hear the door when it opened, only when it closed again. The double click of the lock turning. The heavy thuds as Dad kicked off his shoes. The faint sound of the hanger, his footsteps up the stairs. He lay down beside her without a word, without touching her. She began to cry.

"Say something." Her voice was hoarse.

"I don't know where to start."

Silence again. Ida's nose was running, her eyes were running, but Dad still wouldn't touch her.

"I don't know how we're going to afford it. I don't even know what it costs to fix a car like that."

"I will—"

"You will nothing."

"Dad—"

"You should be glad he might not press charges. He pointed out that his insurance will only cover the repairs if he files a report, but if we pay for the damages he doesn't have to. If he files a report, you will absolutely be charged. Because you are above the age of criminal responsibility. You understand that, right? You can't..."

Ida was shaking with sobs. Her ears were buzzing. Dad continued.

"But even if he doesn't file a report... it wouldn't surprise me if the prosecutor decides to charge you anyway, just to make a point that there will be no special treatment for me, no sir."

"I know it was wrong," she managed to say. "But..."

"Wrong? No shit, it was wrong." Dad was sort of panting, he seemed out of breath. "We don't have that kind of money—a *Porsche*, Ida? I don't understand—" He lost steam. His voice began to catch. "What happened? What the hell is going on with you?" He cleared his throat and kept going, a little louder now. "You have to talk to me, and you have to start now."

She was still crying. But even so, her rage got the upper hand. Dad didn't have a clue. He didn't want to understand. He just took for granted that this whole thing was her fault.

"Don't interrogate me! I'm not a suspect for you to question!"

"No!" Dad was almost shouting now. He had risen from the bed and was towering over Ida. "I'm your father, dammit. That's what I am. And you will answer me when I ask you questions. Because I'm the one who has to clean up this goddamn mess, and I deserve to know why. So I will ask you again. What happened?"

"I can go back to my old school again, Dad. I'll go back."

He didn't respond to that. He didn't point out that they didn't want her there, that what had happened had only made it even more impossible for her to go back. She knew that, and so did he. But he didn't say so. He simply left the room.

She stayed away from school for a week. On Monday, Mom let Ida call in sick when she said she had a headache, and for the rest of the week she played hooky. But on Friday, a teacher called Mom, and when one of Dad's colleagues found Ida down at Central Station, where she had lain down to rest, she was taken to the psychiatric emergency room. They thought she was hysterical, maybe having a psychotic episode or at risk of suicide. That's what one of them said during intake. Ida protested, but it didn't make a difference. And when she got mad, they asked if she wanted a sedative. Then they found her a bed at a pediatric psych clinic in the city. She got to spend that night at home, but Dad drove her to the clinic the very next day. She would stay for a few days, they said, maybe a few weeks, for evaluation. Ida wondered how they treated psychos like her. Would they tranquilize her, force her to strip naked, take medicine that made her all weird? Would they give her electric shock therapy or look into her eyes with special tools? But she didn't ask. Anything was better than going back to school.

At the clinic, she had to change into hospital clothes and pee in a cup. The nurse asked about the marks in the bends of her knees and on her forearms, but since there were no fresh wounds, the nurse was satisfied when Ida said she didn't do that anymore. The nurse hadn't noticed the ones near her groin. If she didn't shave her bikini line, you could hardly see them.

Ida had a roommate. She said her name was Sanna, and she looked like she wanted to talk. But Ida put her earbuds in and pretended to be listening to music, so Sanna left her alone.

For the first few days, nothing much happened at the clinic. It was nice. Boring, but nice. The grown-ups spoke in soft voices. A teacher came to see her. There were classes, but not regular classes. The teacher helped her do exercises in the textbooks and told her which pages to read. There was no whiteboard in the room where the classes took place, and Ida wasn't allowed to use a computer. They had taken her phone too. It didn't make her as angry as she had expected. She didn't want to know what was happening on her phone anyway.

When she wasn't having class, she spent time in the cafeteria or her room. Sometimes she met with a psychologist, but she didn't have much to say to him; he did most of the talking. And in the afternoons and evenings there were group activities. Ida was one of the chillest kids there, so the staff were nice to her.

It wasn't Ida's fault when all hell broke loose the first time. It was another girl who flipped out. Ida and Sanna had just sat down with their meal when a tray flew across the room like a giant frisbee. The food fell in an arc, a potato landed between Sanna and Ida, and the glass and plate hit the floor behind Ida with a dull thud. They didn't break, because they were plastic. Two big guys in black tracksuits with keys on their belts marched in, picked up the girl, and carried her out. She didn't make a sound.

"Are they allowed to do that?" Ida asked.

Sanna laughed. A tinkling, joyful laugh. But she couldn't be happy, could she? No one was happy here.

"They love strapping kids down here," Sanna said smugly. "You'll see."

After a week had passed, her parents were invited to come in for their first family therapy session. The psychologist who talked more than Ida did had explained what it would be like. He said he would ask them to express their feelings about what had happened, one by one.

"I'll be here to help you listen to each other," he said.

Ida could have told the psychologist what would happen. She knew her parents; he didn't.

Mom will cry, Dad will be furious. Mom will ask questions, Dad will offer explanations no one asked for. Mom will want to hold my hand, Dad will have to stand up now and then so he can breathe, when he gets too mad and has trouble keeping himself under control.

And that was almost exactly how it went. The psychologist didn't even have time to start helping anyone express their feelings. Or read them the doctor's referral or go through her records. Mom cried, and Dad was mad. But this time it wasn't Dad who started explaining things no one asked for—instead, Mom began to speak. Because she had been talking to other moms from Ida's school, and she had talked to her sister and her best friend. Helena's mom had called her, she said, and her voice was shrill and she was talking fast, but the psychologist seemed to be listening, and Ida's mom had met up with Helena's mom, and they'd had a discussion, and now Ida's parents understood what had happened, what had made Ida so angry.

"It's not really any wonder," Mom said. "What happened, I mean. In fact, I don't know what I would have done, myself."

And then Ida's dad spoke, and he was so mad that there were tears in his eyes, and he said, "This doesn't excuse what you did, Ida, there is no excuse for what you did," but it was clear that both he and Mom were talking more to the psychologist than to her; she could tell they thought it was important for him to hear about everything they had found out. She could also tell they no longer thought she was insane, they understood, they understood why she'd done it, and they would forgive her, and there was no explanation that could make what she'd done go away, or make the money for the car magically appear, but this explanation had brought the warmth back into their eyes. They smiled.

"It's going to be okay," Dad said.

"Everything is going to work out," Mom said.

And Ida wanted to smile back. But the psychologist wasn't smiling. He looked annoyed. For several moments he sat there looking at Ida and her parents without saying a word. He picked up his notepad and leafed through it, apparently reading something on a different page than the one he intended to write on today. Then he put the notepad down again. He stroked his chin, as though he were only just realizing he should have shaved. There was an uncomfortable silence as no one said anything. But Mom thought it was about time for him to speak up.

"You agree, don't you? That it's no wonder Ida reacted the way she did?"

The psychologist nodded slowly. But he didn't agree. Not at all. Mom could tell. She looked at Dad, suddenly worried. And Dad put on his cop voice, deeper and slower than his regular voice.

"I would contend that there aren't many adults who could tolerate being provoked to that extent without reacting in some way."

The psychologist ignored him. Instead, he looked at Ida as he began to speak. His voice was soft. He was almost whispering.

"There's no need to stop reacting," he said. "No one is saying you have to stop feeling your emotions."

Ida swallowed. She swallowed and swallowed. She shoved her hands under her thighs. The psychologist went on.

"You're here at the clinic because you lash out when you're angry. At your last school, you hit your friends. You hit your siblings. You hit your mother—"

Mom cut him off.

"That's not..." But that was as far as she got. The psychologist ignored her as well.

"Your parents love you. I'm sure that's why they don't want to believe that what you did, what you've done, is completely unacceptable."

Ida tucked her hands even farther under her thighs. Her chest felt tight. Her ears were buzzing like the spring leaves of a birch tree. She stared at her lap. Her legs were jouncing as though they didn't belong to her anymore. The psychologist's voice hissed through the room.

"You're not here because you have feelings, you're here because you can't control yourself. This isn't the first time you've ended up in a situation you didn't know how to handle. Is it, Ida? And life is full of situations like that. What happened at your friend Katti's place... you didn't hit anyone, you didn't hurt a human being like the last time, but it was still wrong. What your friend and your boyfriend did was also wrong, we all understand why you were angry and sad, but being angry and sad doesn't give you the right to break things. Your anger doesn't give you the right to harm anyone or anything. You need help to understand that, and to stop giving in to violent urges the way you tend to do. And when your parents say they agree with me that your feelings don't excuse your actions, it sounds like they *are* excusing your actions, and I think that's part of why we're here now."

Now it was Dad's turn to try to say something, but the psychologist simply raised his voice.

"Your parents saw to it that you changed schools when your old school began to hold you accountable, when they told you your behavior was unacceptable and you had to start dealing with your problems. I'm sure your parents made that choice because sometimes we believe the best thing for people we love is to let them get away with things. But that's not right. We all need to learn to accept the consequences of our actions. Your parents don't know how to help you. And that's where I come in."

The psychologist never seemed to run out of words.

According to the referral from the emergency room doctor who hadn't wanted to look her in the eye, Ida had "anger management issues." The psychologist at this clinic agreed. Ida didn't feel like those words had anything to do with her. They had nothing in common with the fights she'd gotten into at her old school. Which weren't her fault. Everyone at that school was an idiot. Nor with Katti and the golf club incident. Which also wasn't her fault. Fredrik and Katti had known she was there. But they made out with each other anyway. She hated them.

The psychologist kept talking.

Ida lifted her gaze and saw her dad. He still looked angry. Mom was crying again. It made her look so ugly. Dad stood up. Now, finally, it was his turn to talk, but Ida didn't hear what he said or what the psychologist replied. The words were melting together. They turned into mush, and Mom was talking too now. Everyone was talking over each other, about her. As if they understood. They didn't understand. No one understood. It was all just words. Words words words.

She stood up. She opened her mouth. But no words came out. Her mouth screamed, a wordless scream. That shut them up. The psychologist stood up. He backed away.

She hated him. Her hands freed themselves. And her hands did what they always did when she got like this. Her hands were stronger than she was. They belonged to someone else when they hit, when they tore. Someone better, someone who could be seen and heard, who meant something.

Dad grabbed her, but she got away. She took hold of the psychologist's ugly desk and flipped it. Mom tried to catch her, but Ida's fingers became slicing claws, and they squeezed into hard fists that hit, hit, hit. She saw her mother's lip start to bleed, she hated that her mother bled so easily, nosebleeds, cold sores, scratches, she was so weak. Her parents couldn't stop her, they couldn't do a thing, they were so fucking stupid.

The door was open now. The people in black tracksuits rushed in. They locked her arms and stuck a syringe in one, and she collapsed. They caught her and lay her down.

Her body went to sleep even though she was awake. Her muscles stopped working. But inside she was still strong, still brave. She couldn't scream anymore, but she could be seen and heard and she would never stop. No one could make her stop. This was her. In the instant before the injection put her to sleep, she caught her mother's eye.

Don't worry, honey. Everything will be fine.

She had made Mom understand. It wasn't her fault. Of course they knew that.

LILLAN

CRIMINAL CODE 15:7

The snow has come and gone this week. Winter is having trouble making up its mind, leaving the ground unpredictably slippery. But the darkness has no qualms; it's gathering ever earlier, and the spotlights on the schoolyard have already been on for over an hour when the dismissal bell rings and the children pour out of the vast double doors of the building's main entrance. The parents of the youngest children are there to meet them and take them home. Some older students linger for a few minutes by the smoking corner that's not allowed to be called a smoking corner because the school has a no-smoking policy. A couple of others head down to the bus stop. Three eighth-graders loiter on the footpath that leads down to the metro station, they stand there trying to look like they know what they're doing, but when they get too cold they move on. In the hour that follows, the staff begin to trickle out, sometimes in pairs or small groups. They go to their cars in the staff parking lot or trudge down to the metro.

It's been two hours since her last class ended by the time Sofia emerges. Her mother and father call her

Lillan—Little One—and she has blond hair, a grubby coat, and shoes that are too big.

No one is concerned about her. Not the principal, going through unread emails at his desk; not her Swedish teacher, sitting at the bus stop cradling a backpack and waiting to head home. No one looks up when Sofia stops halfway down the stairs and gazes up at the sky. No one calls *goodbye, see you tomorrow.*

To be fair, the school janitor usually notices that she doesn't go home when she's supposed to, but he doesn't really think about it. He has four years left until retirement. For over forty years he has worked at this school, watching the children come and go. There have been girls like Sofia in every class. He is well aware that she is supposed to go home, but in his mind the school's biggest problem is not students who stay too late, it's all the students who don't come to school in the first place.

On this particular day, the janitor is venturing into the schoolyard to gather up some forgotten playground balls as Sofia leaves. Just as she reaches the middle of the schoolyard, the spotlights go out with a gunshot-like bang. Both she and the janitor jump, but they don't look at one another. He could watch Sofia until she's almost to the pedestrian street that leads up to the big square. But he doesn't. And she pulls up the hood of her down coat, shoves her hands in her pockets, and keeps going.

Once she's turned the corner, she starts running toward the metro station. She really doesn't need to take the train, she lives just a quarter of a mile away, yet she wrestles her SL card from her schoolbag, slips into the station, and steps onto the elevator that leads down to the platform.

She takes a pair of earbuds from her pocket. She found them in the corridor right before lunch. They look like they'll work, but it's hard to know for sure. Now she notices that the tiny holes where the sound comes out are full of yellowish gunk from someone else's ears. After making sure no one is looking, she drops the earbuds over the handrail of the escalator. They slide down and fall to the ground at the bottom. When she reaches the end and gets off, she stomps on them, hard, with her heel. The crunch as the earbuds break sounds like when you squash a fat blowfly with your thumbnail. But there are no blowflies at this time of year. She boards the first train that arrives on the platform. Maybe she won't go far, or maybe she will.

Sometimes the apartment is perfectly silent when Lillan gets home. On those days, she takes the keys from her bag so cautiously that they don't even jingle and opens the front door extra slowly. Even if Mama or Daddy isn't home, it's almost always just the bottom lock that's on, which means she doesn't have to stand on tiptoe to reach. She turns the key until it stops. After that she can open the door, slowly so no one will hear, not even the neighbor who always peppers her with angry questions she doesn't know the answers to.

This evening, when she steps out of the elevator, her door is wide open and it's almost ten o'clock at night. It's not just the front door—every door in the whole apartment is open, letting loud noises pour out from inside. Adult-size shoes and jackets litter the floor of the front hall. Lillan can see all the way into the living room. Her mother is dancing, swinging her hips back and forth and waving her hands in the air. A man is sitting on the sofa watching her, but he's not dancing. Lillan knows the man, his name is Magnus but people call him Mangler. From the other side of the hall, in the kitchen, she can hear her father and some other grown-up voices she doesn't recognize. They're talking way too loud, it sounds like they think they're talking about something important, her dad says the same thing several times, someone answers, "I know, it's fucking awful, it's a damn shame." Exactly what is a damn shame, Lillan doesn't hear.

She pauses. She doesn't want to go in, but she's hungry and there's milk and cereal in the kitchen. But if she goes in there, her father will want her to sit on his lap, and he'll say over and over *look at my little girl, she's getting so big, my little girl, look at her*, and then he'll get tears in his eyes and hug her way too tight.

Lillan is not only hungry but tired. She could go straight to her room. If she walks as fast as she can through the hall, past the kitchen and living room, and into her bedroom, she can lock the door with the key she keeps hidden in a sparkly box in her desk drawer. If she has time to lock the door, none of Mama and Daddy's friends will be able to get in, or Mama and Daddy either. Then she can listen to music and turn up the volume until she can't hear them. If Mama or Daddy wants her to open the door, she can just yell that she's sleeping, adults always like it when children are sleeping. She can have that cereal for breakfast. By then, they'll all be asleep.

A little while later, she's still standing out in the stairwell and trying to decide if she should just turn around and go back to the metro, but it's snowing and she's so tired and her bed is so close, just feet away.

I shouldn't do it, she thinks, *kids my age aren't supposed to be riding the metro all alone at this time of night.* So she makes up her mind, the way you do when you don't have a choice, because everything has to work out, everything has to be fine.

"Just as long as I can get to my room," she murmurs as she steps into the hall and kicks off her shoes without untying them first. She gingerly closes the door behind her. "It's going to be fine. Totally fine."

But that's as far as she makes it.

"Lillan!" Mama's voice cuts through all the other noise. She sounds overjoyed. "Lillan, honey, where have you been?"

At school they call Lillan "Sofia," but Mama always calls her Lillan, not just when she's using that happy voice. Once when she was even younger than she is now, she told a teacher at preschool that they should always say Lillan. "My name is Sofia," she had explained. "But I *am* Lillan." Mama loved that story, had told it a thousand times. And it was true that Lillan felt like her actual name at the time. But now, at school, she doesn't want to be Lillan. At school, she doesn't want to be reminded of who she is.

Now Mama dances out into the hall to greet her, moving her hips in time to the music as she keeps talking.

"My wonderful little Lillan, little cute cutie-pie!"

That's not Mama's early-part-of-the-night voice, but it's not her end-of-the-night voice either. It's the voice she uses when people are listening and she wants to be the fun but attentive mother. When she's had too much to drink, but not yet as much as she's *going* to drink. Mama doesn't get that anyone who might be listening is there to party and really doesn't give a hoot whether she's an attentive mother. All they care about is having fun.

Mama's voice is still for them, not for Lillan.

"Where have you been, sweetheart? I've missed you. Did you have a good day at school?"

Lillan lets her mother hug and kiss her, those wet kisses, those too-tight hugs. When Mama is done, she drags her into the living room. There, Lillan says hello to everyone she sees.

"Hi," she mumbles, even to those who don't greet her back.

"This is my daughter!" Mama shouts, to be heard over the music. "My wonderful, darling daughter."

Mangler, on the sofa, nods and responds: "Hi, daughter."

He raises his bottle of beer in a toast. But Lillan has nothing to toast him with.

Mangler is always at their house when there's something to celebrate, he's one of the people who never misses her parents' parties. His wife is here too, lying on the sofa next to him, but she seems to be asleep. Her feet are in his lap, her back is facing the room, and her face is pressed into one of the sofa cushions. Mama hugs Lillan again and tries to pick her up, but she makes herself heavy and Mama has to let go.

"You're getting so big, little Lillan."

A grain of irritation has found its way into Mama's tone. Lillan hears it and gives in, returning the hug. But it's too late—Mama pushes her away. Lillan holds her breath. But just as suddenly as it appeared, the angry tone is gone. Mama's attention has moved away from Lillan as a new song comes over the speakers, one of her favorites. She tears off her hoodie and tosses it on the sofa, where it lands on Mangler's wife's butt. And there it stays.

"Dance with me, Lillan," Mama cries, reaching out her arms, then throwing them in the air so her tank top rides up and shows her belly. The music thumps in Lillan's chest. Mama spins around and around, faster and faster. She stumbles and has to grab onto Lillan to regain her balance. In doing so, she makes Lillan take a funny step. It hurts.

"I don't want to dance," Lillan mumbles. She whispers as loud as she dares: "I just want to go to my room, Mama, please, please, Mama, to my room, okay?"

But Mama doesn't hear. All she hears is the music, and all she's looking at is Mangler. And he's looking back. He wants to see them dance.

"Two hot chicks is twice as good as one hot chick," he says, chuckling a *heh-heh* from the sofa.

Lillan's mother is delighted to be one of two hot chicks along with Lillan. She grabs Lillan's hands tight. Time to jitterbug. Lillan tries to pull her hands back, but it's hard to refuse to jitterbug with someone so much bigger. Mama twists her arms until she's forced to spin.

Mangler fishes a fresh beer off the floor next to the sofa and opens the bottle with his teeth. He spits the cap out, and it lands a few feet away. Lillan tries to keep up with the dance as best she can. It will only be worse if she leaves the room when Mama is this happy. Because she knows when her mother is at her happiest, she is also on the very edge of flying into a rage.

The music was loud even before Mama's favorite song started. Now Mangler turns the volume up a little higher. Maybe the neighbors will call the police. Sometimes things calm down a little when they do. One time, almost three months ago now, Lillan went to her room, sat behind the bed, dialed the number she had learned by heart, and asked the person who answered to send a policeman to her house because she was scared. She won't do that again, because the policeman took her away in one car and Daddy in another one and Mama started crying and screaming and Lillan had to sleep at another family's house where it smelled like dust and cold fish sticks. She stayed there for three days and had to talk to a social worker lady a bunch of times. The social worker was called Simone and she was the one who drove Lillan home. Lillan had promised first her mother and then her father that she would never call the police again.

"No fucking way that goddamn Frenchwoman is coming in my house again," Daddy said, and that made Mama laugh instead of cry, so Lillan hurried to start laughing too, even though she didn't know why Daddy called Simone a Frenchwoman, because she spoke perfectly ordinary Swedish. The main thing was that they were laughing and pretending the whole incident was just some funny story.

Lillan knows she should pretend this is fun too. But she doesn't want to dance, and the music is giving her a headache. If the neighbors call the police, she can hide in the closet in her room when they come. She can sit at the very back, behind all the clothes Mama has stuffed in there because she doesn't want them anymore. Lillan has hidden back there lots of times. As long as she's not visible, Mama can say she's not home, that she went to Grandma's house and will be staying there for a week.

When the neighbors call, the police don't try very hard to look for her, they don't pick up any clothes, and sometimes they don't even open the closet door—only the door to her room—and they don't check to see if Lillan really is staying with her grandmother.

Mangler has turned the volume up even louder. It can't go any higher now. The speakers rattle in protest, it sounds like something is broken, like something has come loose inside them. But Mama keeps dancing. She sings along to the lyrics and spins Lillan in circles. She doesn't know all that many jitterbug moves, but the ones she does know she repeats over and over. Lillan's head is spinning. *This song will never end*, she thinks. Mangler's wife is still sleeping on the sofa behind them. She has turned over, and now her head is hanging halfway off the cushion. Her mouth is half open.

Lillan's mother is dancing and laughing loudly, and her hand is tightly clasped around Lillan's, but she glances constantly at Mangler. She tosses her hair and one strap of her cropped tank top slips down, and with that Mangler wants to dance too. As he gets up, his wife's legs slide off the sofa and she awakens, sitting up just as Mangler takes Lillan by one hand and her mother around her bare midriff. Now they're both twisting Lillan's arms and forcing her to spin even more in the same direction. But now she's upset, she can't hide it any longer, and tears spill from her eyes, she can't help it, and when Mangler's wife notices she staggers up from the sofa and turns off the music.

"Leave the fucking kid alone," she shouts, loud enough to summon other people into the living room. And when Daddy steps in and sees Mangler with his arm around Mama's waist, he starts yelling too.

"What the hell are you doing?"

From then on, everything happens very fast. Mangler's wife storms out of the living room, grabs a coat and a pair of shoes from the floor of the hall, throws open the front door, and runs out of the apartment and down the stairs. Daddy starts yelling even louder. Mama yells back. When Mangler finally lets go of Lillan's hand, Mama takes her by the arm and hauls her into the kitchen.

"Leave me alone," Lillan's mother sobs. "Leave me alone, I said."

She says it over and over, even though neither Daddy nor Mangler have followed her, and even though Lillan would be happy to leave her alone if she would just let go of her arm. When they reach the kitchen, Mama opens the fridge.

"You need to eat," she tells Lillan. She's still angry and her voice is still thick with tears that want to come out. "You need to eat, you haven't eaten, you need to eat. It's late. Did you eat yet?"

Before Lillan can answer, Mama gets even madder.

"Who the fuck ate all the food?"

She throws open the freezer and all the cupboards, the pantry and the cabinet where they keep plates, and she slams their doors shut again so hard they fly right back open and stay that way.

"Who the fuck ate all our fucking food?" Mama is panicking. "Who the fuck...," her voice breaks and she begins to sob uncontrollably. "You haven't eaten. You need to..."

Lillan knows that there never was any food to eat, just the milk from this morning, and it's actually still right there waiting in the door of the open fridge. But she doesn't point this out. When Mama gets like this, Lillan knows, she needs to scream and cry and you just have to let her do it. But Daddy's three friends who are sitting in the kitchen do respond to her.

"Are you saying I'm a damn thief? Don't fucking call me a thief, I'm no goddamn thief."

"Shit, I'm out of here."

"Fucking bitch. You've lost your damn mind. You trying to start something with me, you goddamn fucking bitch?"

They leave—first the kitchen and then the apartment. They slam the front door behind them so hard that the doorbell goes *brrring* even though no one pressed it. This makes Mama even angrier. She lets go of Lillan's arm and takes something from the fridge and throws it in the direction of the hall, even though Daddy's friends are already out in the stairwell, halfway down the stairs. Lillan can't tell what Mama threw until it hits the doorframe and falls to the floor. It's a can of beer. It gets a dent and releases a trickle of foam.

"Get out, for Christ's sake, get out of here, I don't want you here, Jesus Christ, just go!"

The only one who can hear her is Lillan, but she doesn't have time to respond. Her mother's sobs get louder.

"What am I going to feed Lillan? I can't stand it, she needs to eat, she's my little girl, what am I going to do, I can't take this, it's always the same story, it's always my responsibility, everything is always up to me, no one else, I can't take it."

There is no adult left in the kitchen to hear her, and Lillan tries to take the opportunity to sneak away, but Mama notices. She follows. But instead of grabbing Lillan, she walks past her and back into the living room. Then Lillan must be the one to follow her, because she sees Mama run over to Daddy and start tearing at his clothes. Lillan knows she's the only one who can calm Mama down when she's this mad at Daddy.

"Mama, please, please Mama."

Mangler has taken a few steps back and is staring at Lillan's mother as she tugs at Daddy's sleeves.

"Come on," Mangler says. He's pretending to talk to Lillan's mom, but Lillan knows he actually wants Daddy to hear. "Where the hell did you take off to? We were dancing, you and me."

That only makes it worse. Things start to happen very rapidly, like when you fast-forward a film at quadruple speed. But also time seems to slow down, as if everyone weighs ten kilos more than they did a minute ago.

The four of them are the only ones left in the apartment. Mama, Daddy, Mangler, and Lillan. Lillan could have gone to her room and locked the door. Afterward she will wish she had. Instead, she's there, with Mama and Daddy and Mangler and the knife. She doesn't see it at first, but when she does she's not surprised. She doesn't have time to get scared. She doesn't have time to stop what happens.

It happens too fast for her to feel or do anything. But she sees it all. Very precisely, exactly what happens, as if in slow motion. She sees who is holding the knife first, who grabs it next; she sees the part that means it's all over. And when everything is over, and time is once again quiet and still instead of going too fast, the police arrive. And the ambulance. And a second police car. They move in slow motion too, it seems to Lillan, but she doesn't see them, she only hears them, because she's hiding in the closet, under all the clothes. Nothing sticks out, not even a teeny bit of her foot. The police find her anyway.

A woman with regular clothes, ugly shoes, and a flowering vine tattooed around her wrist came and stood outside the closet.

"Hey, sweetie, could you come out here to see us?" she said.

Lillan climbed out. It was hot and cramped in the closet, and it had been hard to breathe. The smell of what had happened was caught in her clothes.

The woman called over a man in an ambulance uniform. He crouched down and looked in Lillan's eyes and felt her wrists, extended her arms and legs, and ran his palm over her belly, pressing his thumbs there.

"Does anything hurt? Did anyone hurt you?"

The woman stood beside them, watching. When the ambulance man straightened up, she looked at him with a face that meant a question, and the ambulance man nodded and stood up. Then he turned around.

"I'm a police officer," the woman said, taking Lillan by the hand. "Could we sit down?" she asked as she headed for Lillan's bed.

When the ambulance man opened the door to leave her room, Lillan could see right into the living room, she could see plain as day what was happening to Daddy in the next room, even though there were so many people in the way. They were sticking a giant needle into his knee, way bigger than any shot Lillan had ever seen, but he didn't even react, his leg and his whole body were all floppy. The policewoman tried to move Lillan away from the door, guiding her farther into the room.

"Come with me," she said. "Maybe you could show me your toys."

This was the silliest thing Lillan had heard in a long time. The policewoman wasn't a friend who had come over to play. She wanted to get away from her and go to her father, but the woman caught up with her and just grabbed her harder, from behind, pinning both arms and lifting her off the floor, and Lillan kicked and they carried Daddy off on a stretcher and then she saw Mangler on the sofa, right where his wife had been sleeping, he had buried his head in his hands, which were inside brown paper bags now, and she couldn't see his face anyway because a police officer was in the way. And she couldn't see the knife either.

"There, there," the policewoman said, and she lugged Lillan away from the door and all the way to the bed and pressed her down onto it.

"There was a knife," Lillan said once she caught her breath. Because the police had to take it away, the knife was somewhere nearby and it had to go away and when she thought about the knife she started to cry.

"I know," the policewoman said. "I know there was. But we have it now."

Then everything was quiet. The door to Lillan's room was closed again, and only the low buzz of voices remained. She curled up on the bed, trying to make herself as small as possible. She screwed her eyes shut. The policewoman kept a hand on her shoulder. She spoke to someone who entered the room.

"Sofia," she said after a while. "Can you sit up?"

Lillan did. Now there were three grown-ups in her room. The policewoman and the cop with a uniform and another lady, she had tears in her eyes and was squeezing her own hands, one finger at a time, spinning her rings, feeling her wristwatch, bracelet, fingernails. The policewoman took out her phone and set it down in front of her.

"I need to ask you a few questions," she said to Lillan. But then she didn't ask any. "I am recording this."

The lady sat down on a chair, it was a chair from the kitchen and they had carried it in. The policewoman sat down next to Lillan on the bed without asking. Lillan didn't want her to sit there. She didn't want anyone to sit on her sheets. They were dirty. But she didn't say anything.

Maybe you could show me your toys? It seemed the policewoman had forgotten about that question. Lillan understood, of course, that they didn't care about her toys. But she did have some. Even if she didn't have any friends to come to her house and play with them.

The policewoman sitting on Lillan's bed rested a hand on her knee. Lillan recoiled and shifted away. Daddy was going to the hospital in an ambulance with a needle in his leg and wouldn't work anymore, not at any job. Lillan's mother used to work at a hospital. But then she got sick and didn't have to work anymore. Lillan's father was never sick. "I haven't had a cold since the eighties," he liked to say, and Lillan knew "the eighties" was a very long time ago, hardly anyone she knew was old enough to remember what went on back then.

"Is my daddy dead?" she asked. But really, she didn't have to ask.

"Sofia . . . ," the policewoman said, because the police always used her real name, and she moved closer again and took Lillan's hand and looked at it. "Your daddy . . ."

Lillan could tell from her voice that she was going to tell the truth. She was surprised. Grown-ups usually weren't honest when it came to serious stuff. She snatched her hand back as fast as she could. She didn't want to be touching the policewoman when she learned what she already knew.

"My name is Lillan," she said instead. "I'm Lillan, not Sofia."

A drunken stabbing doesn't make the news. No one cares. A wounded wolf gets more media attention, or at least it does if it limps onto a playground somewhere in Stockholm County. But Lillan was given a sandwich and a glass of milk at the police station. Everyone she met said they were sorry.

"Our condolences," they said. It made her feel almost like an adult; she didn't think people said this to children very often.

Lillan's mother had been taken to the same police station, the policewoman told her. But she wasn't allowed to be in the room when they talked to Lillan.

"We need to be able to talk to you in peace and quiet," the policewoman had said. But it wasn't *that* quiet. There was a camera in one corner. The Frenchwoman had joined them; she was sitting across from Lillan. She looked agonized. Her dark pink handbag hung from the back of the chair. It was the same handbag she'd carried each time Lillan saw her. Sometimes she would draw it close and press it to her chest, as though it contained her deepest, darkest secrets and she was afraid they might fall out and betray her. But not today. Today it just hung there, light and empty, like a scrap of flesh from a slit belly.

Once the questions began, it felt like they would never stop coming.

"Can you tell us what you did today? Start from the beginning, this morning, if you like."

Lillan had brought Mama a cup of coffee in bed before she went to school. She had used the cold coffee that was left in the pot and warmed it up in the microwave. It bubbled and was scalding hot, but she added some milk. Mama said *put the mug there*, and Lillan knew she meant on the floor next to the bed.

Daddy was lying next to Mama, sleeping, and Lillan knew what would happen if he woke up. It was Mama's birthday. Mama's birthday was an event Daddy thought "called for a celebration." And of all Lillan's least-favorite things, Mama and Daddy's parties were maybe the very worst. Soon she went to school. She had stayed there all day, had gone to every class except gym.

Lillan liked to wait in the bathroom for as long as she could after the last bell. The bathroom always smelled bad at the end of the school day, there was wet toilet paper on the floor, with shoe prints on it, and sometimes there were streaks of poop inside the toilet bowls. But Lillan didn't mention any of this to the police.

"It's Mama's birthday today," she said instead.

"Mmhmm," said the officer who was asking the questions. "I know. Did you and your father celebrate your mama this morning?"

Lillan nodded.

"A little," she said. "Then I went to school."

"Do you like school?"

"It's okay."

"And what did you do after school?"

"Home."

"You went home?"

"Mmhmm."

They lived on the third floor; their balcony had a view of other apartment buildings down the hill from theirs. Lillan had her own bedroom, but the only view from there was the building next door. They hadn't lived there very long; they usually didn't stay in one place for much more than a year. Daddy got mad at pain-in-the-ass neighbors, and Mama got mad at Daddy for being a pain-in-the-ass himself.

"Were you at school all day?"

"Mmhmm."

And that was true. She hadn't left school, not even during the double gym hour, although she did spend that part of the day hiding in the auditorium, where she sat on the floor and played on the iPad she had borrowed from the library and never returned. The auditorium had really good wi-fi, and when the cleaners came to mop the floor they never made a fuss when they found her sitting there. They just swabbed their damp, long-haired mops around her as if she were a heavy flowerpot that no one could move.

Lillan could tell that the police didn't believe her when she said she had come straight home after school.

"I went straight home," she repeated.

"Did you really, Sofia? Think back."

"Mama wants me to, she wants me to come straight home after school. And so does Daddy. Daddy says it's very important. It's important, Daddy says. Daddy wants..."

When she told them what Daddy wanted, they looked down. The policewoman cleared her throat and pretended she had to write something on a piece of paper.

"Are you doing all right? We can take a break if you'd like."

Lillan shook her head.

"Naw."

The policewoman studied her for a moment. There was a little wrinkle on her forehead, but then she looked back down at her papers.

"Can you tell me what it was like at home when you got there?"

"There was a party."

"Hmm."

"For Mama's birthday."

"Mmhmm."

"Mama was happy."

"Okay?"

"I think Daddy was happy too, at first. But I don't know."

"That's okay, you don't have to know everything. Who else was there, besides your parents? Anyone you knew?"

"I didn't know him."

"...Who...?"

"The man Daddy got mad at, I didn't know him. Maybe I've seen him before, because maybe he has been to our house before, but I don't know him."

Lillan didn't want to talk about Mangler. She didn't want to tell them that he'd called her a "hot chick"; she didn't want to say that his wife had been there too, but at first she was asleep and then she left; she didn't want to talk about him even for a single minute.

"Mmhmm," the policewoman said in a sad voice. "Okay."

But then Lillan thought she should share what she knew after all. That she should tell them everything they wanted to know all at once, as fast as she could, so they would stop asking questions, but when she started to do it the tears came. Tears always seemed to come out of nowhere, never when you wanted them to, hardly ever when you thought they would.

"Daddy wants...," she whispered. "Daddy doesn't want...," but she didn't know what to say next.

The Frenchwoman leaned over the table and placed a hand on her arm. And Lillan got mad.

"Daddy doesn't fight. It wasn't his fault."

She didn't know why she said that. No one responded. They just looked at her, their eyes sad. Lillan hated them for it.

This wasn't the first time she'd seen her father in a fight. It wasn't even the first time she'd seen her mother fight. They fought. It happened. Sometimes they fought with each other. Sometimes Daddy fought with other people. Mama had fought with other people too, a few times, but not as many times as she had fought with Daddy and definitely not with as many people as Daddy had fought with. When they argued with each other, it usually ended with Mama crying and Daddy walking out and not coming back for a few days.

Mama and Daddy didn't fight with her, but that was probably because Lillan didn't fight with them. They had hit her a time or two, but definitely not very hard. Should she mention that? Not right now. Maybe later, some other day.

"Where am I going to live now?" she said instead. And when no one answered, she added, "I don't have a grandma." And, softer, so no one would hear: "Either grandma." She hoped they would believe her.

The policewoman didn't respond; instead, she looked at the Frenchwoman. Presumably she figured it was up to her to say *now, sweetie, you'll be staying with another nice family for a few days, while we try to figure out what happened to your daddy*. But the Frenchwoman pretended not to catch on. So the policewoman continued:

"We don't quite know yet. We need to have another talk with your mother, so she'll probably have to stay with us for a while. Your grandma, your father's mother..."

Lillan startled. She shook her head wildly. The tears came back.

"I don't want to..."

The policewoman hesitated.

"But she couldn't... We'll find a good place for you, I promise."

"Am I going to go to school?" Lillan asked next. She knew she wouldn't, but she wanted the police to say it out loud so there wouldn't be any discussion later on.

But the policewoman asked, "Do you want to?" Lillan found that a little strange.

"You can stay home from school tomorrow," said the Frenchwoman.

"We'll pick this up again tomorrow," the policewoman said when Lillan started crying for the third time. "There's no rush, you need to get some sleep, we'll talk more tomorrow."

The mother of the family that was going to take care of her while Mama stayed with the police was called Annelie. She was the only member of the family who was awake when Lillan arrived. Her hair was mussed, and she smelled like apples and brushed teeth. She looked grave as she said hello to Lillan. When she looked at the Frenchwoman she seemed annoyed, as if she were disturbing them. The Frenchwoman didn't come inside and only said, "Well, this is Sofia, she's called Lillan and I bet she's very tired, it's been a long night." Annelie nodded. After the Frenchwoman left, the expression on her face looked more normal.

"You haven't had any dinner," was all she said. She didn't sigh or look like she was about to start crying.

Lillan didn't mention the sandwich she'd been given at the police station, and Annelie took her to the kitchen, sat her down on a chair, and warmed up gluey macaroni and meatballs in a saucepan.

"Would you like ketchup?" she asked as she set a deep plate in front of Lillan. And she poured a big glass of milk and didn't call out that Lillan had taken way too much ketchup, so much that you couldn't see the white macaroni noodles underneath anymore. The meatballs didn't taste like the ones at school.

When she was done eating, she was given a towel folded into a square. On top of it was a brand-new toothbrush.

"There's toothpaste in the bathroom, on the sink," Annelie said, and then she let her go into the bathroom by herself.

Lillan squeezed toothpaste onto the brush, then rinsed it off under the faucet. She didn't like to brush her teeth. When she came out, Annelie was waiting for her. Lillan followed her into a room with three beds. Another child was in one of the beds already. A nightlight glowed in one corner, and Annelie sat on the floor next to Lillan's bed after she crawled under the covers.

"If it's all right with you, I'll sit here for a little while," she said. It wasn't a question.

Lillan fell asleep almost immediately. The sheets smelled like apples too.

When she woke up the next morning, Annelie was in the kitchen with her hair freshly washed and a muffin top that didn't fit inside her jeans. At the table where Lillan had eaten the meatballs sat two children, a boy who was much smaller than Lillan, maybe six, and a girl who was starting to grow breasts and already had zits. A man was sitting there too. He was even fatter than Annelie. The man was the only one who said hello. His name was Göran and he was in a hurry; he took a cup of coffee to go and went out to a white van that said "Göran Jansson, Plumber" on the side. He backed out of the driveway and waved before pulling out into the street. The boy waved back. The girl was eating toast with a ton of cheese and the boy was stirring and stirring a bowl of cereal and the cereal had turned to mush.

Annelie didn't ask whether Lillan was hungry today either.

"Do you like cheese?" was all she said. And when Lillan didn't say no, she said, "Have a sandwich. We aren't in a huge rush, but we need to hurry a little."

Then she set a glass of milk on the table and sat down next to it with a cup of coffee. This was the first time Lillan had ever used a cheese slicer, but Annelie didn't mention it, didn't shoot her an odd look, even though her slice of cheese turned out more like a lumpy blob.

First they dropped the boy off at daycare. They just let him into the yard there, and he waved without turning around.

"Bye, Mom," he called. He didn't say anything to Lillan. Then Annelie said they were going to the police station. In the car on the way, Lillan asked what the children's names were.

"Kristine and Petter," Annelie said.

"Are they your real kids?"

At first, Annelie just smiled. Lillan assumed that meant she was annoyed by the question. *How am I supposed to know?* Lillan thought. *After all, they don't look like you.* But then Annelie answered, and she didn't sound angry—kind of the opposite.

"Petter has lived with us since he was two weeks old. When his first mother died, we got to adopt him, Göran and me. Kristine stays with us pretty frequently, at least a few days a month ever since she was four, but sometimes she lives with her mother, Maria. But this time she's been with us for seven months in a row, and she'll be staying for at least..." It sounded like Annelie didn't want to say more, but then she went on. "Maria, her mom, is in prison, and Kristine can visit her every Saturday and Sunday if she wants to. She'll stay with us until her mother gets to move home again and has settled in and everything."

Annelie parked the car and they went to the reception desk for a voucher, which Annelie placed on the dashboard. Then they went back into the station. They had to go through a security checkpoint, and Annelie set her purse on a conveyor belt. On the other side of the checkpoint sat a police officer who greeted her as though he knew her. Then they went into the same room they'd been in the day before, and waiting inside were the same people Lillan had already met. She would have liked for Annelie to stay, but she didn't. She just said, "Bye, see you later, I'll be back to pick you up," and then she left. But not before she pulled the policewoman aside by the door and muttered something. Lillan couldn't make out what it was but knew it was about her.

"Where is my mama?"

Lillan didn't know why she'd asked, because the fact was she knew exactly where her mother was. But no one else was saying anything and that made her nervous and she couldn't think of anything else to say.

"Your mama is fine," the policewoman replied. "She wanted me to tell you hi and that she misses you, but she has to stay with us for a while until we figure out exactly what happened to your father. But don't worry. You can see her soon."

Lillan didn't ask any more questions about Mama after that. She would have liked to ask if Mama really said she missed her, because she didn't believe it. And she would have liked to say that her mother obviously was *not* fine, because wasn't she in jail, screaming and crying and sad about Daddy? And maybe a little bit sad about Lillan too. But she didn't bring up any of this. It would only have made everything worse.

The policewoman flipped through her stack of papers for a while. Lillan said yes please to a glass of juice and took a cookie from a platter in the middle of the table. She ate it as though she were a cartoon mouse—nibbling a little at a time, around and around, so it got smaller and smaller until there was just a tiny piece of the center left. She popped the rest into her mouth. Then she took another cookie.

"I know this is hard," the policewoman said after Lillan had finished her third cookie. "But I'd like you to tell me what was going on when the fight started."

Lillan didn't respond. Instead she reached for another cookie.

"Do you think you can do that?"

At first, Lillan didn't respond to this either. After the awkward silence grew too long, she said, "Mama and I went to the kitchen when they started fighting."

"Mm," said the policewoman, nodding. "Who started fighting?"

"Daddy and..." She shoved the whole cookie into her mouth.

"Do you know who else was in the room when the two of you left?"

Lillan shrugged.

"Everyone had gone home, I think."

"But your dad wasn't alone in the living room, was he?"

Lillan shrugged.

"He was there too."

"What did you do in the kitchen, you and your mama?"

Lillan shrugged again.

"Then we went back by Daddy."

The officer nodded.

"Was your daddy fighting with someone then?"

"Mangler," Lillan said.

The officer looked up. Lillan had forgotten that she'd said she didn't know his name. But now it was too late to take it back.

"Your daddy was fighting with Mangler?"

Lillan nodded. But that was all. She didn't want to talk about the rest. Why would she need to? Kids shouldn't have to talk about stuff like this.

"Ask him," she managed.

The officer had moved her chair closer to Lillan. Her voice was soft now, as if they were going to whisper secrets to each other.

"We are."

"And Mama?"

"We're asking your mama too. But unfortunately, we need to talk to you as well. So everyone who was there can tell us what they saw."

"What did he say? What did he say he did?"

"I'd like you to tell me what you saw. Can you do that, Lillan? I know it might feel scary, but it's really important for you to tell us."

Lillan knew it was important. She knew why they didn't want to tell her what Mangler had said. Grown-ups told lies too, and shifted the blame. They did it all the time. Her daddy was always saying that someone else had spent all his money, or that someone had stolen the things Mama was looking for, things Mama knew Daddy had sold. Mangler was definitely the same. Mangler must have gone to jail tons of times—maybe even more times than Daddy. But just because he had gone to jail before didn't mean he wanted to go back. So why would he tell the truth? And why would the police believe Mama's story, since they already knew she lied about almost everything? But Lillan didn't want to. She really didn't want to talk about it. And she hated to cry, and now the tears were coming again. So she didn't say any more, she didn't say a word, not even in a soft secret-voice.

That evening, they sat in the den together. They ate chips. The kids each had their own bowl; Petter's was the smallest. Göran and Annelie shared a bowl. Göran mostly dozed and Kristine checked her phone four times a minute. Petter wasn't looking at the TV either, just his iPad, but he sat on the sofa with them and no one asked Lillan any questions about her mother or her dead father. She wanted to ask Petter about the game he was playing, because she'd never seen it before, but she couldn't because Petter was just a little kid.

"How old are you?" she asked instead.

Petter held up five fingers. She definitely couldn't play his game. It was for little babies.

At ten, Annelie said it was time for bed. Kristine and Lillan shared a room. Petter had a bed in there too, but he had fallen asleep on the sofa and Göran carried him to his and Annelie's room. Kristine didn't have to turn out the light, she was allowed to stay up later than Lillan, and the music coming from her headphones was super loud. But Annelie kissed her goodnight anyway and tucked her in, then sat on the floor next to Lillan's bed again.

"Is there anything you want to talk about?" she asked.

But Lillan shook her head. And Annelie didn't say more, just sat there until Lillan fell asleep, even though it took a very long time.

The next day, they hadn't put out any cookies at the police station. But instead there were crayons and paper on the table. The Frenchwoman was wearing different clothes.

"You can draw, if you want to," the policewoman said, and then she went out in the hall to talk to Annelie.

Lillan would have loved to know what they were talking about. But she couldn't hear. So she reached for the crayons and drew a horse's head. She had seen the other girls in her class do that. But even so, she was awfully bad at it, especially making the ears look like real horse ears.

"What's the best part about being a police officer?" Lillan asked when the policewoman came back. Grown-ups liked it when you asked them questions that let them talk about themselves. "Is it fun putting people in jail?"

Right away she knew she shouldn't have said that last part. The policewoman was suddenly very serious and quiet. It took her a long time to answer.

"Being in jail doesn't have to be terrible, actually. I know you don't believe me, but it's possible to get help with certain things when you're . . . and sometimes it can . . . you'll get to see your mom again soon. I promise. Whatever happens, I promise you'll get to see your mom."

Lillan didn't talk about what had happened to her father on that day either.

On the third night, a bad dream woke her up. The nightmare left her sweaty and out of breath. Once her heart stopped pounding, she got up to pee. When she reached the bathroom, she could hear Göran and Annelie. They were in bed, talking. Lillan didn't turn on any lights and sat down as close to the wall as she could to listen. She realized that Annelie was talking about her parents. She had a colleague who knew Lillan's mother, she said. They had worked together, back when Lillan's mother still had a job.

The voices were perfectly clear, almost as if they were in the same room. "Always on something," Annelie said. "She put the patients in serious danger. Stole anything she could get her hands on that would get her high. Didn't even bother to hide it. She would take the patients' opioids herself and let them suffer. Four times, she was reported. But each time, the inquiry was closed." She sounded angry. "Can you explain this to me? Can you tell me why Lillan was still living at home? Is that normal? Was it in her best interest to stay there, with parents like that? No. No child should have to..."

Lillan moved her ear away from the wall. She didn't want Annelie to be mad at Mama. She sounded sad too, but maybe she wasn't, Lillan wasn't sure. Her voice grew softer now, but Lillan could still hear clearly as Annelie told Göran what the police had told her.

"Are they really allowed to tell you that stuff?" Göran asked.

"Of course not," Annelie said.

Then they talked about Mangler. Annelie thought Lillan was afraid of him, and that's why she didn't want to talk about what had happened.

"Or maybe," Göran said, "he's not lying."

With that, Annelie's voice got so low Lillan could hardly make out her words.

"I don't want...," she whispered. "She can live here, with us. Right?" Then it sounded like she was crying. She blew her nose, then continued, her voice firmer now. And that was when she said it.

"In some ways it would be a lot easier," she said, "if it was Lillan's mother who did it."

Lillan was so shocked she almost bolted off the floor. Annelie's voice wasn't as clear now that Lillan wasn't leaning against the wall, but she still heard everything.

"Why does it have to be this way, Göran? Why do those bastards have to either die or end up in prison before we can stop them from ruining their kids' lives? How come we can't help until it's too late?"

The next morning, Annelie looked tired. Lillan got bread and butter and cheese and made a sandwich all by herself. The slice of cheese came out perfectly, so she cut another. It was almost as good.

The police didn't know who had killed her father. Both Mangler and Mama had cuts from the knife; both Mangler and Mama had held it. The police had told all of this to Annelie, and Annelie had told Göran, and now Lillan knew too. But they didn't know the rest of it.

The only ones who knew the truth, aside from Mama and Mangler, were Lillan and Daddy, and Daddy was dead so he couldn't tell, and what Mama and Mangler told the police didn't matter, because the police didn't trust them.

"Can you finish that in the car?" Annelie asked. She cupped Lillan's cheek. "We need to go. I'm sorry, it's my fault, I woke up late."

Lillan's cheek felt cold when Annelie took her hand away. Lillan got up as fast as she could and followed Annelie to the front hall. It was only a few yards from the door to Annelie's car, but even so she stuck her hand in Annelie's, and Annelie let her. When Lillan got in the car, Annelie leaned over her to make sure the seatbelt was fastened properly.

"Do I have to go home?"

It was the fourth day, and they were in the car on the way back from the police station.

Annelie didn't say anything for a moment. Lillan could tell from her voice that her smile wasn't real.

"When your mama is allowed to come home," she said, "You can live with her again."

This was the first time she pretended not to understand what Lillan was really asking.

"But do I have to?" Now she was whispering. Annelie didn't answer. Lillan could see her face in the rearview mirror; she was staring intently at the road.

Lillan's mother often pretended she didn't understand. Or that she didn't hear. But Lillan didn't want to think about her mother anymore.

"We need your help," the police had told her. "We need to be sure we know what happened."

They didn't ask if she needed help. They didn't ask what she wanted most of all. They just wanted to know all about the knife. But Daddy was dead, and nothing Lillan said could change that.

If she told the truth, Annelie would never reheat dinner for her if she got home after everyone else had eaten, she wouldn't get to watch TV with her very own bowl of chips, and maybe Mama would get help paying the rent, but probably not; and maybe Mama would buy the cereal Lillan liked, even though Daddy was the one who always used to do that, and maybe Mama wouldn't want to party anymore now that Daddy was dead, but she liked having fun and always had, even when Daddy wasn't there and even when Lillan cried. Her mama didn't smell like apples. She never sat next to Lillan's bed until she fell asleep.

"Are you all right, sweetheart?"

The car was stopped at a red light. Annelie met Lillan's gaze in the rearview mirror. Her eyes looked worried. When the light turned green, she reluctantly focused her attention back on the road.

"We're almost home," she said. "We're having chicken stew with rice for supper. Do you like that?"

Lillan nodded. She had never eaten chicken stew.

"I love it. It's super yummy."

The next morning, Göran drove Lillan to the police station. He asked her to put some good music on the car stereo and handed her his phone so she could pick whatever she wanted on Spotify. But when she put on her favorite song, no more than two seconds passed before Göran whimpered, "Are you nuts? This isn't music."

At first Lillan was afraid he was mad for real. But then she saw on his face that he wasn't angry, he was laughing. He groaned like he was in pain.

"Make it stop, Lillan! Stop pulling that cat's tail! This is animal cruelty!"

When he put on his playlist instead, and began to sing along to lyrics about someone with golden-brown eyes, it was Lillan's turn to laugh; she couldn't help it. She hadn't laughed since what happened with Daddy, and when she realized as much, she stopped. But she was still smiling when Göran parked the car and the music ended.

"I thought we could talk a little about Mangler," the policewoman said after they sat down in the interview room and the camera was on.

"I think it was Mama who took the knife from the kitchen," Lillan replied.

She didn't say so to lie, or to make up a story. She just wanted to find out what would happen if she said so. She didn't say a word about the other part. Not a word about what happened in the living room. She just said that Mama might have opened one of the kitchen drawers and taken out the knife before the two of them joined Mangler and Daddy.

At first, nothing happened. They all just got very quiet. The policewoman didn't even look up from her papers. The Frenchwoman cleared her throat and shifted her chair, but she didn't say anything.

I'm not making it up, Lillan thought. *Maybe she did, I might remember wrong, I don't know, maybe I just didn't see.*

Then they recovered; the policewoman moved a little closer to Lillan and cleared her throat.

"Did you see it? Did you see your mother take the knife from the drawer?" she asked.

"Maybe," Lillan said.

"Then what did she do with it?" the policewoman wondered.

But Lillan wouldn't say more; that would have to do.

For the first time that night, she had a dream about Daddy getting stabbed in the stomach and dying. It was a weird dream. Because right before she woke up, she was the one holding the knife. And she thrust it into Mama's stomach, which was very soft, but there wasn't any blood at all. Mama laughed her bestest laugh. And then Lillan stabbed the knife into Mangler's stomach and then she realized it was Daddy's stomach and when she pulled it out, Daddy laughed the way he did when he was really happy, and the laugh was catching, so when she woke up Lillan felt a laugh bubbling in her throat and she had to gulp hard and cough to keep it from coming out.

On the fifth day, Lillan was driven back and forth to school in a taxi. On the way home, the taxi driver had the radio on, but it wasn't music, just talk about stuff she didn't want to listen to. She sat in the back seat, wishing she could listen to music on her phone, but that only worked when there was wi-fi, because Mama hadn't paid the bill. So instead she looked out the window. It was as dark as night, and it was raining, but only a little.

"Goodbye," Lillan said to the driver when he pulled up in the driveway.

He rolled down the window, stuck his hand out, and waved in response. Once she had been let into the house, he backed onto the road and drove off.

"How was it?" Annelie wondered. "Was it okay?"

Her voice was cottony soft.

When Lillan shrugged, Annelie rubbed her shoulder, and that was soft too. Lillan didn't startle, didn't walk off, let Annelie keep her hand there. It was as if the cotton had moved from Annelie's voice into Lillan's body, and it settled around her heart and in her belly and made it easy to breathe.

Both Petter and Kristine were at the table when they walked into the kitchen. Kristine moved over so Lillan could sit in the far corner of the kitchen bench. *That's my spot now*, she thought. Supper was fish sticks. But not straight, skinny ones; these ones were knobby and fat and much bigger than the storebought ones. It smelled like melted butter and Lillan could tell the food was good before she even tasted it.

"Have some salad," Annelie said.

But then Petter and Kristine got mad at each other and the cotton disappeared. Lillan didn't know why, but she noticed these things, she could sense when someone was about to yell and fight before it happened. Kristine was angrier, but Petter hit first. Before Lillan could take a single piece of lettuce, he stood up on his chair and swung his little fist and then he grabbed Kristine's hair and pulled.

Kristine shrieked. Lillan clapped her hands over her ears as tightly as she could. Kristine shrieked even louder, and Lillan wanted to get away, disappear, be gone as fast as possible, but she was trapped.

Annelie rushed to the table. She took hold of Petter's hand and forced him to let go of Kristine's hair.

"Stop it," she said. Lillan knew that a grown-up who didn't sound mad could still be super mad. She just wanted to get out. But everyone was in her way, so she cowered in the corner of the bench, curling herself into a little ball.

Kristine shouted, "He's crazy, I hate him!" and Annelie picked Petter up, but Lillan didn't know what else Annelie was about to do and she had to get away, away, away, and she tucked her knees closer to her chest, and now she could hear someone else screaming, screaming like a maniac, and Lillan was on the floor under the table and the screaming was getting louder, she could see arms reaching under the table and grabbing her body to pull her out, and she tried to get away, but she couldn't. She couldn't get away no matter how much she flailed, and the arms were much stronger than her, and they pulled her out and picked her up off the floor and carried her away, out of the kitchen and into the bedroom.

Lillan kicked and kicked, she cried and screamed, she realized the person screaming was her, the crazy screams were coming from her, but the arms held her so tightly, so firmly, and soon there were no more screams, just tears, and Annelie was hugging her to her chest and Lillan leaned against her soft body and let Annelie's arms embrace her, brush away sweaty strands of hair, and when her sobs grew softer she heard Annelie mumbling in her ear, "sweetheart, oh my sweetheart, everything is okay, you're safe, don't be scared, everything is all right now," and Lillan's body went slack as if every muscle had stopped working, and Annelie's lips were breathing *you're safe, everything is fine*, and Lillan breathed back *don't go, don't go, please don't go, don't go*, and Annelie rocked her in time with her heartbeat *I'm not going anywhere, everything is fine, you're safe.*

When the very last sobs had left her, Lillan fell asleep. With her clothes on.

She woke up because she was too warm under the heavy comforter, and she went to the den.

When Annelie saw her, she lifted the blanket that covered her lap and Lillan sat down on the sofa between Annelie and Göran. Annelie cupped a hand over her head and pressed her lips to her forehead. Lillan let her. She didn't pull away; she rested her head on Annelie's chest.

Göran went to make her a sandwich. Kristine put down her phone.

"It was nothing against you," she said. "I'm sorry... it was just Petter, he was annoying me so much."

"It's okay," Lillan said. Her voice was hoarse.

"They argue like that sometimes," Annelie said, her hand still on Lillan's head. "But it's not dangerous. Silly and unnecessary—" she looked up at Kristine, who rolled her eyes— "but not dangerous. Just the kind of bickering that happens between siblings. It's not dangerous, I promise."

Lillan thought about her dream. In some ways, it was as strange as what had really happened. Because the more she didn't think about what had happened, the less she remembered. Where had the knife come from? Did she know? And did Mangler really take the knife from Daddy and stab him in the stomach? It all happened so fast. Maybe she hadn't been watching the whole time, maybe she had looked away, or maybe she had seen something completely different from what she thought. What if she had dreamed it all? What if her eyes had been closed the whole time, and she didn't see anything at all? Or what if what she saw was wrong?

The next day was Saturday. All five of them went to the shopping center to get groceries. Göran and Annelie each took a cart. Petter was too big to fit in the child seat, but Göran lifted him into his cart. Kristine dragged Lillan over to the makeup aisle. Lillan got to pick out her own shampoo. Kristine grabbed a bottle next to it.

"You need conditioner too. You can't use mine."

That evening, Lillan said she wanted to talk to the police. It was late, but Annelie called the policewoman anyway. She wanted Lillan to come in early the next day, even though it was a Sunday. Göran drove her there. He waved to her as she entered the interview room.

"I'll wait here," he said as the policewoman closed the door.

Lillan didn't even get a glass of juice before she began to talk. She ignored the crayons; she didn't say hello to the

Frenchwoman. But as soon as the policewoman sat down and started the video recording, she said what she had to say all at once so she couldn't change her mind.

She looked at the policewoman, stared her right in the eye without blinking. She didn't look at the Frenchwoman, but she could hear her gasp as if she was shocked by what Lillan was saying, as if what she was saying was worse than what had already happened.

"My mama picked up the knife," Lillan said. "Mangler had it first, but he dropped it and Mama picked it up."

And as she told her tale, it felt more and more like it was exactly what had happened, and not that other stuff.

"Mama picked up the knife from the floor and she stabbed Daddy even though Daddy was shouting *no, stop* so she wouldn't do it, but she did it anyway and she killed him. I saw it. I saw her do it."

The grown-ups nodded slowly. The policewoman hesitantly cleared her throat. She shot a quick glance at the camera on the ceiling, as if to reassure herself it was working.

"That must have been difficult to see."

"Yeah."

"Were you scared?"

"Super scared."

And now they were both nodding. Lillan's words had caught up with them. The policewoman's voice became firmer.

"Can you tell me exactly where you were when your mother did that?"

"I was next to her."

"Okay. Were you sitting down or standing up?"

"I was sitting on the floor because someone shoved me, but then I got up and I was standing, I pulled on Mama to make her stop, but she didn't."

"Do you think you . . . ?"

"I saw it all." Lillan knew what they wanted her to say. "I was right next to her and I saw and I'm not forgetting, I remember. I remember exactly what happened."

The policewoman wasn't sure what to say.

"I want to go home now," Lillan said, as plainly as she could. "I want to sleep."

"But . . . ," the Frenchwoman ventured, sounding hesitant. "You can't . . ."

"We can take a break if you want to," the policewoman said.

"I don't want a break." Lillan was crying now. "I want to go home."

The Frenchwoman stood up. She opened the door and called Göran over. He appeared in the room so quickly that Lillan wondered if he had been waiting right outside. Without asking for permission, he sat down next to Lillan and took her hand. She cried even harder.

"Hey," he said softly. "Would it be okay if you came home with me instead? If you stayed with us for a little longer?"

Lillan nodded. She realized she had said the wrong thing. That the grown-ups didn't understand what she meant.

"Mmhmm." She raised her voice. "That's what I want."

Göran turned to the Frenchwoman.

"Perhaps we can agree that this isn't the right time to move her."

"Absolutely," the policewoman said. "She needs peace and quiet."

"Peace and quiet," Lillan mumbled. "I need peace and quiet."

Göran placed his other hand on her head. Lillan let it stay there.

"We'll do that," the Frenchwoman said. "If you can keep her for a while longer?"

"She can stay as long as she wants," Göran said. "If it were up to me, she would—"

He stopped, cutting himself off abruptly. But Lillan knew what he meant. She made her voice big and strong. Everyone had to hear.

"I'm going to stay. For as long as I want."

LYDIA

CRIMINAL CODE 3:9

It was cold outside. Later, when Lydia read the investigation documents, she would learn that it was twenty-five degrees and skies were clear with a moderate breeze. At the start of the evening, she had been wearing only a T-shirt and a hip-length jacket. Even so, she couldn't recall feeling chilly. She only remembered his warm hands. How they felt as they stroked hers, the soft dry skin, fingertips with blunt nails, as they took her hand, a steady, sure grip. How he had let go. How empty her hand had felt without his.

Lydia Seger was in her third semester of law school at Uppsala University. She was only a half-hearted student, had already had to retake one exam, and she was waiting, without high hopes, to learn the results of the most recent one.

His name was Ted, and he was already a third-year student. He told her so while they were plodding through those obligatory initial questions: What program are you in? Where are you from? When did you start? Where do you live? She had responded evasively, as she usually did, to any questions that didn't have to do with the here and now. He didn't seem to notice and told her that he was studying medicine; he made it sound so serious Lydia laughed at him.

"You don't look like you spend your days with your nose buried in an anatomy book," she said, even though she actually had no idea what medical students did or what they typically looked like. The only med school students she'd met before were a pair of twins who were members of the choir in her same student union. They were always wearing their university coveralls decked out in fake medals, and they behaved as though they had never spoken to a woman they weren't related to. Ted was the opposite of those twins. They looked like middle-aged, row-house residing fathers of three. Ted had a small tattoo on his upper arm, almost up on his shoulder; he had dark blue eyes, worn out shoes, and thick, wavy ash-blond hair that was a little long in back. She wanted to stick her hand under his shirt to see if his stomach was as smooth as his arms. She wanted him to press his hand against her skin, between her T-shirt and the waistband of her jeans.

"Are you really going to become a doctor?" she dared to add. By then, Ted had placed his big, wide hand on the back of her neck and leaned in close to whisper in her ear.

"I'm a natural."

His hot breath made her blush. It felt like her whole body was blossoming with shame or lust or both. She wanted him to undress her and tell her the Latin names of each part of her body. *Femur, sternum, clavicle.* And explain to her what happened when the blood surged through her veins and made her skin a thousand times more sensitive than normal. But he let go of her and walked away. She didn't follow.

For all intents and purposes, Lydia was an only child. Sure, she was the youngest of four siblings, with two brothers and a perpetually angry sister who spent more time with animals than she did with other people. But since she was eleven years younger than her next-oldest sibling, she hardly knew any of them. Her sister had lived at home the longest, but she moved out when Lydia was twelve. She didn't mind being an only child. While her sister still lived at home, the two of them could go days without seeing each other, and they never talked about anything of consequence when they did.

There were thirty-nine, or possibly forty, or maybe just thirty-eight rooms in the house where Lydia grew up. She had tried to count them one especially rainy summer when she got old enough to count that high. But the two top floors were closed off. In the part of the house that was still heated and cleaned regularly—by a dejected full-time maid who looked confusingly similar to the dejected live-in maid whom she had replaced—there were thirty rooms. Lydia's mother lived in one of them; you would find her father in another. Only occasionally did her parents wake up in the same room.

Lydia's bedroom was across from her mother's, and each room had a tile stove and a window seat, a parquet floor, and a large portrait of a horse with beefy legs and a flying mane. Her bed was wider than it was long, and Lydia had been sleeping in it ever since she was old enough to move out of her crib.

She had elected to study law because she thought it seemed like a good option if you had no idea what you wanted to do. Her high-school grades were excellent, among the best in her school, so getting accepted was no problem. At the welcoming assembly, the vice-chancellor, who was also a professor of law, had given a speech.

"Jurisprudence," he had said, "has been developed by generations of lawyers and politicians in order to address the general public's demand for revenge, stricter punishment, and the philosophical idea of the value of the individual. Our book of laws is the code we depend on to offer solutions to our very worst human conflicts. You will be tasked with putting this code into practice. Don't forget that. You must solve the conflicts of others because we are so bad at solving our own." He paused briefly, then leaned over the podium to gaze at the audience and added, "Perhaps the very best lawyers are those who are most conflict-averse in their private lives."

The students had laughed at that. Lydia included. But she hardly understood what he meant. Conflict was foreign to her, not something she was ever drawn into. She had never had to resolve disputes, not even between other people. She didn't have to worry about arguments at home, because there weren't any. Her siblings were seldom there, and her parents never fought. They were too polite.

Lydia's most frequent companions when she still lived at home were the family dogs, Nelson and Klerk. They were Labs, one black, one yellow. They were too old and weary to fight, even with each other, and Lydia had never heard them bark unless there was a hunt underway. Klerk had bad hips, but Nelson loved to jump onto her bed, and he would fall asleep stretched out beside her, dreaming wild dreams that made him howl and paddle his feet. She liked to pet the dogs, even though they smelled bad and it made her hands vaguely sticky. Once in a rare while she would take them for a walk; otherwise, they mostly ran loose around the grounds. When her father took his morning walk, they came along; Nelson twenty yards ahead of him and Klerk just behind.

Each morning, Niklas the groundskeeper would drive her to school, twelve miles away. When the school day was over, she took the bus home again. It was about a mile from the bus stop to the house, and if Mom or Dad or one of the staff didn't pick her up she would walk. Sometimes she brought a friend home; if the friend slept over Mom might come tell ghost stories about ancient relatives who climbed out of the family portraits to rummage through the kitchen cupboards, fry pork until the smell of it spread through the rooms, or overturn a Greek pitcher or Chinese vase in a room no one had set foot in for years.

Lydia lived at home until it was time for high school, and then she went to boarding school. It wasn't like she didn't make any friends there, in fact, she always had at least one best friend, sometimes two, but she couldn't remember ever fighting with them or having a falling-out. Or at least none that were too serious.

If Lydia got mad at one of her friends, she would just stop speaking to her for a few days. She got it out of her system by talking behind the back of whoever she was upset with. And after her feelings settled, she would resume the relationship as though nothing had happened.

Beyond being free of conflict, Lydia's childhood had also been free of ambition. Her family made no demands of her. Her oldest brother was supposed to take over the estate, and her sister would take care of their parents. Her middle brother was like a backup for the eldest brother. No one knew what Lydia's designated role should be.

Lydia's oldest brother had always been a stranger. When he came for a visit, it was as though they were entertaining royalty. He joined them for dinner, never asked Lydia any questions, and spoke only if someone asked him a direct question. Their father conversed with him as he did with the groundskeeper; the only difference was that he wore a look of greater concern. When Dad drank too much cognac, he sometimes raised his voice and wanted to pontificate on the dangers of clear-cutting the forest and remind his son never to sell off any land, not even Lillgården, the little manor, which they hadn't been able to rent out in over twenty years.

"No holes in our cheese," Dad said. And Lydia's brother nodded. He never contradicted his father.

Although her middle brother's only worth was as a spare in case the important, firstborn brother were to up and die before producing an heir, his affairs often attracted attention. This attention was largely negative in nature, given that Lydia's middle brother devoted himself to the sorts of activities a spare with no intrinsic value tended to pursue: drinking, bad investments, and destructive relationships. But their parents never discussed it, at least not with Lydia. The only reason she knew he was a problem in the first place was that she eavesdropped on her sister when she was telling her boyfriend about it over the phone. Lydia had nothing to prove. It was nice that she got good grades, but it wasn't important. Her parents came to watch school plays and last-day-of-school ceremonies, but they weren't the least bit disappointed when she never got a leading role and was never awarded any honors. She didn't like any particular sport, never developed any special hobby, but this didn't seem to concern her parents either.

Lydia had understood from a young age that this family hierarchy, with her at the bottom, was good for her. That it made her free, and not just the most ignored. She supposed the only problem was that she couldn't figure out what to do with this kind of freedom. She didn't want to become an artist or an actor; she didn't want to write a book. Music was something you danced to or listened to when you wanted to avoid talking to strangers on the bus. There was nothing she wanted to create, no intellectual pursuit that awakened her soul. She didn't long to get away or discover the world. Lydia didn't want to keep every door open; that would only make it drafty. To put it simply, she didn't quite *get* life. But not even that caused her any notable concern.

The second time she talked to Ted, he walked into the kitchen of the club with a beer in hand and sat down on the floor next to the dishwasher where she was working. Ted wasn't a member of her same student union, but each Thursday since the first time they'd met he had shown up there. She had seen him. They had acknowledged each other, but only from a distance. Stockholm's Nation was the student union everyone went to on Thursday nights. Even him.

On this evening she had started to look for him as soon as they opened. It wasn't clear whether what she did here could be called a job, because she didn't get paid for it. She had signed up to be one of the Nation's club workers during her second semester, but at the time all the spots had been filled. Now she was finally part of the crew in charge of Thursday nights, who took care of everything from cooking to—yes—dishwashing.

She spotted Ted at a distance a few times that evening, but he didn't come say hello until after closing time. Then he waited while she bent over the wide sink and washed up, soaping and rinsing both face and hands.

She wanted to get rid of the food smell; that seemed more urgent than preserving what little makeup she still had on. Besides, she felt brave, letting him watch from just a few yards away as she cleaned up. The water trickled down her face and got the neck of her T-shirt wet. She felt sexier than all the times she had stripped, more embarrassed than seductive, for guys she liked; she felt boundless, as if anything was possible now. When she was done, she looked him straight in the eyes while she dried off with a clean kitchen towel, her hair, down her neck, under her T-shirt. She could see exactly what it did to him. In that moment, she thought she knew how this night would end. In that moment, she longed for it.

And then they walked out into the winter night. It wasn't just the two of them at first; there was a big group leaving the Nation all at once. But to her it felt like they were alone. He was the only one she was looking at, speaking to.

He looked more at her friends than at her, talked more with the others than with her, but it was an active sort of avoidance. She couldn't have explained how she knew this, but each time he ignored her or laughed at someone else's joke, the magnetic field between them grew stronger. When he replied to everyone else, he was actually addressing her. When she was quiet, it was because she wanted him to have to listen more carefully. Everything that was happening was between the two of them; everyone else in their group was just an extra.

The plan was to go to someone's place and keep the party going there. They were presumably heading to Studentvägen; there was always some corridor in the student apartment complex with loud music and beer on offer. They walked alongside the group for a while. No one seemed to notice the sparks flying between them, the feeling they would give in to soon, very soon. After a couple hundred yards he bumped her arm. A few minutes after that he took her hand, just for a second, as if to say *we're heading this way*. He only touched her, no one else. Each time he brushed against her she wanted to laugh, she had to force herself not to giggle hysterically. She was usually tired after a Thursday night at the Nation, but this time she was more energetic than she had been in months. His skin tickled, the thought of his skin tickled, his gaze, his scent, the back of his neck. As they approached Studentvägen, Ted stopped to let the rest of the group go ahead of him. He didn't have to ask her to stay, it was the only thing to do. No one seemed to notice that they lingered outside.

Lydia remained at a slight distance. She locked her eyes on his as their friends disappeared, and they didn't move until they were all alone. Then Ted took two steps toward her, intertwined his fingers with hers, and they began to stroll back into town, away from the rowdy corridors full of students, back toward the cathedral. When they reached the cemetery, he kissed her. Just once, a quick peck. Then he took her hand and started running. After a moment she made him stop, pulled him close, kissed him again, in the light of the full moon, longer this time. He cupped his hand around the back of her neck; she slipped hers under his shirt. When they parted, they were out of breath, him more so. She giggled when she saw the way he was looking at her. Then they walked on.

It was her idea. She insisted. He didn't want to. There was construction scaffolding against the façade of the cathedral; parts of its exterior and roof were being renovated. He was hesitant, but she took his hand and pulled him close. "Don't be a wuss," she said. "Come on," she said. "I have a surprise for you," she whispered. It felt brave to say so. And he smiled tentatively and gave in, climbing up slowly after her. She was moving quickly. He struggled to keep up. She turned around more than once to help him. “Come on, come on, come on!”

They could see the full moon again. It was unusually large, blurry at the edges but shining bright. On one of the ledges—maybe the third level of the scaffolding—he stopped with his back facing out, turned to her, pulled her close, and howled, tilted his head back and howled. Then, finally, she let herself laugh. He didn’t join in, but he smiled. Right then, he smiled. Had his uncertainty vanished? Close beside her, so close that she stopped breathing.

“Come on,” she whispered, because she had to make him feel the same incredible rush, so she took the lead again, she kept climbing and he followed her. They had to be quick, so they would be able to go home afterward, to a place where it could all start for real. Where his skin would touch hers and nothing else would matter. Now and again she turned around to make sure he was behind her. He was. He was with her all the way up, and she didn’t chicken out even a little bit. When he stopped, she lured him on. Are we really . . . ? Come on!

When they climbed past the tarp that shrouded the scaffolding, she could see how far they had come, how incredibly high they had climbed, but she couldn’t break the spell, it would ruin everything, she refused to, she couldn’t let him go now, so she left the scaffolding, having reached the top, and stepped onto the roof ledge. Now a different feeling took over the tingling in her skin. This was dangerous. For an instant, the magic was gone, but she didn’t say anything and when his hand reached for hers, she laughed and took it and then she sat down on the ledge, leaned against the façade, and the edge was far away but there was a pull low in her belly, same as there always was when she experienced vertigo.

"This is fucking insane," Ted whispered. From the way he said it, she could tell he thought this was insane for real, and Lydia knew he was right. Even so, he stayed, sat down beside her, his back firmly pressed to the façade, far from the edge.

He draped his jacket over her shoulders, on top of her own jacket. They smoked up. Lydia'd had the joint in her pocket, and she lit it, but he was the one who took the first hit. First him, then her. Then him again. Lydia didn't know his last name. She didn't ask. It wasn't important; she didn't care right now. Fear had no place here, everything was expanding, now she was truly alive. She had never been a brave person, but she wasn't about to wuss out now. Ted handed her the joint, but she didn't need any more, so he kept it, smoking it down to his fingertips.

He didn't seem high, Lydia would say later. She didn't say so to lie, or to protect Ted, what would be the point? But she would lie about whose joint it was to protect herself. She wouldn't say that it was all her idea, that they'd climbed up at her insistence.

When he stood up, she protested. She wasn't misremembering, was she? She had protested, right? Hadn't she said *sit down!* in a serious, sharp voice?

The part of the roof they were sitting on was level; a few yards away from them it began to slope down, not much, but it was so dark out. Not pitch black, but close.

Was there frost? Must have been. It felt chillier up there than down on the street. *Isn't that where I started to feel cold?* Lydia would think. *Was it the wind blowing harder? Or did I already know what was going to happen?*

"Sit down," she said. *She said that, right?* She tried to shout. *Didn't she?*

"Sit down, Ted, I'm serious."

Or was it like in all the nightmares to come? That her voice wouldn't work? That she had to force out every word? Was she creating a false memory? Was she trying to remember things that had never happened? Maybe she didn't say anything. Maybe she only laughed. Because she *had* laughed, she remembered that, she would never forget it. She wanted him to think that she was brave, that nothing could scare her. Was that why he thought she wanted him to keep going, just a little farther?

Ted began to walk. He took two steps, or maybe three, across the roof. And then another giggle escaped her, where had it come from? Was that why he reached out for her, was that why it looked like he wanted to dance? How was it possible for her body to laugh while she was so terrified that she had lost the ability to cry out, or say quit that, stop it, come back? Why didn't she tell him to stop? She never asked him to stop. Why did she laugh and make him think she wanted him to keep going? He didn't understand that she wanted out of there. How could he? Ted was walking toward the edge, but she couldn't move, could only press her back against the façade, hear the laughter leave her body, like spasms, epilepsy, something she had no control over. Was that why she didn't stand up and pull him back? *Come on!* She was the one who brought them all the way to the roof. She was the one who talked him into it. He'd been hesitant at first. But not anymore. *Come on, Lydia!* Ted was high, she could see it now. The way he moved was too precarious. But he reached out for her as he backed up, trying to lure her over. He didn't see how close he was, it was dark, she couldn't see either. Was that why she didn't scream? Was that why she didn't stop him?

It happened fast. He made a noise, it wasn't a call for help, it didn't sound like any noise she'd ever heard another human make. His head sounded hollow when it hit the scaffolding. And then he was gone.

Did she hear him hit the ground? She didn't think so. But she curled up into a little ball as Ted's scream echoed deep inside her. It was deep and dull and grew louder in strength. It didn't even last a second. It would stay with her forever.

She rattled off the emergency number, one-one-two, one-one-two, but she couldn't get her phone out, it was like every move she made had to be tiny, or else she would fall too. She crept toward the scaffolding, she climbed back down, one step at a time, and as soon as she reached the ground, she would make the call. *Oneonetwo, oneonetwo.* But she knew there was no one she could call who could make the world make sense again. She didn't know how long it took to shuffle down, slide down, one level at a time. But she reached the street and kept her eyes on the asphalt and began to walk away, away, away from him.

She fled from him, fled from the place where Ted lay. She didn't hear the ambulances until she was crossing the cemetery, she hadn't made the call, her phone was still in her pocket, untouched. Then she noticed she was still wearing his jacket. She pulled it tighter and kept walking, away, away, home, she didn't turn around. Her laughter was still gone, as was her voice. Now she was just cold.

She was sleeping when the police knocked on the door; she didn't know how she'd managed to doze off. But she was still wearing all her clothes, even her shoes. She kicked them off before she answered the door, but she had to put them on again.

"We'd like you to come to the station with us."

That's not what they led with, of course, they said they'd been told she and Ted had wandered off together just a few hours ago.

"You were with Ted last night."

It wasn't a question. They already knew.

So someone saw us, someone saw what happened between us. And then they asked if she knew Ted was dead. But that wasn't really a question either.

"Could you tell us what the two of you were doing, Lydia?"

She shook her head as best she could.

"No," she whispered. "No, I don't know. I don't know anything." But she began to cry; there was no hiding it.

The officer was a woman, and she spoke to Lydia as though she were a child. Was she a child? It felt that way. She wanted her mother. When she realized she was still wearing his jacket, the tears began to fall. "He didn't want me to be chilly," she said. "It was cold out."

"You can have something hot to drink at the station. But we have to go now. We'll talk more when we get there," said the policewoman.

And Lydia nodded. She stuck her hands in the pockets of the jacket. There she found her lighter. She placed it on the hall table before she left the apartment. The policewoman put an arm around her, guided her out of the apartment, down the stairs. On the way out of the building, Lydia buried her nose in her collar and sniffed tentatively. She was sure they would take the jacket away from her when they realized it was his. But for now, they let her be. She pulled up the zipper and allowed the policewoman to lead her to the street where the patrol car was parked. It was still chilly out, but the full moon was gone now. The sun was coming up. She wasn't cold anymore.

MIKAELA

CRIMINAL CODE 3:5

Whenever I bring my son home to Mom, to the house where I grew up but never played hide-and-seek, he crawls into a cupboard or wriggles his way under a sofa or hides behind a curtain before Mom even has the chance to lock the front door from the inside and return to the living room. Lukas is flexible as a rubber band and tough as a leather belt, and he always wants to play. New games, old games, listening to new stories, reading the same book a hundred times. Running farther than he ever has before, crawling, climbing, jumping. He thinks dark caves are exciting and heights a challenge. He's brave; I'm a scaredy-cat. He does everything exactly the way he wants to; I can hardly manage to do the stuff I absolutely have to. He's everything I'm not. How I ended up with a child who knows how to be a child is the greatest mystery of my life.

My mother's name is Lena, and she's an alcoholic. This is nothing new, quite the opposite. Still, her alcoholism is always the reason Lukas and I have to go see her. We never drive the hundred-plus miles to celebrate a birthday or enjoy Christmas together or hunt for Easter eggs in her yard or even just eat Sunday dinner. My mother never nags me to give her more time with her only grandchild, she never asks if we'll be moving closer so we can get together more often. My mother never misses me or Lukas, and she's always annoyed when we show up, even for a planned visit.

On this particular day, she knew we were coming. We weren't trying to surprise her; it wasn't an intervention. Still, she hardly even said hello as she let us in, just nodded curtly before turning around and going back to her room to lie down. She wasn't drunk when we got there, just tired. Lukas, though, he was like a fully charged battery when I set him on the floor. He had only thrown up once in the car before dozing off, and all his nerve endings seemed to crackle with energy.

My plan was simple. I would check the mail and take Mom to the doctor. I didn't expect that to be a problem; Mom loves doctors because they listen to her and feel sorry for her. Sometimes they prescribe pills, which she'll either take or sell in exchange for what she really wants: alcohol.

As Lukas dashed into the house, I looked at the clock and figured I might as well tidy up a bit before we left. We had time. That way I wouldn't have to do it when we got back, and it would be perfect if Mom napped for a while. So I emptied the dishwasher and started to fill the sink with hot water so I could hand wash what couldn't go in the dishwasher. I had only made it through a couple of pots and an ashtray before I heard Lukas chatting to himself in Mom's bedroom.

"Gamma's candy. Gamma's candy so yummy."

That was what he said. The doors between us were open. I heard him clearly. The ashtray I was holding crashed to the floor as I whipped around and ran to him. I shouted, "No touching Grandma's things!"

I didn't want to kill my son's joy, or quash his curiosity, I would give anything to keep him from becoming anxious and cowardly like me. Still, I roared like a maniac when I saw him standing by Mom's bed with that object in his chubby fist. The voice that came out of me was so loud I hardly recognized it. *No touching Grandma's things!* I scared him, even though I didn't mean to.

In a millisecond, he dropped what he was holding and burst into tears. His whole little body stiffened, his plump lower lip trembled, and he was so scared that he didn't even scream, he was just wracked with silent, powerful sobs. He's sensitive to loud voices, I suppose all kids are, but I wasn't thinking rationally. I thought he had found a bottle of pills, some sort of medicine. Mom is always leaving them open, full or half-empty, tossed on the floor or forgotten on the sofa. Sleeping pills, maybe? Or something even worse. I was shaking so hard. I had relaxed when I saw she was sober and it's always worst when you're not prepared, when disaster sneaks up from behind. Maybe that was why I lost control; maybe that was why I did what I did later on.

As I scooped Lukas up, he threw his arms around me and clung to my chest. Mom was lying in bed. A crumpled cigarette lay in the ashtray on her nightstand; it had burned out on its own. She didn't react to my screaming or to Lukas. How could she have slept through such a racket? It was astonishing. But it didn't look like she was faking. Her arms stuck straight out from her body as if she'd been crucified, and her belly was so swollen that you could barely see her face, just her pale, doughy breasts slipping out of the threadbare nightgown. It took a long time for the quivering air to settle after my outburst. But Mom just kept snoring.

"There, there, buddy, you're okay," I said to Lukas in a soothing voice.

I sucked in air as if I couldn't breathe and pressed him tight to my body. Slowly, he began to relax as my pulse found its way back to normal; his panicked tears subsided into brief sobs, and the sobs into breaths, gentle lapping waves.

I bent down, still holding Lukas, and picked up the object he'd found.

It's not Mom's pills, I thought, relieved. I almost laughed. *It's her fucking dentures.*

The teeth were yellowed, with a semitransparent pink palate. Our grocery store sold bulk candy in the shape of teeth; it had been a hot-ticket item during Halloween. I had taken Lukas trick-or-treating with the neighbor kids just a few weeks ago, and we came home with pounds of candy; I had to take more than half of it away from him. I brought a huge bag to work, to share in the break room. Even so, we had tons left at home. I'd eaten some of the candy dentures myself.

"Sweetheart," I whispered, to mitigate my earlier shouting. "Wow, you really scared Mommy. It's okay, Lukas-boy.

Mommy was just a little scared, but everything is fine now. But you aren't allowed to open Grandma's drawers, those are her things, not yours."

I placed him on my hip. He's getting big and pretty heavy, but I can still carry him. I woke Mom up. I had to shake her for a long time before I could rouse her.

"Get dressed," I said. "It's time to go."

Then I left the bedroom and went back to the kitchen. Lukas stuck his thumb in his mouth and grabbed the neck of my T-shirt, just like he used to do when he was a baby. I set him down on a kitchen chair and gave him a slice of apple from the plastic container I'd brought. Then I rinsed off Mom's teeth and placed them in a glass of water. Lukas stuck the apple in his mouth and sucked on it as he glanced back and forth between me and the glass, looking suspicious, as though he was worried I might still be angry.

After only about fifteen minutes, Mom came out. She was dressed and wearing that expression she often has when she's sober. *The day after. The hours before.* That mean look.

When she noticed the glass, her eyes flashed. But before I could say anything, she plunged her hand in, pulled out the teeth, and popped them in her mouth.

"Why do we have to leave already?" she asked. "The doctor's appointment isn't for another forty minutes."

"Lukas needs to eat something," I said. "I want to stop on the way."

She nodded at that. She didn't protest. I chalked it up to her wanting to get to the doctor as soon as possible.

Once the appointment was over, she could come home again and start drinking. *Maybe that's why she's sober*, I thought, *she doesn't want to be drunk when she sees the doctor*. It's easier for her to get their attention, arouse their sympathies, if she seems somewhat put together.

Mom used to have stretches of calm, but they're increasingly rare. I can't remember the last time she had one, and these days it's like a never-ending plane crash where she's the crew that won't stop freaking out and screaming, and I'm the pilot who can't fix a thing because all the engines have flamed out and the controls don't work and red lights are blinking hysterically all around me.

Mom calls me at all hours of the day, drunk and incoherent or drunk and sad or drunk and panicky. Whenever there's a few days of peace, I can expect a call from a neighbor or some "friend." I don't know who they are. Her friends never stick around long. But they usually demand that I *do something* because *it can't go on like this*, and they're never interested in hearing what I have to say, they just want to reassure themselves that Mom is my responsibility. They want to ease the guilt that creeps up on them when they get sick of dealing with her.

Over the past few weeks, I'd gotten an unusual number of calls from people who claimed to be Mom's friends. I'd even heard from one of my old teachers who saw her hanging around the city center.

"She didn't appear to be in the best shape," he said. In a voice that meant: *Why don't you do something?*

That was why I had offered to give her a ride for today's appointment. Not because she wanted me to, and, in fact, not even because I thought it would help. I only offered because I couldn't think of what else to do. Of course I wanted to plead with the doctor to help me. I wanted to demand help. I wanted to refuse to leave until they agreed to do something. But I also knew what the doctor would say—that there was nothing they *could* do, not as long as Mom refused. I've heard that answer a thousand times already, and my questions and the doctor's responses have turned into automatic exchanges, each line a domino that can do nothing but fall. Even so, I planned to try again.

Sometimes it actually makes me feel better. The best doctors get this look on their face, one that says they too can see how pointless, how hopeless my situation is. Maybe this doctor would be one of them. One of the ones who, for a brief moment, relieves the feeling that I'm crazy not to give up when I should. There was no sense in talking to Mom—that ship had sailed long before I was old enough to know what to say.

She's my mom, is my usual refrain when someone asks how I can bear it. Maybe they think that means I love her. Maybe it does mean something about love. But I'm not sure. Maybe it's about the guilt I would feel if I didn't point it out. She's my mom.

I've asked for help from more than just doctors. A few years ago, I contacted a lawyer. I wanted him to help me have Mom declared incompetent, to take away her ability to spend all her money on alcohol, because each time her early-retirement pension payment arrives, it's gone within a few days.

"That isn't possible," he said.

He explained that the law had changed a few years after I was born, and people could no longer be legally declared incompetent in Sweden. So then I asked if we could force Mom into rehab.

"She isn't sick or dangerous enough," was all he said, as if he had any idea how sick or dangerous she might be, even though he'd never met her. When I contradicted him to say that she definitely was, he asked me to describe her behavior, and I tried to explain, but I could tell that he'd made up his mind before I even started talking.

He suggested I go to a meeting of co-dependents anonymous, so I did. I thought there might be someone there who could give me practical, useful advice. There were seven women in total, and we met in a school gym that smelled like rubber and middle school memories. The leader was the only man.

"She needs help to find the motivation to help herself," he informed me when I tried to explain what I needed help with. I wanted to ask him if he embroidered such words of wisdom onto wall hangings to bring in a little extra cash on the side. But instead I fell silent, didn't share more, didn't ask any questions, and left while the others were standing in a semicircle around a plastic table and drinking lukewarm coffee from paper cups and eating dry shortbread cookies. Nothing could force me to go back.

Mom can't be motivated to quit. She loves to abuse substances. She smokes in the shower and would happily die drunk. She's only happy when she knows she has at least three days' worth of alcohol at home, and nothing but solitude ahead of her. Nothing could make her give it up.

I want her every right to make her own decisions taken away. That was what I wanted to say to the doctor when we met. The doctor should be able to see that Mom is plenty sick and dangerous. It's obvious to anyone who encounters her often enough.

Mom was first into the front hall, and I followed with Lukas. I helped her put on her shoes before I helped Lukas. I helped her into her jacket before I wrestled him into his snowsuit. We went out to the car, I opened the door and put Lukas in his car seat. But I buckled Mom's seat belt before I strapped him in. Then I drove to the nearest shopping center. I didn't ask her any questions, because most of the time questions only upset her, so I chatted about Lukas's new preschool and Stefan's plans to build a deck. She didn't answer, but it seemed like she was listening. She hardly ever talks when she's sober.

I do have good memories of my mother, of course. When I was little, wine made her more cheerful, helped her chill out. She turned into the fun mom who told stories everyone laughed at, who wanted the kids to sit with the grown-ups at the table and never go to bed. With some wine in her, she turned into the mom who played the best music and didn't care if the neighbors complained. If there was a party, she also turned into the prettiest mom, with the right color eyeliner, always smelling of the nicest perfume, wearing clothes my friends wanted to borrow.

I don't remember when things started to change, I only know that once I did notice, I was ashamed. I should have realized earlier how cringy she was, what a drunk she was. I should have seen that she was no longer someone who had a glass of wine to be social, to enjoy the sunshine, because it was Wednesday or Friday or a birthday or a special evening. But I hadn't realized. According to Mom, there was always a good reason to drink. Her explanations were perfectly rational. Work and Dad's illness and Grandma dying and the hot-water heater breaking. *Because you're worth it.* Because everything was easier with a glass of wine or two, even the kind of stuff that was really, truly hard.

Mom was put on sick leave long before we began to talk about her drinking as an illness. We called it other names for years. *Stress. Burnout. Depression.* Her friends were fake, whiny, and old-fashioned. The divorce wasn't her fault, Dad was the one who wanted a new life, who betrayed us.

But then it wasn't just her own friends and my father who couldn't stand to be around her anymore. My friends didn't want to come to my house, they no longer laughed at her jokes or looked flattered when she asked where they'd bought that sweater or blouse. They whispered behind my back, shook their heads at her when they thought I couldn't see. And that's when I finally saw it. She had become a mom who took her glass of wine with her to the laundry room, drank beer while she was vacuuming, enjoyed a port during *Bolibompa* and sherry with *Midsomer Murders*, who drank ice-cold vodka straight from the bottle, hiding behind the open freezer door. Who threw up first thing in the morning and last thing before bedtime.

Mom had noticed this too, of course, that she had stopped being the cool mom. It made her furious, mostly at me. My friends were idiots, she liked to say. And no wonder, she would add, because their parents were even worse. She stopped wanting to drive me to school, and she was usually drunk when I got home at the end of the day; she canceled parent–teacher conferences at the last minute, forgot about dinner, stopped working, started sleeping in the afternoon, the morning, all day long.

After that, it happened very fast. She became shrunken and swollen at the same time, her skin gray and wrinkled, her hair sparse and dry as straw. But she kept wearing the same plunging necklines, kept making eyes at the same men, wanted to dance, sit on laps, whisper and giggle, no matter their age and even though her makeup was always smeared and her upper lip glistening with sweat.

It didn't take very long to get to the shopping center—maybe ten minutes. I parked and asked Mom to wait in the car. I was just going to run inside and grab a yogurt drink and maybe a banana. Did she want anything? I asked. No, she said. Was she okay watching Lukas, I asked. If she waited in the car with him, he could stay in his car seat. Running into the store would be much faster that way. Yes, Mom said, no problem.

Five minutes later, or ten max, I returned to the car to find that Mom was gone and Lukas was still in his car seat. She had left the passenger-side door cracked, maybe to give him air or maybe so she wouldn't activate the alarm. I handed Lukas one of the bananas, unbuckled him, and picked him up. He was able to point which way Grandma had gone. Even though he's so little, he already knows that you have to keep an eye on Grandma. She was at a restaurant a few hundred yards away.

"I got hungry," she said as we approached her table. But there was no food on the table, only beer. "Can you get this?" she added, handing me the check, which had already been delivered. "I left my wallet at home."

Lukas tried to wriggle out of my arms as I talked to Mom. A server came over to us. She asked if everything was all right. A family at the next table stopped talking to watch us instead. I settled the check. There was no point in refusing; either way, I was going to have to pay it. I asked Mom to come with us. She refused. We left without her.

On the way back to the car, I canceled the doctor's appointment. Lukas began to cry as I strapped him into his car seat. I gave him the yogurt drink, which he threw down. Most of its contents ended up on the floor of the car, but a few drops spattered on the windshield. I wiped them off with the back of my hand and tried to play Lukas's favorite song on the stereo, but it didn't work. He screamed all the way back to Mom's house.

The lawyer I'd contacted about having Mom declared incompetent had asked if I really wanted to have that kind of authority over my mother.

"I think it might not be such a good idea to have that sort of relationship with a parent," he'd said. He had thought having power over her was what I was after.

But I don't want to control Mom—that's what I want to avoid. In a perfect world, I wouldn't have anything to do with her. That's my dream. My second most secret, shameful dream after the worst one: that she would just die. My greatest wish after that is for someone else to be in charge of her money, her prescriptions, her expenses. If she could no longer freely access her pension, I wouldn't have to be the one who paid her rent and her electric and phone bills after she spent all her money on alcohol. I wouldn't have to find the collections notices unopened on the floor of her front hall when I come to clean her apartment. If someone else could just take care of all that, I would do the rest, I would do it without complaining.

I've asked to set up direct debit for the most important expenses, I've forged Mom's signature a few times and forced her to sign documents other times, but whenever she has a couple of decent weeks, she cancels the automatic payments so she can withdraw the money the minute it lands in her account.

"Your mother is an adult," the lawyer had told me, as though I wasn't well aware. "Everyone enjoys the same rights. Everyone has equal value. Every adult must be allowed to make their own decisions in life. Even if you don't approve, even if it means they ruin their life."

I wanted to ask this guy too if he embroidered motivational words on pillows. I wanted to ask him if there was some snappy way to say that it was more important for Mom to be able to drink herself to death than it was for me to have control over my life and my money. Some legal precedent, maybe, to explain that all the rules and rights are there to benefit Mom, not people like me. Rights are not for those of us who do everything right, only for people who don't deserve them in the first place. I wanted to tell him to go to hell.

When Lukas and I got back to Mom's house, I carried him inside, sat him down on the sofa, and turned on the TV. He stopped fussing now that he was out of the car seat and could climb around on the sofa instead. After he got tired of that and plopped back down to sit, I went into Mom's bathroom to give it a quick clean. I knew she would come home once she had finished what I'd paid for at the restaurant. It wouldn't be long, she had no money and they would stop serving her if she couldn't pay.

There were no pills in the bathroom. But I did find a photo album at the very back of one cupboard. I'd made it for her when Lukas turned one. Somehow I had imagined that she would show pictures of her grandson to her friends. But it was shredded, scribbled full of her drunken ramblings, impossible to make sense of. It looked like she had drawn a Hitler mustache on Lukas in one picture. I took the photo album to the kitchen and tossed it in a black garbage bag from a roll I'd brought from home. I shoved it down as far as I could so I wouldn't have to think about it. One of the pictures I saw before I realized the album was ruined was of me, taken almost four years ago. In it I was pregnant, and I can still remember how fat and ugly I felt. But in this photo, I could see how cute I'd been, cheeks rosy as if I'd been skiing for hours, clear skin, happy eyes.

These days, I avoid cameras. Lukas is only three, but I've gotten fat, my breasts are twice as old as the rest of me, and I'm always tired. It doesn't bother me that Stefan has trouble getting hard, that we barely even have sex anymore. I get where he's coming from, and I don't want to nag.

"My mom came down with something," I told the receptionist who answered when I called to cancel the appointment. I'd considered saying she was hung over, but there was no point, they wouldn't catch that it was a barb.

"That's too bad. I hope she feels better soon," the receptionist responded.

If what my mother has is an illness, then why don't you treat her? I would have liked to add. There is medicine that can help. She refuses to take it. There are treatment programs. She won't go. There is help to be had, but she only pretends to accept it. Why don't you make her? Why is she allowed to make these decisions, when I'm the one who has to deal with the consequences?

But I didn't say anything. Mom's appointment was rescheduled for two weeks later.

She can go by herself, I thought. *I don't give a shit anymore.* I don't give a shit about any of this. Not her filthy sheets, her collections notices, her dirty apartment, not the smell when you open her front door. I don't give a shit about her. Let Social Services deal with it. Or how about her fucking friends—why don't they do anything?

Almost two hours passed before Mom came home. I had to open the door for her because she couldn't manage to get the key in the lock. She was totally plastered, one hand clutching the doorframe so she wouldn't fall over, the other holding the remains of a hotdog.

"So you had some money after all? Or did one of your friends show up? Someone buy a round?"

"Go home," she said. "Just go to hell, I don't want you here, leave me alone."

I didn't respond. Instead I went to the living room, where Lukas was still watching TV. Mom followed me.

She glared at me. *That drunk look.*

"I don't want you here. Do you hear me?"

I gazed at her but said nothing. She had what looked like impetigo around her mouth. She was all puffy. She could hardly button her coat, since it had been over a month since she was admitted to the hospital to drain the fluid from her abdomen. Her skin was turning yellow. All her internal organs were corroded by her drinking. I wondered if she was going to puke up the hotdog. Her esophageal sphincter is far too slack to keep food down. She smelled like old cigarettes and dirty underwear. She had oozing sores on both arms because when the alcohol left her system, she got itchy all over, and she can't keep down enough alcohol to black out. *She's my mom.*

"Get the hell out of here. Are you listening to me?"

I'm the one who takes care of her, who makes sure she doesn't have to sleep under a bridge. Yet she's the one who gets after me? *You're-so-fat, shouldn't-you-be-at-work, what-on-earth-are-you-wearing?* And I just stand there and take it. *My mom.*

Mom staggered, then nodded at Lukas.

"How long is that kid gonna suck his thumb? He'll have braces until he's a teenager. You get that you're going to have to pay for that, right? Maybe you think it's cute? It's not fucking cute to have a mouth full of barbed wire. Stop treating him like a baby. Who knows, maybe he'll finally stop wearing those fucking diapers."

Lukas was startled. He gazed anxiously at his grandma and then at me.

Mom laughed. Lukas still wears diapers at night. Sometimes he asks for one when he needs to poop. I don't know why I told her that, or how she can even remember hearing it. But I didn't point out that she should *start* wearing diapers again, that adult diapers would considerably improve her hygiene.

"Mom," I said instead, with the calmest of voices. "I don't want you to talk like that. It scares Lukas."

A therapist I saw a few times, because Stefan thought I should, asked me how old I was when I first understood that Mom was a drinker. I couldn't bring myself to explain that Mom had always been a drinker, but that it wasn't a problem at first, so instead I chose a random memory: a day I came home from school with a friend and Mom was vacuuming in the kitchen with the radio on full blast. I was fourteen at the time, and that was about how old I was when I began to feel ashamed of her drinking. But I had been aware of it for years. That day, there wasn't time to throw out the beer cans before my friend saw them. I told the therapist that I was more ashamed of having left the beer can mess than I was of Mom.

Therapists love stories about children hiding empty bottles and cleaning up and being responsible even though they're little. This gives them a chance to make use of the special courses they took in college; they get to try out different treatment methods they've read about in American psychology journals, it lets them stake out goals and teach you mantras to recite. There are tons of methods like these for us codependents—we're not treated like the alcoholics, incapable of shouldering responsibility. On the contrary, we are expected to take control of our lives. Set boundaries. Learn to deal with our emotions. Take responsibility for our codependence.

No one seems to realize how ironic this is. That codependence—a condition where you're always putting other people's needs above your own—is yet another thing you're supposed to take responsibility for, presumably because if you don't, that responsibility will fall to someone else. But being dependent, now that's an illness you can't help having.

I told the therapist about the time Mom was vacuuming while sloshed as if this was the first time I had realized she drank, but the truth was that by that point Mom and Dad had already been divorced for two years and deep down, I knew long before Dad moved out why he didn't want to live with us anymore. I didn't mention that part. The therapist looked very pleased with what I'd said and didn't wonder why I was concerned about hiding the empty cans if I didn't already know that Mom was a drunk, so I kept quiet. I like to make therapists happy; I always have.

"But who the hell knows if that will even help," Mom said with a cough. "You wet the bed at confirmation camp, even though I trained you out of diapers and your pacifier before you were two. He probably got it from you."

Lukas squirmed on the sofa. He was looking at the TV, but I could tell that he was listening to Mom, that he could hear what she was saying. I think that was when I first knew what I had to do. Lukas's anxiety made me feel calm, determined, focused—the way you might feel before a competition. My rage let go of me and was replaced by something else.

"You're scaring Lukas," I said again, louder this time. "Do you hear me, Mom? You have to stop. I'm not kidding."

She looked at me. She seemed to be smiling. A vague, absent smile.

"I've told you a thousand times." My voice was its normal volume now. "I don't want you to upset Lukas."

At that, Mom shuffled over to Lukas on the sofa. She grabbed his elbow and pulled on it slowly until his thumb popped out of his mouth. His eyes moved from the TV to his grandmother. He smiled hesitantly. But Mom didn't smile back. She had no intention of turning this into a game.

When murderers describe how it felt to kill someone, they often say something like *everything went black*, they *don't remember*, they did what they did *as if in a trance*.

But when I did what I did to Mom, I wasn't in any sort of trance. Nor was I acting in self-defense or by some weird kind of reflex. Maybe I was still shaken up from thinking Lukas had swallowed some of her pills, maybe I was mad about the photo album, upset that she had left Lukas alone in the car, that she had scared him, but it wasn't like there was any one thing that was the last straw, there really wasn't.

First of all I picked Lukas up off the sofa—carefully, almost slowly. I went out to the car, strapped him into his seat, started the engine, and turned on the heat. I opened his favorite game, handed him my phone, and walked away. I didn't do any of this quickly, there was no panic, I wasn't out of breath, my heart was beating normally. When I came back inside, Mom was still sitting on the sofa. The children's show Lukas had been watching was still on.

"Stand up, Mom," I said. Then I took her by the arm and pulled her up. She swayed. But I held on to her.

"You're such a fucking remarkable mother," she blurted. "You'd think you were afraid of him. You've always been afraid of everything. Are you afraid of your son too?" She laughed. "Have you ever told him no? Anything that kid wants..."

The first blow got her in the cheek. It was a hard hit, not least because I was also holding on to her with my other hand. But Mom mostly just looked surprised. The next blow landed even better. I had let go of her arm, and she fell back onto the sofa. I grabbed her by the hair and pulled her up again. When I did that, she made a noise—not quite a scream, not quite a sob, but something in between.

One whole side of her face was red, swelling up, maybe she'd even end up with a black eye. I held her gaze as I hit her one last time, on the other cheek. The pain in my fist made me gasp. I thought it only hurt to get punched; I didn't know it hurt to do the hitting.

Mom's lower lip split. Her teeth slipped out with a dull pop, like when you uncork a bottle. I tried to catch them but missed. I left them on the floor where they fell.

"Stop," she whispered, making her voice feebler than she needed to. She does that a lot; she likes to play the weakling. I wanted to spit on her. But I didn't.

When I lowered my hands, there was blood running down her chin. A lot of blood. I went to the kitchen and washed off in the sink. There was a dirty pot on the stove, so I scrubbed it and put it to dry.

Before I left, I placed a five-hundred-kronor bill on the coffee table in front of her. She closed her hand around it before I could turn around. You can stay drunk for days on that much money, if you don't care about the quality of what you're drinking. It's been years since Mom stopped demanding wine and started to make do with hand sanitizer and mouthwash when there was nothing else around. One time, when Lukas was a newborn and I invited her over, she drank my perfume while I was taking a shower. It didn't get her very drunk, just enough that we would have to drive her home.

Mom wouldn't call the police to report me. Even if she wanted to, she couldn't resist the compulsion to drink up all that money. And by the time she woke up on the other side of that bender, she would have forgotten it all. Or at least her memories of what had happened would be too fuzzy for her to do anything about it.

If she tried to tell, no one would believe her. I do everything for my mother, everyone knows that, of course I wouldn't hurt her. They would think someone else did it. Absolutely anyone could end up in a scuffle with her. Drunks fight, especially with each other. Mom is always falling out with her friends over the tiniest things. *Did the match end 3-2 or 4-3? Who played the lead role in* Pretty Woman*? You're wrong, I'm right, I'm gonna kill you, you bastard.*

Lukas glanced up at me as I got into the driver's seat. Then he went right back to my phone. On the way home, I got hungry. I had to stop for hamburgers. Two for me, a kids' meal for Lukas. He only ate three fries; I gobbled down the rest. Later I had to pull over to throw up. But by then Lukas was asleep, so he didn't notice.

"How was she?" Stefan asked as I got in bed and let him cuddle close to me.

I pressed myself against him and pulled his arms tighter around me. He'd helped me bring Lukas in from the car, but he hadn't asked why we had come home a day earlier than planned.

"Same as usual," I said. "I don't feel like talking about it."

"Mikaela, honey," was all he said. He took my hand and brought it to his lips. I had a scrape the size of a postage stamp on my right knuckles. But he didn't mention it. We just lay there together, not saying anything. It took over ten minutes for me to start crying. But once I started, I couldn't stop.

I heard the rain and the wind outside the bedroom window as Stefan murmured words meant to comfort me, as he assured me he loved me no matter what I did.

"I hit her. More than once."

"You'll never do it again," he whispered.

"How do you know?"

"I just know, you're not that kind of person."

But he was wrong. Because I didn't regret it. For the first time I had forced her to listen to me—that was how it felt. When I hit her, she reacted. I got through to her. She was drunk, but she couldn't ignore my punches.

"What happened?" he whispered.

Instead of answering, I cried, because it was easier.

The therapists who didn't get it, the ones who asked when I first understood that Mom was a drunk, they were asking the wrong questions. They should have asked when I understood that I was a prisoner, how old I was when I realized I would never be free of her, that I could try for the rest of my life and never succeed. Mom will always control me; it will never be the other way around. She has all the power: over me, my feelings, my actions, everything. Mom decides.

Everything I do might as well be screaming into a black hole.

Stefan lulled me as though I were a baby, held me, told me I didn't have to see Mom ever again, that I didn't owe her anything, that I had to forgive myself. That only made me cry harder. I cried until I was out of breath and recovered it again. I cried until I realized we were breathing in rhythm, just like Lukas and I had earlier that day. Only then could I stop. Only then could I tell him what had happened.

I started by telling him that Mom had left Lukas in the car by himself. I talked a lot about the doctor's appointment I'd had to cancel. I waited until last to tell him about the dentures Lukas had found. He laughed at that part, so suddenly and spontaneously that I started to chuckle too. It was a funny story. We could tell it to Lukas when he was older, add the time he almost ate Grandma's teeth to the collection of family legends. We could tell that story instead; we could forget the rest of it.

"You don't have to go back," he told me. Then he fell asleep with one hand on my breast. He snored. I couldn't fall asleep. Lukas had napped for so long in the car that he would probably wake up in a few hours. I needed to get some sleep while I could. I had to doze off soon and wake up rested; there was so much I had to take care of.

Tomorrow, I thought, *I'll go back without Lukas.* It stresses me out to bring him along. Maybe I can even reschedule that appointment for this week, I can explain that it's urgent, that Mom truly isn't doing well. That she's worse, that things got much worse very quickly. I can explain and make them see that this time, it's genuinely a crisis. She's my mom, I will say. *She's my mom.*

I know they'll understand.

ANNE

PENAL LAW ON NARCOTICS § 1

Anne got a seat at the very front of the gallery. Aside from her, there were only two others there to listen. Tommy wasn't one of them.

This was her fourth time attending court proceedings, if she counted Jonathan's detention hearing, but her first time in this district court. A glass wall separated the courtroom from the gallery. The two ladies who'd come to watch as her son's life was ruined were chatting with one another. To them, this was free entertainment, Anne thought. She wondered if they would soon pull out their knitting.

She wriggled out of her coat and draped it over her lap. The prosecutor had placed a binder on the table, but only one, and it was fairly slim.

"We should be done not long after lunchtime," Calle the attorney had said. "By four at the very latest."

The presiding judge announced the case, and the door to the gallery was closed. Then Jonathan and his attorney entered the courtroom. The attorney was a guy with gelled hair and a tie as wide as a table runner. He'd asked

Anne to call him Calle during the detention hearing a month ago. Today, they'd only met for the briefest of moments in a room adjacent to the courtroom.

Neither Calle nor Jonathan had asked her why Tommy wasn't there. Even though Calle had said at the detention hearing that it would be smart to show the judge that Jonathan had a family who was there for him. Anne had relayed this to Tommy, but he just shook his head as though she couldn't have said something more idiotic.

"I was there the first time we were supposed to show the judge we were there to help him get clean. No judge is so goddamn naive that they'll fall for that again."

Anne hadn't pointed out that this would actually be Jonathan's third trial. She had, however, explained in detail what they would have to do so that Jonathan could be sentenced to home confinement with an ankle monitor rather than to prison. That there were certain demands she and Tommy must fulfill in order for that petition to be granted. She had memorized what Calle had explained to make sure she would sound knowledgeable.

"Jonathan doesn't have a place of his own, and he doesn't have a job to go to or schooling to complete. All he has is us. And in order for him to have an ankle monitor at our place, we need to be on the same page. We have to sign papers and attest that we know what's involved."

Tommy just kept shaking his head. He said it didn't matter what the hell they did. Jonathan would never be able to stay clean and so he would end up behind bars whether they let him try home confinement first or not. He didn't get how important it was for Jonathan to avoid prison, how everything would only get worse if he was locked up.

The seating in the gallery reminded her of a movie theater. But there were no cup holders, nowhere to put popcorn. Even so, one of the two women in the row in front of Anne's pulled out a bar of chocolate. She peeled away the wrapper, popped a square in her mouth, and offered the candy to her friend. The friend shook her head. Before the woman returned the bar to her purse, she broke off another row. Having stuffed that in her mouth too, she licked her fingers clean.

The presiding judge sat behind a long, half-moon table. She was wearing a dark suit and lots of hairspray. Next to her were the lay judges; two on one side and one on the other. At the far end of the same table was the clerk, a girl who couldn't be more than twenty-five, with a pinched mouth and nervous hands. Anne didn't like lawyers. Of course, the lay judges weren't lawyers by training, they were more like politicians, but that certainly didn't help. In any case, they didn't look like the presiding judge, who reeked of money and inborn superiority.

Anne's social circles weren't exactly teeming with rich people, but she knew a few. None of them were pleasant. Take her boss, for instance. He had a summer home in Mallorca, drove a Tesla, and was generally an idiot. And Tommy's wealthy cousin was some kind of engineer and lived in a big house in Saltsjöbaden. Not only was he rude to them, he hardly talked to anyone when he showed up to family reunions. And to read what rich people wrote about their lives on Instagram, you'd think they automatically turned stupid the moment they didn't have to worry about paying the bills anymore. *I love autumn, red wine, and warm jackets! Help me choose the color of my new kitchen cabinets: Should I go with ivory, eggshell, cream, or vanilla? Can anyone recommend a good spa near Auschwitz? It is soooo important for our kids to learn about history, but it would be nice to relax a little afterward.*

Rich people's problems were never actual problems, and their feigned guilty conscience about things they did seemed absolutely ridiculous to Anne. Flight shame and charity and hashtag solidarity. How could anyone take it seriously? People who pretended to care about children dying in wars on the other side of the world and bragged about donating money to fight famine. Who shook their heads and said things like *where is this country headed* and *isn't anyplace safe anymore* after burglars hit a neighbor's house and made off with an oil painting or two.

"It feels like I'm going to die, Mom," Jonathan had said the last time she visited him in jail. They were allowed to sit in a visiting room, just the two of them. He cried. "I'm going to die in here, Mom." His cell was tiny. His agony was so overwhelming that she could hardly breathe. "I can't live like this."

"It's going to be okay," she replied. She tried to take his hand. With that, he stood up and asked to go back to his cell.

None of the people in the courtroom today had children who were terrified of dying. None of them had to argue with their husband about whether they should attend district court to watch their son be judged by people who didn't understand who he really was. None of them knew how it felt to get a call from the emergency room a week after their child was found unconscious under a bridge. They didn't know what the visiting room of a jail looked like; they didn't know how it smelled in an apartment full of addicts.

If the judge had children, they were probably kids who did party drugs and microdosed to cure the winter blues. The judge surely wouldn't think this was a problem. She would consider that kind of drug use very different from Jonathan's. She would discuss the issue calmly and sensibly with her rich friends during dinner parties at her big house, but no one would become upset; no one would raise their voice.

All this moral panic about opioids, isn't it kind of bourgeois? Shouldn't we get to have some fun as Swedish taxpayers? I enjoy a nice spliff, anyone offering? If I live to be eighty, maybe I'll start doing heroin, haha.

The presiding judge turned on her microphone again. Now she cleared her throat and looked down at her papers. It seemed she had to remind herself whose insignificant life she would be ruining today. Then she angled the microphone closer to her lips.

"Welcome to Case B 2219-23," she said in a bored voice. "I will begin by making sure everyone who should be here is in attendance. Jonathan Olsson? You're here with your attorney, Carl Hammar?"

This ugly-bitch judge didn't have any kids who risked overdosing because they got their hands on a bad batch of drugs. Her children would never get caught; they had their drugs delivered to their home, and there were no raids in the places where they partied. If there was a security camera outside her huge mansion with its ocean views, that was because she had put it there. No plainclothes detectives were sent into the clubs her children went to. And her kids wouldn't run away from home to get their hands on what they needed to tolerate life. They would keep having fun and living their lives however they pleased, with no cops or idiot lawyers butting in.

Tommy thought it was silly when she brought up money. It made him angry; he took it as criticism. *We have enough to get by*, he always said. *It's not as if we're welfare cases.* But Anne knew everything would have turned out differently if they were rich. Jonathan would have been more resilient in the face of setbacks, wouldn't have needed to get high the same way, and even if he had started doing drugs they could have gotten him better help. With more money, they could have moved away from the friends who were a bad influence. But that made Tommy even angrier. Almost as furious as he was when they discussed the ankle monitor.

All their fights started and ended with Jonathan. They'd argued about him when he was little, when he was a teenager, when he became an adult. About why he was the person he was. What should they have done differently, what should they have avoided? Accusations, faultfinding, bitterness, and anger. But now, perhaps, they'd had their last fight. Because Tommy had given up.

He didn't want anything to do with Jonathan anymore. He wanted his son to go to prison. He thought that it *was probably the best solution.*

"I don't have the energy to fight anymore," he'd said. "I don't have the energy to be angry." His voice droned inside her head each night when she went to bed.

She had tried to remind him that Jonathan would be clean when he came home from jail. They wouldn't have to babysit him through the worst of it—he'd already gone through withdrawal. But Tommy wouldn't listen. He just said the same thing over and over.

"You have to stop protecting him. We have to stop helping him. We have to stop. You have to realize the kind of person he's become. You have to realize who he is."

So Anne had asked Tommy to move out. Everyone who lived in the household where Jonathan and his ankle monitor would stay must sign the piece of paper from the prison service, so that was the only solution. Tommy couldn't stay. And he hadn't even protested; he had packed his bags the very same day. And two days ago, she had received divorce papers in the mail. As soon as the trial was over, she would sign them.

Today's trial began just like the first two had. The prosecutor started off with a brief explanation of the charges against Jonathan. There was the usual one, possession of narcotics. But there was also the other one. He had been arrested on the grounds of his former school, and the prosecutor claimed that he was selling to the children there. Anne didn't believe it.

"Jonathan is no dealer," she'd told the attorney. "He would never be able to pull it off. You have to be organized and focused, and Jonathan... there's no way, he can't be dealing."

She hadn't meant it as a joke, but the attorney laughed. Not for long, and it wasn't a very cheerful laugh, more resigned than anything. He mumbled something in response, yet Anne didn't understand what he was trying to say. But she hadn't said anything more.

In the courtroom, Jonathan sat side-on to her. If he were to turn his head slightly, he could easily meet her gaze. But he didn't try. His eyes were downcast, he wasn't looking at her or the judge or anyone, just the tabletop. Anne could feel his agony through the glass; it made her heart clench. She knew how he was feeling. It was like his pain belonged to her—not symbolically, but physically. The ache he awoke with every morning originated inside him, like coming down with the flu. She could feel it too. So she understood. She understood that everything he took was so he could survive the day, to overcome the panic that made him want to die. But she also knew that it only helped for a little while, a little bit; it smoothed the sharpest edges but didn't take away the fear.

"He won't stay home just because he's wearing an ankle monitor," Tommy had said. "You know that. It will never keep him from doing what he always does. And if he does what he always does, they will lock him up."

She hadn't responded; there was no point.

The first time the police caught Jonathan with drugs on him, he was sixteen. They hadn't charged him that time because he had overdosed and ended up in the hospital. He'd spent a month as an inpatient, and after that everything was fine for a year. He almost got well. But then it started again. Worse than before, as if he needed to make up for lost time. His first conviction came when he was twenty. The second time he was charged was just over a year ago. He'd been lucky to get probation both times. He wouldn't be so lucky this time.

Anne was familiar with the trial process. It followed a set framework; she even recognized the words and phrases. The prosecutor spoke first, and Jonathan's attorney had a chance to respond. Just as in the previous trials, it seemed unfair that all Jonathan could do was protest. But no amount of protesting would help this time.

"I will do my best to convince them that ankle monitoring is appropriate," Calle the attorney had said. He sounded resigned, as if there wasn't really any point in trying. "The prisons are overcrowded, so maybe it will work. But no promises."

The prosecutor's first witness was the officer who had arrested Jonathan. He was in his thirties, and he stated his name but Anne didn't catch it. He was a fast talker.

He wants to get this over with, she thought. She imagined he wanted to be doing something else, maybe getting back to a homicide he was investigating or to his hardcore training for the Vasaloppet, for he seemed the type to enter the ski race with his friends, and it was only a few months away.

"We were out on another call," the police officer said in a nonchalant voice. "I actually work in Violent Crimes, but we spotted him as we drove by the school and decided to bring him in."

"What made you decide on that course of action?" the prosecutor asked.

The officer couldn't help himself—he scoffed.

Just say it, Anne thought. *I dare you to say it.* But the officer cleared his throat and adopted a more mature tone. He knew the difference between what was proper and what he could only say outside the courtroom.

"The defendant was obviously under the influence," he said at last. "As we drove by, we noticed him staggering around up by the basketball courts. This school has occasionally called in to report individuals under the influence loitering nearby. I know the kids at that school well, and they typically—" He cut himself off. "When we heard over the radio that the incident we were responding to had been handled by some of our colleagues in Violent Crimes, we decided to drive back."

The prosecutor thanked the officer. Jonathan's attorney turned on his microphone, leaned forward, and asked if the witness had actually seen Jonathan make a sale. He emphasized the word "actually."

"No," the officer replied as he inhaled and checked his fitness watch.

"Thank you," said the presiding judge. The officer was allowed to leave.

The prosecution's second witness was a teacher from the school. As she took the witness oath, she looked so anxious that Anne thought she might burst into tears.

"I see him all the time. You know, at the school, I mean. He's always... he always looks like he's on something. We've discussed him with the principal, you know, and the janitors and everything. And the police, of course. We can't... he can't... we can't have people like him on school grounds, obviously." She nodded and looked beseechingly at the presiding judge; it seemed important to her for the judge to share her views. "It's very important. For safety and security, and... our students..."

She ran out of steam when the judge didn't nod back; she simply took notes on her legal pad without looking up.

The attorney asked her the same question he'd asked the police officer, whether she'd seen Jonathan selling anything, but when she hesitated to answer he cut her off. He sounded angry—even furious. As if it was her fault, as if she had been the one to bring it up.

"You must be absolutely certain you saw him selling, if you're going to sit here in court and claim such a thing."

She wasn't absolutely certain, she managed to say, and the attorney wanted to end there. But the prosecutor asked the judge for the floor again. Calle the attorney stared grimly at his notes, paging through them as though it wasn't even worth listening to what was about to be said. Anne dug her fingernails into her palms and bit the inside of her cheek so hard she tasted blood. She wanted to walk out of the gallery; she didn't want to hear any more. But she stayed.

"Could you tell me a little more about what you were thinking when you noticed he was spending so much time around the school, even though he doesn't go there and he's so much older than your students?"

This gave the teacher a fresh burst of energy.

"Obviously I was thinking *why is he talking to our kids? Why does he come to the school every day?* He finished school a long time ago. Why does he keep coming back? Of course I knew he was dealing." She turned to the attorney as though she knew he wanted to say something. "I know he's an addict, he used drugs even back when he was a student at our school. And sure, maybe I didn't see it, the transaction itself, or whatever you call it, but I knew what he was up to. We all did. What else would it be? It's not like he's a pedophile."

Calle became upset; he almost bolted up. The presiding judge nodded in his and Jonathan's direction.

"No one has accused the defendant of—" It seemed like she didn't even want to say the word.

Jonathan cut her off. He spoke so loudly that Anne could hear him through the glass wall, even though the light on his microphone was red, which meant it was off.

"I'm not a fucking pedo!"

"No one is saying you are," the judge said again.

Anne felt ill. Jonathan was dealing. To children. She never would have expected it, not in her worst nightmares. In her imagination, she went back and killed the people who sold drugs to Jonathan when he was young, she would dream of their heads exploding with her bullets, of closing her fingers around their necks and squeezing harder and harder until they stopped breathing. She would dream of seeing them on the street when she was driving, hitting the gas and running them down, reversing over their fragile backs, hearing their bones splinter. Now Jonathan was one of them. Now he was the one tearing lives apart, injecting poison into children's bodies, luring them in with euphoria but spreading death. Slow, tortuous, inhumanely grim death.

Jonathan had no one to testify on his behalf when it came to the accusation itself. But the attorney had called in a psychologist Jonathan had seen a few times. Anne had seen him too; she and Tommy had had to pay nine hundred kronor to listen to him mutter from behind a scraggly beard that failed to make him look any older. He couldn't talk to them about Jonathan, because he was "prohibited from doing so." Instead he rattled off the various methods and theories he "made use of in his therapy practice."

But today he did talk about Jonathan. He looked as if he was delighted for the opportunity, smiling broadly as he talked about Jonathan's poor mental health and how tough his life was, and when he said that Jonathan was "working on recovery" he began to nod. Up and down, up and down, like one of those ceramic cats you see at Chinese restaurants. Calle had explained that the point was to encourage the judge to decide it was better to sentence Jonathan to care instead of prison. But even if that didn't work, it would still increase the odds that he would be sent home with Anne with an ankle monitor.

The judge didn't seem convinced. She leaned forward, peering intently at the psychologist over her glasses.

"In what way is he working toward getting better? Would you give a few examples of steps he has taken in recovery? In concrete terms."

The psychologist's smile vanished.

On only one single occasion had Jonathan gotten the help he needed, and that was after his overdose. He couldn't stay clean more than a few hours, even if he'd spent time locked up and unable to get his hands on what he needed. But that overdose had landed him in the hospital, where he'd been forced to detox and then follow a treatment plan. The hospital staff had been able to get through to him. No one else had.

"Has he followed any particular program?" the judge persisted.

The psychologist shook his head sadly.

"No . . . ," he said after a few seconds. He paused. "Jonathan hasn't found a suitable program yet."

Anne wanted to leave, to stomp loudly out of the gallery to show the judge what she thought of her questions. But she didn't. Instead, she listened as the judge announced a recess and directed everyone to leave the courtroom.

Anne was the first one out the doors. She inserted her card into a coffee machine just for something to do. But the coffee cooled in her cup as she waited to be allowed back inside. Calle had said he would relay Anne's determination to have Jonathan live with her under ankle monitoring; there was no need for her to speak in court. But Jonathan was going to testify. She thought she knew what he would say, but there was no way to be certain.

During his very first trial, Jonathan had told the judge he began to smoke marijuana when he was twelve, and was trying amphetamines and hash within a year. Anne was so shocked that she started crying. She hadn't noticed his problems, or at least hadn't understood what they were, until he was fifteen. She'd thought he was still a child at the time, and to learn that he'd started three years earlier than that was mind-boggling. When he was twelve, she was still kissing him goodnight, she could remember the feel of his smooth cheek, his soft hair. She still helped him cut his fingernails, because he found it tricky and was afraid of cutting them too short. His left thumbnail was thinner than the others and the skin around it was often chapped, even though he claimed to have stopped sucking his thumb when he was seven.

That was the only time she cried during his trials; she had been so unprepared. But she could tell that Jonathan was telling the truth that time, that he wasn't making any of it up.

When she went back into the courtroom and took her seat, she was alone in the gallery. The ladies who'd been sitting nearby were gone. Anne found this surprisingly annoying. They probably didn't think it was *exciting enough.* Those old bitches didn't have to wait for the judge's pronouncement to know what would happen. They knew Jonathan would be going to prison.

Her son's fate was the judicial equivalent of a movie that closed soon after its premiere. *Predictable and boring*, the reviews would have read.

It was Jonathan's turn to talk. The microphone was on now, but he wasn't speaking clearly, Anne had a hard time making out his words; he was mumbling, rambling, and she could tell from his back that he was lying. The judge asked more questions.

Anne knew what the truthful answers would sound like. He had no job, he had no plans for his life, and he lived wherever he happened to pass out. Then the judge asked if what the psychologist said was true, that he'd tried to get off drugs, and he said yes. But it was clear that he was lying.

Jonathan's hands flew through the air, he first rubbed them over his thighs, then through his close-cropped hair, over the back of his neck. His hands were wide, full of marks, his cuticles bitten to shreds.

His hands had nothing in common with those sweaty little-boy hands she used to hold when they needed holding, or simply when she felt like it.

When did he get these other hands? she thought. *When did he stop holding my hand when we crossed a busy street? Or when we were watching a scary movie? Did it happen overnight? Why can't I remember the last time it happened? Why didn't anyone tell me to enjoy it before it was too late?*

She looked at Jonathan as he spoke with the judge. The judge wasn't asking direct questions anymore, but she was talking about the qualifications for serving a sentence with ankle monitoring. She didn't call it an ankle monitor, though; she said, "restrictive surveillance."

Why, Anne thought. *Why is she talking about the penalty already? Isn't she supposed to pretend she hasn't prematurely convicted him?*

"You know," the judge said, "that one of the requirements in order to be a candidate for restrictive surveillance is that you must stay clean. You are aware of this?"

They had discussed it. Tommy had declared this one of the many reasons the whole thing was a bad idea.

"Why would we fight to have him at home when we know it will never work?"

Calle the attorney had said the same thing, just a little more evasively.

"I speak for you and your wishes," he'd said, looking at Jonathan. "What do you think? Do you want me to try?" Jonathan had shrugged. But he also nodded.

He was nodding now too, even though his gaze was fixed on the tabletop.

"Sure," he mumbled. "I'm clean now."

The judge didn't respond, just eyed him over her reading glasses.

"If you can get him an ankle monitor," Anne had told the attorney, "We'll deal with the rest as we come to it."

She remembered how Jonathan's baby body felt in her arms, how he seemed to become heavier once she finally managed to quiet him, when all his tense muscles relaxed and he fell asleep. At the same time, he was easier to carry that way. She remembered his jaw moving in his sleep. His hands grabbing for her, hands that were so strong, with nails as sharp as puppy teeth, grabbing her necklace and not letting go even after he was asleep, fingers she had to pry open before she could put him down.

"It's going to be all right." How many times had she told him that? "Everything is going to be okay."

His diaper butt. The dimples in his chubby knuckles and knees. His wavy, dark blond hair—when he was little, she let it grow out so long that his bangs fell in his eyes and he would blow on them to get them out of the way, or he would brush the hair aside and tuck it behind his ear with such concentration that she had to laugh.

These days, he fiddled with his hair when he was actively lying, or when he was caught in a lie. When the prosecutor asked Jonathan why he had so many drugs on him when he was arrested, he scratched behind his ear.

"Can you explain to me why you spend so much time at the school? Why there, and why not, I don't know, somewhere you can meet people your own age?"

Anne didn't hear Jonathan's reply, but it didn't escape her when he stroked his hand over his scalp seven times—she counted.

The judge nodded as Jonathan spoke. And she jotted something on her legal pad. Then she asked if there was anything else Jonathan thought they should know. He shook his head. With that, she turned to the prosecutor and he was allowed to speak again and then it was Calle the attorney's turn and then it was all over.

"You may all wait outside," the presiding judge said.

Jonathan and the prosecutor and attorney waited in a room of their own. Anne wasn't allowed to be there. Ten minutes later, the loudspeaker crackled and the doors of the courtroom opened so she could go in.

Not even now, she thought. *Not even now can they pretend Jonathan's fate is worth careful consideration.*

"You will be notified when it is time to begin serving your sentence. You are prohibited from traveling abroad, you must remain available, and be prepared for the call to come soon."

He got restrictive surveillance. An ankle monitor. Calle the attorney looked like he wanted to high-five Jonathan when the judge announced the verdict. But then she turned to Jonathan.

"As I have explained to you, this all depends on whether you can remain drug-free. You will have to be tested before you begin serving your sentence, and you will be tested regularly throughout your home confinement. If you do not stay clean, your restrictive surveillance will be revoked immediately, and you will be transferred to a correctional facility. So I suggest you use the time before you begin serving your sentence to deal with your addiction."

She made it sound no more dramatic than a visit to the dentist. She began to collect her things before she was even done talking.

Anne waited outside the courtroom until Calle the attorney and Jonathan turned up. The attorney shook her hand and clapped Jonathan on the shoulder. Then he said, "Bye, we'll be in touch," and Jonathan got a bag from some room Anne wasn't allowed to visit, and then they walked outside together.

Jonathan still wouldn't look at her as they got in the taxi; Anne got into the back seat so he could sit beside her, but he took the passenger seat instead, even though the driver had dumped a bunch of stuff there that had to be moved. Jonathan waited. He would rather wait than sit beside her.

They didn't speak in the taxi. Anne stared at the back of his neck from the back seat, the blond hair, the collar of his T-shirt. His ears, covered in downy fuzz. He had gotten his ears pierced when he was fourteen, without asking permission first. Three holes in one; four in the other. He wasn't wearing any earrings right now. Maybe, she thought, he'd had to take them out in jail.

"Do you need to stop by and grab anything?" she wondered. Jonathan waved his hand in a way that presumably meant *no*, but he didn't reply. So Anne didn't say more, because she didn't want to talk about jail, didn't want to say the word out loud or talk about what would happen next, because the taxi driver would hear and this was none of his business. Jonathan didn't say anything either.

When they reached the house and stepped into the front hall, he dropped his bag on the floor. His jacket landed on top of it. He kicked off his shoes, which flew in different directions—one landed under the radiator, the other outside the guest bathroom. Then he went to his room.

Anne picked up his shoes and placed his jacket on a hanger. Then she started dinner. She was going to make real food. There was hamburger and a package of half and half in the freezer. She defrosted it in the microwave and mixed it with sauteed onion, carrot, one egg, and three crushed rusks. Mashed potatoes and meat patties. They didn't have wine with the meal. Just water.

"I know a place," Anne tried. "I could try to get you in there." But it came out no louder than a whisper. And he didn't respond.

Jonathan ate two servings. He hardly ever had much of an appetite. But today he scarfed his food down without chewing. When the food was gone he became nervous—she recognized that nervousness. He paced, swinging his arms, scratching everywhere he could reach, looking anywhere but at her. They tried to watch a movie. But he couldn't sit still on the sofa.

"Mom," he whispered at last. "I can't. I'm not going to be able to do this. I have to go."

She knew it. Of course she did. But this time was going to be different. She had planned for this—of course she had. Tommy had needed to move out so she could offer Jonathan the chance to ask for ankle monitoring. But that was only the first part of her plan. She knew exactly what she had to do, and Tommy couldn't be here. She would get Jonathan to the hospital. It would never work otherwise. At the hospital, he could go through withdrawal. They were the only ones who could help him. And then he would agree to treatment. The hospital staff would get him to accept it. His fear would help him. Fear would make him do as she wanted. But he had to do it before he began to serve his sentence. He had to get to the hospital before he could forget how miserable he was when he was locked up. Otherwise, this would all be for nothing. She had to hurry.

And he wouldn't have to steal, or buy the cheapest stuff he could find. Today he would get what he wanted from her, and just a little more. He would fall asleep, a little too deeply, as if he were wound in cotton—every inch of skin wrapped up and protected and hidden. And then she would call for help.

"My son is overdosing," she would say. And then the hospital would do the rest.

She asked him to follow her upstairs. Before they went into the bathroom, she took a deep breath. She had placed the items in a metal tin that used to contain cookies, then hid it behind things Jonathan wasn't interested in: pads, tampons, lotion, and shampoo for dyed hair.

Buying what he would need hadn't been a problem. She knew everything she needed to know, Jonathan had taught her—not because he meant to, but because she had always been there, steps behind him, right afterward, too late, too far away.

As she stepped into the hall she heard him tear frantically into one of the boxes. He didn't need water to swallow the pills, he could do it dry. Then, silence. He mumbled something, it sounded like he couldn't believe his eyes. How had she gotten hold of all this? How was it possible?

It took him two hours to fall asleep, and afterward she went in and sat on his bed. Now it was her turn. Now she would do the bit that would put him over the edge.

She stroked his cheek, smoothed his hair, bent down and kissed his forehead. Then she took his hand and closed it around the syringe she'd filled. He woke up and looked into her eyes, saw what she was about to do, smiled wanly and closed his eyes again.

No one would know it had come from her, no one would imagine she could do something like this. They wouldn't suspect a thing. This was just what happened to addicts who had spent time in jail. It was easy to take too much when you'd been clean for a time.

She had always been on her son's side. Loved him, helped him, no matter what. Now she was going to save him. Now everything was going to be okay.

You have to let go, Tommy had said. *You have to let him fall, or he'll never get back up again.* But she would never leave her son. She would never let him die. She would never give up.

She sat beside him and counted slowly to one hundred; once, twice, three times. Then she called the emergency number.

"112, what's your emergency?"

"My son has taken an overdose," she said. "Come quick. He needs help. You have to come right away. He needs help. Come quick."

The voice on the other end sounded distant.

"Do you think you can tell me—how do you know he took an overdose?"

She said it again. Louder this time.

"He needs help. You have to come right away."

Anne could hear the dispatcher clearing their throat. She could hear the sound of other calls in the background. A second passed, then two, three, and four, before the voice returned.

"I don't have any units in the vicinity right now. We're getting a high volume of calls. We'll send someone as soon as possible."

VICTOR

CRIMINAL CODE 10:5

Victor was twenty-nine years old and five foot nine, and he lived with his partner, a woman five years his junior who couldn't cook. Her name was Veronika, and they'd been together for almost four years. She and Victor both had whitened teeth and highlights in their hair, but they went to different clinics for their treatments. Victor thought he was hotter than Veronika. He wasn't. But he had thick, medium-blond hair and dark blue eyes, and one year after he met Veronika he ended up in fourth place on a list of Sweden's best-dressed men. Veronika was the one who bought his clothes. At first, he had trouble understanding why sweaters should have sleeves of different lengths and look like they were inside out when they weren't, but he stopped complaining once that list was published. He even got used to wearing sandals with suits and pants with a crotch that hung so low he appeared to be struggling with a very full diaper.

Victor's father ordered all his clothes, even socks and underwear, from a tailor on Savile Row in London. London was also where Victor had been born. It was where he had spent his first six years of life, before his parents got divorced and he had to move to Stockholm with his mother on a week's notice. Back in London, Victor's father got a new wife, a housekeeper, a footman, and two nannies who worked in shifts to take care of Victor's twin brothers, who were born exactly three months after the divorce was finalized.

Victor lived with his mother in Stockholm for five years. During those five years, he saw his father seven times. Each time they were together, his father asked the same three questions: How is school? How is your mother? Do you have enough money to get by? Victor answered as best he could, and always in the same way. His answers were always "good," "fine," and "yes." It felt like the safest way to avoid any follow-up questions. And indeed, there never were any; his father didn't seem interested in knowing more. But Victor always thought the third question was odd. Didn't his father know exactly how much money Victor and his mother had? The other kids at school said his dad was rich and his mom had gotten tons of money in the divorce, and when he came home and reported this to his mother, she didn't deny it.

"He deserved it," was all she said. "We should have gotten even more."

So one time, when his father asked if he had enough money to get by, he mustered his courage and said, "I don't know. I might need even more?" And for the first time, it seemed like his father actually heard his answer. But instead of getting mad, he burst into infectious laughter. "Exactly!" he said. "How can you be sure you have enough money to get by? There's no way to know. You should always assume you need more." And then he handed Victor a wad of cash, looked at him for much longer than usual, and clapped him a few times, almost lovingly, on the shoulder.

It took quite a while for Victor's father to realize that despite Victor's claims to the contrary, Victor wasn't doing "good" in school at all, at least not in the parts that involved a classroom and especially not the subjects that required any concentration on his part.

In the early years, the issue was mostly homework, and the fact that Victor hardly ever did as he was told. He found it easy to make friends and even easier to land in hot water with teachers and staff, but extremely difficult to complete his schoolwork.

Victor didn't get into fights; he didn't cut class. Even so, the closer he got to the senior grades, the more frequently Victor's mother received concerned phone calls, and a few months before he turned twelve, she got fed up. Telling him he had to shape up was no use, and his grades didn't improve even when she paid a girl to come over every week and help him with his homework. Victor's mother had remarried and was trying to get pregnant; she had torn her Achilles tendon playing tennis and had to rehome the dog she'd bought when it turned out Victor was allergic. She wanted to move to a different part of the city, far from the schools that might be suitable for Victor. In other words, her life was plenty stressful as it was, and she didn't have time to solve all the problems he brought upon himself.

It was decided that Victor would go to boarding school in England. And after Victor's mother sent a copy of his first grades to Victor's father, they found themselves in agreement for once. English-style discipline would whip Victor into shape. It would be good for him to get away from his friends and the social-democratic curriculum of the Swedish education system.

And so, in the middle of fall semester, he was moved to Somerset. The main building of the school had towers and pinnacles and stained glass. It had been a monastery during the seventeenth century, and its picture adorned all the brochures Victor paged through before he was placed on the flight. But when he arrived, it turned out he would be living in a different facility, a one-story sand-lime brick building over half a mile away from the monastery. The classrooms, dining room, and common room were on one end, the dorms on the other. There he would spend every hour of every day until he began Year Nine, more than two years later. Victor was assigned a narrow single bed in a large room with eleven other boys who'd all moved away from their parents when they were six. He had his own wardrobe with nine hangers and two drawers, and he had a nightstand that locked. He wasn't allowed to bring his computer or phone to the dormitory. If he wanted to call home, he had to do it during the scheduled telephone time, which was every Saturday and Sunday between four and six p.m.

When Victor moved to England, he began to see his father more often. He would spend at least one night at his father's place in London at the start and end of every term.

But his father's questions and Victor's answers remained the same, even though his father actually regarded Victor with skepticism when he claimed that school was "good." "Sure," he would say evenly. "If you say so."

Each summer, Victor would fly to Mallorca and spend a week at the house his father had bought with his new wife. Victor had a room of his own there, between his twin brothers' rooms, but they were usually away the week he visited. When the twins were little, their mother would take them to see her mother; when they were older, they were typically away at sailing camp. The idea was for Victor and his father to have a chance to "spend some nice, relaxing time together," but his father's vacations were seldom relaxing. Victor's father liked to spend time with his friends, especially when his wife wasn't there.

Victor never went to sailing camp. His mother insisted he spend time with her during school breaks. And she hated the ocean unless she was enjoying it from a sun chair on a private beach outside Carmel in northern California, or "Carm," as she called it. One of her new husband's companies had offices not far from there.

At first, Victor had a hard time making friends at his English school, but near the end of his second term he found two buddies he got along with: a Norwegian boy named Joachim and an exchange student from Spain named Juan.

Joachim was a year older, had been held back a year, and he convinced Victor to sign up for the rugby team. "Not to play," Joachim explained, "just because it's easier to skip rugby practice than to sneak out of required classes."

Juan was the president of the school's Minecraft club and made, by far, the best grades of the three boys.

Joachim was by his side when Victor drank his first beer; Juan was the one who made sure Victor and Joachim passed math. Juan started dating one of the girls in science club, and it was at her fourteenth birthday party that Victor kissed his first girl. She had braces that cut his lower lip, and Victor thought he was in love, up until a cuter and more popular blond girl from drama club started following him on Instagram. Then he stopped replying to the science girl's texts, and after a few weeks she stopped sending any.

By the time they started Year Nine, the three boys were inseparable. Juan was the best DJ at school, and Joachim was the one who found a local who would buy beer for them and put them in touch with a guy who could get marijuana. Juan was the one who taught them to play the latest and best computer games, and Joachim was Victor's partner in crime when Mr. John, the head of school, caught them smoking behind the dining hall. That time both he and Joachim got "external detention," and Victor had to stay with his father in London for a week. His father wasn't there, but the housekeeper let him order takeout and watch TV as much as he liked. He cried on the train back to school, but when he met up with Joachim later that evening he felt better.

Juan never received disciplinary measures, not even the time all three of them were summoned to explain why they'd all made identical errors on their math test. But the school did give him a warning. Juan was more careful after that; from then on, Victor and Joachim were only supplied with the exact number of right answers they needed to pass the test, never more.

After graduation, Victor began to study business administration at a university in Scotland. It was the only British school to accept him. Joachim took a gap year to do an internship at Goldman Sachs in New York. Juan went to the London School of Economics and moved in with a girl he'd met while working at Roblox over the summer. After seven months, Joachim had not only managed to get hired at Goldman Sachs but also convinced one of his superiors that Victor should be awarded an internship in the same department. So Victor quit school and moved to New York. The plan was to stay for six months, but he stuck around longer. He loved it. The stress that burned out half the interns after a few months was better than any of the drugs he'd ever tried.

After the internship, Victor was hired to work at Goldman Sachs' new office in Birmingham. Joachim stayed in New York, but they saw each other often, either in London, where Juan was working as a freelance game developer after graduating in record time, or in New York. Joachim rented a ridiculously expensive studio apartment. Juan and Victor would sleep on his pull-out sofa bed. They partied at clubs where all the women were six inches taller than Victor but happy for him to offer drinks and cocaine. The guys never got together in Birmingham, of course. Or "Little Pakistan," as Joachim called it. "Everyone's trying to escape from there, no one goes there on purpose."

Victor had been working for almost two years at Goldman Sachs when he and Joachim received a long email from Juan. His girlfriend was pregnant, and Juan had an idea. He'd developed a quality control tool he wanted to sell to one of the biggest game developers on the market, but he thought it was worth much more than he'd been offered. In order to negotiate the best possible deal with the developer, without risking his own know-how, he had to bring in more money. He wanted to be able to hire staff to help him with everything besides the actual content development, wanted his own legal department that specialized in gaming copyright. For that, he needed investors, and wasn't Goldman Sachs one of the world's most prestigious investment banks for a reason?

Joachim flew in from New York and Victor took the train down from Birmingham. They'd received instructions from their bosses to "take their time" and not to "throw money at this Spaniard for no reason." But before the weekend was over, they'd made up their minds. Joachim and Victor would leave their jobs, start their own venture capital firm, find their own investors, and also contribute a hefty chunk of their own personal cash. "Ask your dad, if you have to," Joachim had said. But Victor didn't need to; he already had the sizable fund his mother had negotiated for in the divorce. He would use that. Then they'd go in and bet big on Juan's gaming company. Joachim was almost sober when he took a firm grip on the back of Victor's neck, leaned toward Juan, and declared, "There's no fucking reason we shouldn't be billionaires. Goldman Sachs can fuck itself in its wrinkly old ass." They'd laughed at how furious he sounded, but it wasn't a joke.

The guys' firm did well. Very well, even. In under two years, with Juan's game developing company as a subsidiary, and after finding success with two more start-ups, they built a portfolio valued at two and a half billion pounds. Joachim and Juan were based in London, but Victor moved to Stockholm to handle the Swedish contacts; there were big investors there, the tax system was the most capital-friendly in the EU, and all the Swedes were curious about Victor. Not least because they all knew of his father, the British financier, and his mother, who managed to come out of the divorce settlement with so much wealth that she was practically a legend.

In Sweden, Victor was soon the talk of the town. He ended up on the front page of *Dagens industri* and got to attend a gala where he was named "Rising Star of the Year." That was where he met Veronika, who had just turned twenty and moved down from Gävle to study marketing at Stockholm University. She had come to the gala with some other guy but went home with Victor. And after that first night, she stayed. Victor realized he liked having her there, and although he didn't quite understand how it happened, she took over all the practical details of his life, the parts that had nothing to do with investments. She was in charge of cleaning, she planned his parties, and she proved to be unbeatable at gossip. After a month with her, he knew more about the private lives of potential Swedish investors than anyone else on the market. It was invaluable. He was in love.

Once they'd been together for a little over a year, Veronika convinced him to move from Östermalm, in the heart of Stockholm, out to posh Djursholm. He kept the apartment but let her pick a house on Strandvägen, a stone's throw from Vågaskär, Björn from ABBA's island. That made them neighbors with some of Victor's biggest investment partners. While very few of Victor and Veronika's friends wanted to live outside the city, the couple's parties were legendary, not least thanks to their indoor and outdoor pools. Besides, when Veronika's constant renovation projects got to be too much, Victor could always spend a few nights at the apartment in Östermalm.

On the surface, everything was great. But when Victor was about to turn twenty-eight and Joachim had just turned twenty-nine, "Forbes 30 Under 30" came out, and before it even hit the internet Veronika had informed him of the news. Joachim was on the list. He was named one of Europe's most promising young talents in the "Venture Capital" category. Juan was there too, in the "Gaming" category. Victor's name, however, was nowhere to be found, not even in the description of the company they'd launched together or the fund they had built up thanks to his money.

"It's just a silly list," Veronika said when she called him. "Don't let it get to you."

But naturally, it got to him. It was thanks to Victor, not Juan or Joachim, that they were one of the few new investment funds still holding on despite Brexit, all the pandemic shit, the war in Ukraine, and the Swedish krona crashing as fast as inflation and interest rates were soaring. Sure, Juan was the programming genius who'd gotten the ball rolling, and the gaming industry was one of the few that flourished during the pandemic. And of course Victor knew that outside of Sweden, Joachim was the face of the company. He knew everyone said Joachim had the nose for business, that he was the one who sniffed out the best start-ups, that he was the one who charmed the most generous investors. And Victor knew that everyone in the industry said, behind his back, that he'd only gotten as far as he had because of his father's money and the contacts his father had given him. Even though his father hadn't helped him at all, even though he'd never asked for help or an introduction to a single one of his father's contacts, even though he hardly knew his father, people thought of him as a simple nepo baby, with no drive of his own, no ideas of his own, no money of his own.

The Forbes list was annoying because it provided ammunition to everyone who wanted to talk shit about him. But it was also important, because it reminded him of a crucial fact. It reminded him that it was time to become an adult, sever the umbilical cord, take a step away from everyone who took credit for his accomplishments. He had to do something new, make a big investment, a brave investment, all on his own. And he would have to do it fast, before it was too late to be young and promising. It was high time to show what he was made of.

Times weren't optimal for high-risk investments. The stock market was tanking. And in order to make a major move without Joachim and Juan, he needed a new source of income. He couldn't get more money from his father, who had already made it clear to Victor that the twins would split the inheritance, since Victor had gotten his share back during the divorce. And the billions that were tied up in the trust he shared with Joachim and Juan wouldn't do. He wanted to buy out the penthouse in Palma and the charming, nine-thousand-square-foot mountain cabin in Crans-Montana from the fund. But the interest rates went crazy high when the krona did its Zimbabwe-style plunge, and he wasn't about to become a regular old Joe-schmo millionaire who had to check the balance of his private account at the end of each month—he'd rather get hired by some bank to manage one of their "sustainable funds" with "ethical options" and "socially responsible investments." He would rather die than have to take meetings with new retirees who wanted to find "a safe place" for their ludicrous "savings." He wanted more. Much more.

Victor was no philosopher. He never pondered the meaning of life; to his way of thinking, there was no point. But he knew that a person who earned more money than he had last quarter would never become passé. Money made life complete. No one who could afford their own plane wasted time on flight shame or worried about whether Riksbanken, Sweden's central bank, considered the sky the limit when setting interest rates. Rich people lived longer and were healthier and happier while doing so. In all likelihood, you could buy your way into paradise too. Why not? Hadn't God created Man in his own image? So surely St. Peter was open to having his palm greased.

And as long as Victor continued to earn money, he wouldn't have to think about death. With enough money, he wouldn't need anyone—not his father, not even Joachim and Juan. If he could only get a little wealthier than he already was, he would get the respect he deserved. And no adrenaline kick could match the one he felt when he came across a great new investment opportunity. It made him immortal, confident, and irresistible. And it had been a long time since an investment opportunity had put him in as spectacular a mood as the day he learned about the three-master *Kristina*.

"We're buying a goddamn ship."

Victor's mind had been made up since the birthday dinner, from the moment he learned *Kristina* was for sale. But he didn't say so out loud until he returned home to Veronika that same evening.

"And you didn't even want to go," she replied.

She'd been invited to an "event," so he'd had to attend the dinner solo. He wasn't happy about it. The two of them had been invited because the birthday boy had invested a lot of money in his fund. Even so, Victor had hemmed and hawed until the very last minute. He didn't anticipate being able to squeeze any more out of this particular investor. Besides, the guy was a wet blanket who only hung out with people his own age, middle-aged drips with kids, some of them already on their second marriage.

But Veronika insisted. It wasn't like they argued about it, but she pointed out in a needlessly acid tone that "it's always smart to put in an appearance" and he "should really be better at keeping an ear to the ground" and that "the hosts' kids go to school with the kids of the AI guy who bought that ugly house in Gamla Djursholm, what was his name again?" In other words, it sounded like she was also starting to wonder why he wasn't on that goddamn list. Victor had feared this might happen; she heard all the latest gossip, and of course there were lots of folks with schadenfreude out there, people who weren't about to drop it anytime soon, who would go on and on about that list until the next one came out.

The birthday party was almost unbearable at first. He got trapped with a group of men in their fifties who were having a very detailed discussion about a bicycle that cost 142,000 kronor. He wasn't sure whether they thought that was too expensive, or whether the price was a sign it was a quality bike, and he didn't bother to ask. Victor didn't ride a bicycle and had no desire to.

It wasn't until dinner that the party went from torturous to promising. For some mysterious reason, he was seated next to a woman with A-cups, a wedding ring, and short hair. At first, everything she said was completely useless. Something about the host's ex-wife's curtains, something about a dog the ex-wife had had put to sleep, and a whole lot of complaining about the school the host's son should be attending but which had refused him a spot. Victor listened with half an ear. But then she started talking about a boat—a ship, really—that served as a school.

On only one occasion had Victor gone sailing with his father and his two half-brothers. It hadn't been a fun trip. Shitting in a bathroom the size of a cabinet, showering in saltwater, and sleeping on a mattress one inch thick by two feet wide was not his idea of a good time. He'd also been forced to watch his father and brothers hoisting the sails and shouting inexplicable instructions to one another while he huddled in a corner and tried not to get in the way.

Never again, he had promised himself.

But the boat his dinner partner was talking about was no silly sailboat. It was a ship, built a year before the market crash of 1929, and with its home port in Framnäsviken, just south of the Bridgettine sisters' convent in Djursholm. Victor had seen this ship, had driven past it any number of times. But he hadn't known it was a school.

When she mentioned the owner's name, Victor sat up straight and turned to her so he wouldn't miss what she was saying. He'd been wanting to meet this guy for years, but for some strange reason it had never happened. And somewhere in the middle of her sermon on schools and boats, the short-haired chick leaned closer to him and said, in a voice louder than was necessary, "I heard he's going to sell it all. The entire group."

The guy across from Victor nodded.

"It's true. Sweden's biggest privately owned charter school group. Not just *Kristina*, the whole shebang."

"My husband is calling it an official secret."

"Does anyone know why he's selling?" Victor asked.

The man to his left nodded slowly, with a suggestive smile. He drew his finger across his neck in a throat-slitting gesture. Victor's dinner partner's verbal diarrhea continued with unfettered enthusiasm.

"I really hope they find the right owner. Someone who can take over those amazing schools. We need an alternative to the horrid, socialist public schools."

Victor didn't ask if her children went there, because there was no need. She would tell him either way.

"My oldest will be a second-grader there this fall. I can't imagine the younger ones going anywhere else. My best friend has all three of hers there. They were speaking better English than their parents by grade two."

The guy across the table was almost as effusive.

"They really have the right idea. More teachers for fewer children, special ed support, sports on a whole different level. I asked my kid if I could join their soccer team."

Everyone laughed, Victor with a half-second delay. And conversation continued in the same vein. He was treated to a crash course about a market he'd never considered—*children*. And he could hardly believe it had never occurred to him before. Because inflation, environmental crap, and stock-market crashes might affect consumer patterns when it came to clothing and expensive real estate, but people would always keep popping out children. Women were all the same, their financial situations and ambition notwithstanding. Even Veronika had started to attend baby showers and lie in bed staring at Instagram posts of very pregnant, half-naked women backlit in profile. All chicks wanted to have babies. Lots of them. And kids had to go to school—it was the law. And the older those kids got, the more problems they developed. Problems that had to be solved with money. And unlike other sectors, which depended on luring people in with money, it was primarily the *state's* money that was used to provide children with a decent education. Everyone knew that in times of recession and high interest rates, when private investors became skittish, you should turn to the state. And charter schools did not charge tuition; they were financed from the state education coffers, which paid a certain amount for every child that attended school. Victor hadn't had any idea. He'd assumed charter schools worked like the private schools he had attended. But his dinner companions told him all about this brand-new world. It sounded almost too good to be true. Charter schools weren't a market reserved for people with too much money, like his friends; they served anyone with children, even the poors.

Victor Googled the firm when he went to the bathroom. Sure enough, it seemed to be in trouble. Last year had been their third operating at a loss. Their main competitor was doing much better. It was a smaller company, but even so it had posted profits of almost 490 million kronor. *Half a billion*, Victor thought as he washed his hands thoroughly. *In profits.*

He stood by the towel warmer and brought up a four-year-old interview with the owner of *Kristina*, who was posed in front of a schoolyard full of children. The headline was a quote: "This is the most important investment of my life. Nothing can beat this."

Victor closed the page and tucked his phone in his pocket. So this was more than a moneymaker. Running a successful school business would put him back in the headlines and on the red carpet. Schools were part of everyone's life, in one way or another. "Our children are our future," blah blah blah. You had to respect someone who owned a school, especially if it was a school that helped kids who weren't the offspring of millionaires. He would be admired even by people who didn't understand finance.

As he headed back to his table, he thought about the *Kristina* group. It didn't take a math degree to understand that special ed teachers and tiny classes, state-of-the-art sports facilities, and gourmet food were expensive. But those could hardly be a necessity, or that other firm wouldn't be so profitable. The question was, how much could you dial down the luxury before the parents smelled a rat?

He smiled to himself and took his seat. Victor knew who to ask. One of his mother's best friends' sons was on the education committee of Sweden's second-largest political party. His name was Sixten and they'd seen each other every summer since they were little. His mother liked to organize a long weekend at the house she kept outside Falsterbo and invite all her girlfriends and their kids. According to Victor's mother, the reason the kids were required to come along was that she didn't want to be away from Victor "when he was finally home." But in fact, it was mostly so the mothers could hang out and drink while a handful of au pairs kept an eye on the kids as they jumped in and out of the pool.

That was how Victor got to know Sixten. The reason they'd kept up sporadic contact as adults was that Sixten was always inviting Victor to all sorts of functions, both private and official. Victor wasn't a big fan of politicians, especially ones who wanted to do business; they were pushy. Sixten was no exception. He was also a braggart—he liked to talk like he knew the art of the deal, knew which rules to bend to get where you wanted to be, even though he hadn't made it any farther in life than the worthless Swedish parliament. Victor had never needed his advice before, but now he would prove useful.

When dessert was served, his dinner partner finally stopped chattering. She sipped her champagne and eyed her piece of cake doubtfully.

Victor shook his head and smirked, mostly to himself.

"Who the hell names a boat *Kristina*?" he muttered. "Why would anyone want to call it that? It sounds like a farmwife whose clogs are too big and whose cow has gone dry."

The guy across the table laughed and raised his glass in a toast.

"It's bad luck to change the name of a boat," he said. "So maybe they had no choice."

As soon as dinner was over, Victor went to the wardrobe, grabbed his coat, jogged out through the security gate, and ordered a taxi once he was a few hundred yards from the house. He called Sixten from the taxi and they arranged to meet in the VIP lounge at Spy Bar. Sixten seemed almost ecstatic that Victor wanted to see him. And it didn't take him more than ten minutes to explain how best to make a charter school run at a profit.

"Skip the problem kids. No matter where they come from, and yes, we know where they come from, but whatever, they're expensive no matter what. Find a way to avoid them. Every last one, from dyslexics to droolers, they cost too much. Put together a press release, aren't you dating, like, some PR chick? She's not? Well, she can become one, haha, right? How hard can it be? She can cobble together a plan, like: We will become the most ultramodern school in Sweden, and then you make sure to max out all the expense accounts, IT services, facilities upkeep, materials, library... and you'll be totally transparent about costs so the parents know you're pouring gobs of cash into making this school into the kind of place the public schools can't afford to be, and then you hire your own companies to make it all happen."

"I don't have any IT or cleaning companies—"

"Then start them. You already have the only client you need, and it's one who won't complain. You can tell the parents you're splashing out, making your school better than any other, but no one will actually come check to see what that really means. And if the parents ask why you're firing half the teachers, you just tell them you're reallocating resources."

They had a good, long laugh at that. Victor was starting to like Sixten. *Reallocating resources.* He never would have guessed you could be both a member of parliament and a pragmatist. What was more, Sixten knew all the ministers in government. If they turned out to be half as accommodating as Sixten, Victor would see to it that Sixten brought them by the Djursholm house sometime so they could get drunk and start talking about how to get Sweden and the krona back on their feet again.

When he got home to Veronika he was tipsy but in a chatty mood. He liked to make her feel like she was involved in his decisions, even though she wasn't. At first, she seemed slightly amused.

"What? A school?"

She had been sleeping and seemed miffed to be woken up. But it didn't take long to convince her.

"Don't you get it? The children are our future. We'll make Sweden great again. You'll head up our marketing division and explain the new direction we take. And you can be on the board, if you want," he added. "I'll be the chair, but I need people I can trust."

She liked that. And no surprise, it turned out she had quite a bit of information to share about the current owner. It wasn't just his school that was in trouble. He'd run into a number of major setbacks and had put his house in Djursholm up for sale. His wife was talking about their upcoming move; Veronika thought she'd heard they were going to Croatia, because the wife was Croatian and they had a house there.

"Do you know how dire things must be for them? Who would move to Croatia on purpose? For a week of vacation, fine. But forever?"

The next day was a Sunday. But that didn't stop him from setting up a meeting with the owner of the firm just four hours after his accomplice dug up the right phone number. They met at the owner's headquarters in Mörby. It wasn't a large office at all. The owner introduced himself as Arash, no last name. There was no need for one; although they'd never met they were well aware of one another. The negotiation was the fastest one Victor had ever pushed through. In exchange for a quick deal and complete release of responsibility for the outgoing board, Arash was willing to hand it all over for no more than the listed value.

Victor heard Veronika's voice in his head. *Do you know how dire it must be?*

They decided that the due diligence process must be completed in under two weeks. Victor wasn't worried—scrutinizing a school company that was running at a loss shouldn't be problematic at all.

Included in the sale was one of Sweden's largest charter school companies, with three branches—two in Stockholm and one in Skåne. The ship *Kristina* was a minor part of the operation, but she was recently renovated and, as Arash put it, "brand-elevating." Beyond her three masts, the ship boasted fifty-eight berths in twenty-two cabins, six thousand square feet of sail area, and a mahogany deck. And each year, thirty sixteen-year-olds mustered on the ship alongside twenty-four teachers and teaching assistants, the captain, the cook, and the rest of the crew, to sail to Brest in Brittany and back.

Arash informed him that the boat was used in the education of children with special needs.

"They can't follow the usual curriculum, it's too . . . ," he tried to find the right word. "Demanding, maybe."

"Aha," Victor said. "So it's like a sailing camp for kids who need to get out in the archipelago?" *The type of kid the Green Party wants to send on a luxury cruise to reward them?* he thought, but didn't say. *We'll put a stop to that!*

Arash shook his head. He didn't look amused.

He's an idealist, Victor thought, surprised. *He's sad he has to sell, this means a lot to him.*

"Shall we move on, perhaps?"

It's hard to be an idealist when you're facing bankruptcy.

Arash didn't mention the losses, and Victor didn't bring them up. He didn't have to ask any direct questions about them. The whole firm was one huge losing prospect; even the elementary schools were too expensive to maintain. The vouchers paid by the government didn't add up to enough to cover all the resource-intense needs of the students. But Victor had already drawn up his profit plan. He even knew how he would use the ship to his advantage.

The only problem was that damn boat's name. But that was something he could fix.

I'll come up with something amazing, he thought, *a brand-elevating name.*

"I'd like us to do this together," he told his partner as they were about to get in bed that same evening. "I want us to create a school for guys like me, who maybe aren't the best at school but who want to make money."

Veronika turned to face him as she pulled off her T-shirt and began to unhook her bra.

"What do you mean?"

"And, you know, girls too of course. We'll market ourselves to boys . . . and girls ages fourteen to sixteen who have shown special talent in their studies, or in entrepreneurship."

"Mmhmm." Veronika nodded and stepped out of her panties.

"I'm an entrepreneur, so it's not unusual that I might want to give something back. We can hold inspirational seminars for these kids, and their bored moms can attend if they want to. We'll have to reserve some spots for 'disadvantaged' kids from the west side, or else marketing will be too tricky. The media might come after us. But there must be ambitious boys in that crowd too, right? I got a tip about a new headmaster we can poach from a competitor, one that's turning a much better profit. He and I are going to have lunch, he seems to be really on top of things."

Victor couldn't hold back a chuckle as he thought of what Sixten had explained about unlimited profit ceilings. He let the laugh out and added, "I was thinking of offering the Minister of Education's husband a spot on the board. He's buddies with Sixten and seems like an ambitious little fucker. Already on a couple of boards, but they're so dull he'll probably bend over backward to join this one."

"I have tons of ideas for inspirational speakers," Veronika said, climbing naked into his arms. "They can really make a difference. This is going to be freaking awesome."

The grand opening of Victor's charter school company was held on the ship, partly because it was the perfect setting for a party, partly because the kids who were selected for the inaugural journey after the change in ownership would make for a perfect photo op. Twenty kids who looked just like Victor had at that age, and ten who hailed from other parts of Stockholm but who checked every box imaginable when it came to achievement and educational performance.

One of the princesses was there; her dyslexia foundation had donated a small amount to have their logo included on the charter schools' uniform shirts. To be sure, Victor had fired eleven of the twelve special ed teachers the former owner had hired, but these days there was a line in the budget called "special support measures" that equaled the amount previously allocated for those staff. Exactly what these support measures would entail would be determined "in regard to the students' individual needs" and would be delivered by Victor's own brand-new IT company. That should take care of that.

His newly appointed headmaster was there as well. The headmaster was already a little tipsy when he arrived, but it was a beautiful day, and he'd come from a long lunch with the politician who'd recommended him to Victor. They didn't talk for long, but the headmaster assured Victor that the kickoff weekend he'd held for the key staff had been a success.

"They're on our same wavelength. They get that we're not running a charity here. That we can't stretch in every direction at once. If things get to be too much for one lone student, they can just as well stay home. Habitual truants are cheaper than kids who insist on coming to school and forcing everyone to go along with their screwy demands."

Victor nodded and clapped him on the back.

"That sounds great, I trust you."

But then he wandered off. He had no desire to get bogged down in the details of the operation. As long as the money was coming in as it should, and the schools started turning a profit, he wasn't about to interfere. He was already on to the next big thing. His buddy the Minister of Education had invited him to lunch, where he got to meet the Minister of Justice, who was an exceptional bore. But during coffee, Victor had settled on his next venture: correctional care. Because if the Minister of Justice could implement even half the plans to lock up increasing numbers of ever-younger offenders on considerably longer sentences, Sweden was going to need more prisons around so more prisoners could be crammed into smaller spaces, not to mention facilities that didn't cost so damn much. Fighting crime was a billion-kronor industry; Victor couldn't believe he hadn't thought of this earlier. There was tons of money to make there. Maybe he would buy some of the facilities that used to house refugees and renovate them into correctional institutions. That probably wouldn't cost much. He would make Sweden a safer country and be on the frontlines, raking in profits, while doing so.

Victor gave a speech. As the flag pennants snapped in the August sun, he declared that the ship would be called *Libertas*, like the goddess of freedom, like Lady Liberty who stood in the harbor in New York, raising her torch for the dreams of freedom and the equal worth of all; the dreams of justice and success. Because he firmly believed that anyone could become anything, as long as they put in the hard work. This was exactly what he himself had done, and look at him now: He had more money than he could possibly spend. Everyone chuckled at that. Then he thanked his old teachers for making him hate school, and they chuckled even more. And in conclusion, he broke a magnum of Dom Perignon 2000 against the hull, and vegan appetizers were served at the reception.

Veronika was dressed in white and stood next to him as the applause turned into a standing ovation.

One hour later, Victor and Veronika were kissing in the car.

Their part was over. They could sit back and relax. The only reason Victor might need to visit the schools was to be photographed for media profiles. And there was no lack of interest on that front. One of the TV channels had asked if he would consider participating in a documentary about "the new Sweden." Veronika had instructed him to hold off on responding; she was going to look into what sort of documentary it was first. After all, he didn't want to draw scrutiny this early in the game. He wasn't worried, though.

He couldn't remember the last time he was so pleased with an investment. He was in the center of the action, earning money on what every Swede considered the most important part of life. He could hear the applause almost as clearly as he did the money pouring into his accounts.

"What do you say?" he whispered to Veronika as he stuck his hand under her skirt and ripped her nylons at the crotch. "Want to go home and make a baby?"

ULRIKA

CRIMINAL CODE 4:2

I don't think you want to hear this story. But I don't care. It's not a tidy narrative with a dramatic inciting incident, chapters that are just the right length, and a happy ending. You want to hear that everything always happens for a reason, that doing the wrong thing can sometimes be right, that it's necessary to sacrifice your principles for the greater good. But this is not that kind of story, it's not going to teach you anything, it's not going to open any doors to deeper insights about life. My telling it is not going to make anything better. But I'm going to tell it anyway, although I don't even know how it begins. No one is forcing you to listen. I'm not doing this for you.

I knew I wanted kids eventually, but Johan wanted them first. For two years he wouldn't shut up about how much he looked forward to being a dad. I liked the fact that he had to convince me, that he was the one who felt his biological clock ticking, rather than the other way around. But I was hesitant. Because I knew it would affect my life more than his, no matter how much we pretended *we* could be equal partners in parenting, unlike every other mom and dad in the whole world. I wanted a career, and I wasn't ashamed of it. I worshiped the cult-like atmosphere of the company I worked for. And to know I was one of the chosen ones who got to work there, and not just any old employee but one of the most instrumental ones, one of the people who always kept an overnight bag at the office so as to accept surprise business trips? That only made it better.

I loved everything about my crazy job. The happy hour every Friday, with interns the partners had hired for the sole purpose of hitting on them, the Chinese takeout we got delivered to the office after business hours, the conferences where we drank too much at night and talked shit about our competition, only to get up ridiculously early and spend all day at seminars that mainly functioned as a venue to discuss how great we all were. It was like high school, except with money and friends. I was young, impressionable, and thought I had my whole life ahead of me before I had to grow up. Even so, I agreed to have a baby. Maybe I thought it would take a while to get pregnant—that had been the case for my mom and all my friends. Maybe I was picturing at least a couple years of unwelcome periods, negative pregnancy tests, and visits to an IVF clinic. Two of my best girlfriends had already asked if I wanted recommendations for a good doctor. One of them thought I should try acupuncture.

But my biological functions were in tip-top shape. Two months after I went off the Pill, I was doubled over the toilet and puking. Johan was overjoyed and I felt remarkably proud. Because my body worked, I guess. As if this said something about my ability to parent, as if it was a sign everything would be fine. As if the fact of my fertility was another line to add to my CV.

During my pregnancy, we did all the things expectant parents do. We looked at pictures and diagrams to keep track of the embryo's growth. Waited exactly ten weeks to share the news that we were having a baby, then felt dissatisfied when people's responses were insufficiently enthusiastic. And when we revealed that it was a boy, I felt even more disappointed—mostly with my father, because he was so thrilled. *Isn't the most important thing that the baby is healthy, not that I'm expecting a boy?* I wanted to say. Because this wasn't the Stone Age, was it? And Johan and I argued about how much a stroller should cost, and obviously we took pictures, not just of my growing belly but Johan's too. I started reading about the different stages of pregnancy and saw pregnant women everywhere; I knew exactly which celebrities were in the same week as me, and I followed every dietary guideline scrupulously, not just the ones I was given at the clinic. Meanwhile, Johan and his friends were discussing the best kind of car for a young family.

And despite all of this, despite the fact that we were becoming totally different people even during my pregnancy, we said the same thing every other pair of parents-to-be says: "Our lives aren't going to change just because we have a baby. Things will be the same as always. A baby is just a small person." I think we even believed it.

But you can imagine what happened. Parenthood transforms everyone. You don't have to be a parent yourself to realize this. When Liam was born, the world shrank to the size of a walnut. The moment I saw him, everything changed. Yes, I know it's a cliché. Yes, I know it doesn't make me special, I know it's pointless and silly to say so because all normal new moms feel the same. Nevertheless, it was a shock to me, the way life turned upside down. The way everything I thought I knew was thrown into doubt. It was nuts. I lay in my hospital room that first night, listening to him snore, and I was fascinated to know he could do that—snore, that is. I hadn't expected my baby to do anything except obvious baby things. I'm sure this sounds stupid, but I thought I was prepared because I had packed that hospital bag with diapers and tiny onesies, socks and salves, even a pair of newborn-sized sneakers, which naturally he never wore, not even once. I'd read a few books, gone to all my checkups, downloaded an app, and thought I would automatically know everything about him because he had been inside me. I thought we already knew each other and that he was literally just an extension of me.

I had not expected that I might look at him and have no idea what he was thinking about, or that it would hurt me—as in, real, physical pain—when he cried. And I definitely thought I would be able to control what he did or didn't do, feel, and want, at least while he was a newborn.

But discovering otherwise didn't make me angry. It didn't make me sad, not like that. Once the shock faded, it only made me more focused. I would never again have to wonder about the meaning of life, and perhaps that made me happy. No, I'm sorry. I *know* it made me happier, and

I apologize if that sounds like another cliché, but it's true. Liam is the love of my life, and none of what happened later can change that fact.

At the birth center, everything was simple, and Liam took control of me. My body belonged to him. Breastfeeding went well. The staff praised me, even though he was the one sucking on my body so hard I could feel my uterus contract. He made a fist against my swollen breast, scratched me with his razor-sharp nails, and bit me when the milk didn't let down fast enough. All of this hurt, but it felt right. The pain meant it was important.

Now, I'm sure you think I'm painting a rosy picture here, that I'm choosing to remember the good parts because it all turned so intolerably nasty later. Maybe that's true. But it doesn't mean I'm going to talk about how my child made my life difficult. About how hard it was not to get any sleep at night, how horrible it is to be stuck in an ER waiting room with a child who has an ear infection. Plenty of other people tell those stories. Every other TV show or movie or book seems to be about how awful parenthood is and how it only leads to tragedy. Abraham being ordered to kill his son as a test from God, or Medea killing her children to punish her unfaithful husband. But that's not my story. I didn't develop postpartum depression, and I definitely didn't secretly wallow in disappointment with Liam because he took my life away from me. I've always known that Liam is the most important of all, even at the birth center when he was a mystifying newborn. And no, my job was not a place for mothers who wanted to be with their children.

Naturally, I had to switch to a less demanding job. But I didn't miss my career. It could hardly measure up to what I got to have instead.

Back then, when he was a tiny, newborn baby, it was easy to be his mother. I assumed every challenge I overcame was proof that it didn't matter how hard life might get. I thought I could handle it. I was a mother, and I was stronger than ever—nothing could break me.

Liam was always himself. He was never entirely mine. Sometimes he looked at me with skeptical, almost suspicious eyes. But I loved his reticence, how it felt like he could see right through me, like I had to work for his love even when he was a newborn. And little by little I conquered him. He fell asleep with his cheek against my bare skin; he woke up with his hand still clasped around my necklace.

When he got older, I drew him in with tales of the heroes he wanted to be and the adventures he didn't have the courage to set out on. He was occasionally anxious, often had nightmares, never wanted to play war games, but I could comfort him. With his hand in mine, he found the courage to climb, swing, and jump just like the other kids. And we enjoyed being together. He talked to me about everything, told me about things that scared him, friends who said mean things, girls he had crushes on, teachers who were weird. He came to me with the stuff he couldn't tell anyone else. He wasn't ashamed; he knew I would never judge him.

But even so, I lost him. When he was a teenager, of course. That's when he stopped believing I could help him. That's when he stopped wanting to hold my hand.

I don't think I had a teenage rebel phase. That process of separation that everyone says is so important—I never had to go through that. Maybe I wasn't as close to my parents as Liam was to me. Maybe they didn't want me as much as I wanted Liam, could that be it?

When I was little, and wanted to please my father, I would polish his glasses. It made me feel all warm inside when I handed them back and he put them on, peering at me over the rims to whisper *you're daddy's little girl.* God, I loved that. Daddy and me, you know? I always missed him, even when he was home, and it felt like Christmas and my birthday combined if he happened to laugh at one of my jokes or nod thoughtfully at something I had said.

With Mom, things were uncomplicated. I never pondered how to make her happy, or even wondered if she was content. Her role in my life was clear, self-evident.

I thought Liam would always love me the same way I loved my parents. I thought I would never lose him. But when he turned thirteen, he stopped trying to make me laugh or consider something new. He stopped talking to me; he wanted to be rid of me entirely. He didn't want to see me, hear me speak, be anywhere near me.

To be fair, it was the same with Johan—Liam didn't talk to his father either. But Johan wasn't as bothered by it, at least not at first.

"It's normal at this age," he said. There were a thousand possible explanations, all of them natural. Hormones, a crush, the fear of growing up... or should we call a dermatologist? Our friends with older children had gone through the exact same thing. "It will pass," they said. So we went to dinners and told stories about our kids and laughed, and sometimes it felt like we were competing to see who could tell the funniest joke about feeling like their own child didn't love them. "Teenagers are monsters. It's like being back in school and having a crush on someone who thinks you're the biggest dork in the class. It's not fair that we have to go through menopause and have a teenager in the house at the same time!"

But when we were alone, it wasn't funny anymore. No one was laughing. Liam was unpleasant to be around, and meaner than I'd thought possible. He shouted, he closed himself in his room, he slept until well into the afternoon. I would walk by his door and stop outside it to listen, hardly daring to breathe in fear he would notice what I was up to. Should I go in? I didn't want to bother him, but I wanted to show I was there for him. I wanted to make appropriate demands, set smart limits. But without provoking him, because I wanted him to feel that I respected him.

Back then, in the beginning, I was still worried about that stuff, worried about what he'd think of me. I thought it was important for him to feel that we trusted him. I looked to the future, trying to convince myself I was building up the relationship we would have when he was an adult, when we would respect one another and he would love me in a new, independent sort of way.

Sometimes I asked Johan what he thought, and he said Liam was spoiled. Or did he feel ignored? Maybe he was upset that Johan had started working too much. Should the two of us really take that trip alone together? Only children don't have it easy; could it be something else? Did we need to make sure he knew it was perfectly fine if he was gay?

Johan got mad, he felt attacked, as if I thought it was all his fault. I protested, but he was right. I wanted it to be Johan's fault, I hoped it was, and if I had believed in God I would have fallen to my knees and begged to have someone, anyone, to blame for Liam's rage and grief, as long as that someone wasn't me.

One day I found an empty wine bottle in the pantry and a cigarette butt on the window ledge outside Liam's room. He threw a fit when I asked him about it. The cigarette belonged to a friend, he said, and the wine bottle definitely wasn't his, and even if it was, how could I think he would be so fucking stupid as to leave it in the pantry? When Johan got home, we talked to Liam together. We tried to explain that his actions were normal, that we too had tested boundaries when we were his age. But they were also unacceptable. He had to understand the risks, understand that he was way too young to start drinking and smoking.

The discussion didn't last long. And it ended poorly. Liam fled to his room. When we followed him, he was sitting on his bed and slamming his head against the wall. I thought he was going to crack his skull open. Over and over—I counted five times before Johan stopped him, and he screamed at the top of his lungs as Johan held him tight. When I tried to put my arms around him, he bit my arm so hard it put a hole in my T-shirt. I ended up with a U-shaped bruise just below my shoulder, and it lasted a whole week.

That's when I got scared. More scared than before.

"I think he needs help," I whispered to Johan before we fell asleep. But he didn't answer. Maybe he had already dozed off, but I don't think so. I think he just didn't know what to say. And the next day, Liam was almost his normal self. For several days in a row, he ate breakfast before he left for school. He sat down with us for dinner and answered questions about his day.

Maybe it has passed, I tried to think. *Maybe he's feeling better now.* But that was probably around the time I realized this was only the beginning.

Six weeks after his first big meltdown, Liam came home early from school, locked himself into the guest bathroom, and swallowed two packages of Tylenol.

On my way home from work, I picked Johan up from the train station because it was raining so hard. We got home ten minutes after Liam. His backpack was in the hall, but he wasn't in his room or in the kitchen or in front of the TV, and then we realized the guest bathroom was locked. We may never have been on the same page as much as we were in that moment, Johan and me.

Liam cried when we broke down the door, screamed as I called for an ambulance, he bit me again—this time on the hand, hard enough to draw blood, as I pried open his mouth and tried to stick my fingers down his throat while his father held him from behind so he couldn't get away.

He had to spend two weeks in the psych ward after that. We learned from his doctor that he had suicidal thoughts. That he'd had them for over a year. What did we say to that? I don't remember. Johan cried.

"What do we do?" I asked the doctor.

He said that Liam would be prescribed medicine. A treatment plan would be made. We would receive support, he said.

"What kind of support?" I asked.

While he was in the hospital, we removed the lock from the bathroom door. We took away the key to his room so he couldn't lock himself in there either. I searched his room. Liam used to like playing with Legos. He used to watch Melodifestivalen with his parents, all of the heats leading up to Sweden's entry for Eurovision. The boxes I used to dump all his scattered toys into before tucking him in at night were still under his bed. In them I found two razor blades and a diary. There were two empty whipped-cream chargers in a half-open pencil case on his desk. I read the diary. I checked his backpack. There I found two more razor blades, wrapped in toilet paper. The next day I went to the IT expert at work and asked him to help me hack Liam's phone. He said it would be much easier to simply report Liam to Meta, TikTok, Bereal, and Snapchat and demand that they close his accounts. So I did.

"But you have to take his phone away or he'll just create new ones," the IT guy said. "And his computer."

He looked skeptical, aware that I wouldn't be able to keep Liam off the internet. He knew it was a losing battle.

When we visited Liam at the hospital, I told him I would be taking his phone and computer away from him whenever he wasn't at school.

"Do you hate me?" he screamed. "Do you *want* me to die?"

"Do you hate your family?" I asked. "Why do you hate me?"

He looked frightened. I was scaring him.

"You can't," was all he would say. Over and over again, the same words. "You don't get it, I need to, I can't explain." I don't know what he meant, what he needed to do, what he couldn't explain.

"Try to secure your home," the doctor said as he discharged Liam. "You have to keep an extra eye on him. Call us if you notice that he's getting worse."

"Yes," Johan said. "We will."

"What do you mean?" I asked. "How will we know if he's getting worse?"

We were given the clothes Liam had been wearing when he was admitted. They were in a white plastic bag. They still smelled like vomit. The medicine was in a separate bag. I didn't let Liam carry it. The doctor had told me to make sure he took the right dose. That was my responsibility.

"If he refuses to take it, call us," he said. "And we'll have to admit him again."

Control is a dangerous road to set out on. There's no end to it, no stage at which you can relax, rest on your laurels. You will never have the amount of control you think you want. But you do it anyway, you do everything you can and a little more, you run faster and faster along the precipice until your legs can't keep up and you fall headlong.

Take the phone-tracking app, for instance. I told Liam he was required to keep it on and allow access to his location so I always knew where he was. He did. After the hospital, he did most of what I asked of him. The medication made him tired, and he wasn't as angry anymore. He spent most of his time at home, but the few times he went out, I would spend hours staring at the little dot on my phone that showed me where he was. On the days he was at school, the dot stood still. But what was he doing there? The dot couldn't tell me that. He spent every evening at home. But he would retreat to his room. I could order him to leave the door open, but I still couldn't see what he was thinking. What thoughts were torturing him, why he was in such pain.

"That's your responsibility," the doctor had said. "You have to keep an eye out, in case he gets worse."

Worse than what?

I bought drug tests at the pharmacy and made him take them. I stood behind him in the bathroom and watched as he peed on the stick. They never came up positive for anything that couldn't be explained by the medication he was on. I forced him to show me his forearms, I went in while he was showering to see if he had cuts on his legs. He didn't. But he wasn't getting better. He didn't want to eat, didn't want to leave his room, he said he was visiting friends but instead went down to the laundry room to sit with his hoodie over his head. He pretended to eat, pretended to go to school, stopped working out, and stopped talking, but kept screaming at night, kept wearing long sleeves, baggy clothes, dark hoodies, untied shoes.

But was he worse? I called the doctor for advice. He said it might take some time for the medication to make him feel better.

"Let's wait and see," said the doctor. So we did.

Liam had to go back to the psych ward after his second attempt. That time, he did it in a school bathroom. Almost an hour went by before anyone found him, and Johan and I weren't allowed to see him until the next day after he'd had surgery, something about bleeding in his stomach that needed intervention. Liam was propped up in a bed with its safety rails up when we entered his room. The nurse who showed us in informed us that he was still sedated. He looked cold, so I placed an extra blanket over him. Johan spoke to the nurse in a loud, agitated voice. He wanted to know what had happened; he kept asking why. *Why why why?* I wanted to tell him to stop. Shout *shut up! How is she supposed to know?*

A week later, when we were allowed to bring Liam home, he met my gaze when Johan stopped at a red light. He had gathered everything into that one look. I thought he was going to say something, that he hated me, maybe. That would have been good—for him to express an emotion that wasn't about hating himself and his life, but something different. But he was quiet and then he turned away when I took his hand. He left his hand where it was, though, and it was totally limp.

We started locking his door from the outside when we couldn't be with him, and at night when we wanted to try and get some sleep. Johan fastened his windows shut so they couldn't be opened either. We hooked up his old baby monitor so he could call for us if he needed to get out. But we did lock him in. He became our prisoner.

I took leave from work. More and more often I called the school to report that Liam would be home sick, because I couldn't keep an eye on him there. I took away his phone and his computer, and if he wanted to play games or call someone he had to do it in the den. He didn't ask for his things back. Every evening he sat down to eat with us, and the rest of the time he mostly just slept.

"It's the medication," his doctor said. "It makes him tired."

And a month passed, then two. He spent almost all his time at home. Summer arrived. When autumn came, he had to start school again. He was behind, but it might be reparable, the teachers said when we asked. We cut his therapy sessions back from four times a week to two. After seven months, we stopped locking his bedroom door every night. After eight months, I dared to let myself think, for the first time, that maybe we had turned a corner. That it might all be okay.

For eleven months, we had good days, worse days, days I don't remember, and days I will never forget.

The night before, the three of us ate dinner all together. It was a Monday, it was an early-release day at school, and Liam seemed to be in a good mood. No, I take that back, he *was* in a good mood. I've relived that night so many times, and I wasn't imagining it. We talked about the weekend. Did he want to come along to visit Grandma and Grandpa? *Maybe*, he said. I didn't press him for an answer, but I thought it looked like he was smiling.

At four a.m., I woke up because it was very cold in our bedroom. He'd gone up to the attic. The door that led up there was open. Cold air streamed down through it; no one went up there except to get out the Christmas decorations or put them away. I had been planning to ask Liam if we should fill a box or two with stuff from his room he didn't use anymore, and maybe store it up there. But I hadn't gotten around to it.

Johan got him down, I don't even know how. He started CPR while we waited for the ambulance. Afterward, he said I was the one who called for help, but I don't remember doing it. I got to ride with Liam, and Johan followed in a police car, he shouldn't drive, they all said, it could be dangerous. We arrived at the same time, we watched the hospital staff move Liam from the ambulance stretcher to one of theirs. They ran off with him in a big hurry. *He's still alive*, I remember thinking. *They wouldn't be hurrying if he was already dead.* Then we were instructed to wait in a room and Johan took my hand. I couldn't remember the last time I'd held Johan's hand, but I felt dizzy, I thought I would fall over unless someone held on to me. Johan was still holding my hand when the doctor came back with the news.

"I want to see him," I know I said. And they took us to him. When we entered the room, he was lying on a stretcher. They had lit a candle and pulled a white sheet over him, all the way up to his chest. His arms were down along his sides, and I took his hand. It didn't feel like his skin. He had no eyelashes; he had been in the habit of pulling them out for so long that I usually didn't even notice anymore. But now I could see that they'd started growing back on the left side. He had been feeling better, I hadn't just been making it up.

I turned to the nurse who had accompanied us in.

"He's cold," I said. And she didn't contradict me, just went out and got a blanket. I draped it over him and tucked him in, not too firmly, just right. I don't remember much after that. I don't want to talk about it. If I do, it will become more important than everything else, and that would be a lie. You think this is the last chapter of the story. The tragic end. But you're wrong. Because Liam's story doesn't end with his death.

When he comes to me in my dreams, I can't predict when it will happen, I can't prepare myself or force it to happen, and he's usually about seven years old. He's happy. He wants to cuddle, talk, sleep in my bed. In my dreams he's always close to me, I'm allowed to touch him, I'm allowed to hold him for a long time, letting my finger trace the lines of his face, I'm allowed to press my lips to his forehead, inhale the scent of him. In my dreams, he's alive. And it doesn't hurt, not until I wake up. These dreams sustain me, give me the strength to remember, talk about him, look at photos, touch the things that belonged to him. To never let go of his life.

The most important part of this story is Liam's life. He is the beginning and the end, eternity, everything. Nothing can ever change that.

SARA
CRIMINAL CODE 20:3

Summary: Background information concerning filed report.

Case no.: 0230-K2203-24

Local Police Precinct Björkvalla filed a report with Special Investigations.

Among the duties of LPP Björkvalla, as for many other actors in law enforcement, is maintaining awareness of the current situation concerning gun violence and gang bombings, as well as handling the complex problematics facing Björkvalla.

In dealing with the criminal gang known as the "Björkvalla Network," LPP Björkvalla discovered that a number of cases have faced obstruction from the moment they were opened. These problems were first noticed in late 2023/early 2024. Suspicions were raised that privileged information was being leaked to the Björkvalla Network when obvious discrepancies and cautious behavior were noticed in the suspects under surveillance, after covert coercive measures were implemented against the network. Among other changes in behavior, the telephones being surveilled stopped being used.

This crime is of a nature that puts the entire system at risk, and chief district prosecutor Lena Andersson initiated an investigation under the rubric "aggravated breach of duty of confidentiality." The purpose of the investigation was to determine whether someone provided privileged information to the network, and if so, who.

They picked me up at work. I was in my office. They sent two uniformed policemen, as if I were dangerous, possibly armed. I was informed that they wanted to question me, and then I was driven to the suburbs, to the district court out there. I wondered why we couldn't just do it in our interview room, which is only three floors down from my office. But there might be a conflict of interest, they said, as if I was getting it on with someone in law enforcement, which is absurd. I hardly even say hi to the prosecutors and police officers that come up to our offices, not even the ones I've seen a hundred times. And they definitely don't say hi to me. They don't know my name, and they don't care. How could they have a conflict of interest just because we work in the same building? There's no logic to it.

When we arrived at the other courthouse, I was frisked. Again, totally illogical. Did they think I was walking around with a loaded gun in my fake leather Zara purse? Still, they took out my lip balm, my hand cream, and my leather gloves and turned them this way and that, as if they contained secrets. Then they kept my purse and everything inside it, and we went to the interview room. After we sat down, the prosecutor and the officer on one side of the table and me on the other, they asked if I wished to have a lawyer. I certainly did. I had worked in the courts long enough to know who's good and who to avoid at any cost. Naturally I knew why I was there, and I wasn't about to say a word until my attorney arrived. I understood the gravity of the situation as well, of course, but in some ways I was relieved. *It's finally over*—that was the feeling. *Now B. can get the help she needs.* I'd been thinking for a while that I ought to contact the police, I just hadn't known how to go about it. But now it wasn't my fault, I couldn't be blamed. And the police would understand, they were human, they were familiar with Lubbe and knew what he was capable of. I guess I expected I'd be heading home after an hour or so, the time it would take to work it all out. They needed to talk to B., of course, and maybe put some safeguards in place during the ongoing investigation, but they would realize I wanted to cooperate, even if B. was afraid to talk. But that's not how it turned out.

First I was placed under arrest. Two days later, I was jailed. I was put on restrictions and had a private cell. Phone calls to my family were monitored, and Stefan and the kids have only been able to visit me twice. When they do visit, a guard sits with us to make sure we don't discuss the case. They worry I might sabotage the investigation if they don't keep me locked up, that's what the prosecutor said during my detention hearing, and the judge agreed. I had entered bizarro world. It's like I'm in a bad movie.

I don't know if I could have predicted how my family would react. It wasn't something I'd ever thought about before. But now that I know, it doesn't feel like much of a surprise. Stefan is furious, of course. I know he is, even though he hardly says a word when he visits. He's not an aggressive man, he's never hit me or anything like that. It's been years since he lost his temper and broke something. But now his rage is back. It's not like I have any trouble working out what's making him angry. And it's probably not what I did, or at least that's not the main reason. I don't even know if he understands what I did or if he's learned why I did it. The police say my family isn't allowed to know anything about the investigation "at this stage." But maybe the newspapers mentioned it anyway. I have no idea. But one thing is certain: He's furious that I got caught. That I'm bringing shame upon him. His anger over what the neighbors are saying, what our friends are gossiping about, what the newspapers are publishing—it was so powerful that I could almost reach out and touch it in that tiny visiting room where I got to see him and the kids, Oskar and Ingrid, the day after I was put in jail. The second time they visited me it was almost worse. That time, it was just Stefan and Oskar. And they haven't come back since either. I tried to call a few times, but no luck. Maybe it's just as well. We can figure it all out when I'm free again.

Whenever our friends find something to talk about beyond their aches and pains and new medications and how this person got diagnosed with cancer or how that person got sent to a memory care facility, they get all excited. A fresh, unexpected misfortune like the one that got me, and they rediscover a vigor they haven't had for decades. They love gossip, and the fact that I'm in jail must be the most spectacular piece of gossip our friend group has ever encountered. It's even bigger than the time newly divorced Fredde went to Thailand for New Year's and came home with a wife who was eleven years younger than his oldest daughter and hardly spoke any English.

I'm younger than almost all our friends. I call them "ours," but really they're Stefan's. It's always been that way. My husband and I are twelve years apart in age. Our life, my life, has always been out of sync with his friends'. When I was struggling with diapers and sleepless nights, they were talking about how their kids broke into the liquor cabinet or came home smelling like cigarettes. And now, when I still have a job to go to, they spend their days rushing between golf and bridge. Their topics of conversation rotate between arthritis, grandchildren, and other people's misfortunes. Nothing brings them as much joy as when things go really badly for someone they don't actually care that much about. I'm one of those people, to them, the kind that livens the mood when she makes a fool of herself. Now they can delight over the fact that I'm about to lose my job so close to retirement. I suppose I've never really had close friends of my own, not since high school, anyway.

Obviously I realize that the gossip is impacting Stefan, and he finds it upsetting. All the whispering, all the *did you hear what Stefan's wife did?* Of course he's angry, even if he won't say so out loud. I presume he's yelling at the kids instead, that's what he typically does. Any kind of hardship, anything he can't control or solve by raising his voice or throwing money at it, makes him lose his temper. And that affects the whole family. Maybe that was why Ingrid wasn't there for the second visit, she's my sensitive child, even if she isn't a child any longer. And if by "sensitive" you mean "cries as easily as Stefan gets mad." Women who cry at the drop of a hat have always been one of my pet peeves. When Ingrid sat in the visiting room at the jail, sobbing so hard she let out tiny moans between breaths, I wanted to walk away. But I didn't. I nodded and made comforting sounds and tried to look the way they wanted me to look, even though I didn't know how. At any rate, it wouldn't put a dent in Ingrid's weeping or Stefan's repressed rage.

Oskar is the one who's more like me. He's reserved, doesn't speak except out of necessity. Both times he's been here to visit me, he has only asked me about practical matters. Am I satisfied with my attorney? Are they treating me okay in jail? Do I need help with anything? Am I eating? Sleeping? *How are you doing, Mom?* Oskar hasn't raised his voice once. I haven't seen him cry since he was in elementary school. Even so, I know. I know he despises me and what I did. But I can't explain my reasons, because I'm not allowed to discuss the investigation with them. Everything they'll hear about what happened will come from people who aren't me, and that doesn't seem especially fair. I wonder if Oskar will let me see his and Erika's children once this is all over. Or if it will be too late to explain why I did what I did, once I'm allowed to. I guess we'll see. There's nothing I can do but wait.

Memo regarding case number 0230-K2203-24

Information from the chief of security at Stockholm District Court

Sara O. is an authorized user of STELLA, the court's case management system. Comments have been made to the effect that she has conducted frequent inquiries in STELLA.

Those in charge of decisions regarding covert coercive measures at SDC have private offices. The cabinet where decisions regarding covert coercive measures are stored is in a so-called archive room. Those who handle documents from that cabinet are not required to keep any sort of access log.

SDC has 9 case units and 20 court clerks, of which 4 handle matters involving covert coercive measures according to a rolling schedule.

Records are available of those entering and leaving the workplace. Sara O. is a full-time employee and normally works between the hours of 8:00 a.m. and 4:30 p.m.

Employment history: Probationary employee at SDC with start date 09-01-1996. Permanent hire date: 03-01-1997.

I've worked at district court forever. I started almost thirty years ago, and at the time it was a dream. I loved sitting in on trials when a clerk was out sick and they needed a substitute, or just to listen—every case was equally exciting. I enjoyed the work of registering and archiving rulings and verdicts, booking everything from case-settlement meetings to regular old staff meetings. My job provided just the right mix of challenge and routine. Most of the time, I knew exactly what would happen when I arrived in the morning, but now and then I was surprised. And when the lawyers were discussing especially sensitive cases in the lunchroom, I could join in and offer my opinion—the first boss I had always wanted to hear what I had to say. I liked that about him—he wasn't interested only in statutes and whether a decision was likely to be upheld by a higher court. It was important to him that what he did was "comprehensible." That's what he called it: "comprehensible." And I was happy to be his test case; I thought it was fun. For lack of a better word, he made me feel important, at least some of the time.

My position offered security; when the kids were born, and when they were little and always coming down with something, I could use my parental leave without arguments with some boss who didn't understand that people had lives outside the office.

My current boss, Vivianne Krauss, came on the scene much later, when my kids were teenagers. She's a different sort of person. Not as pleasant. But by then, I'd already taken all the courses necessary to understand the new database systems, and although she's fifteen years my junior, I'm the one who taught her to use them, not the other way around. If she hadn't depended so much on me when she first started, I'm sure she would have had me transferred. She's never liked me, I've seen the way she looks at me, pretending to chat with someone by the coffee machine even though her true motive is to spy on me. Even so, I don't think she's the one who put the pieces together about what I did. Vivianne Krauss doesn't think I'm capable of anything that requires initiative, much less anything that might make a difference. She must have been awfully surprised when the police told her. I wonder if she even exclaimed something like *it figures* or *I always knew something was off about that woman.*

As far as I recall, Vivianne has never asked a single question about my personal life. It's not as if I wish she had; I'm not interested in her life either. I don't want to know what she does when she gets home to her turn-of-the-century house with its ocean views. Problems with the help, or shoveling a path all the way to the garage—none of that interests me. How do I know she has a turn-of-the-century house and paid help? I can tell by looking at her.

I get to work at the same time every day. The court is right across the street from the station; it's the first thing you see when you get off the train. I must have looked up at it thousands of times, but I can't describe the building except in vague, everyday terms. A dingy gray façade, tidy rows of narrow windows, impossible to recall how many stories tall. There is a staff entrance, an unassuming small door that leads straight into a freight elevator.

But I typically come in through the main entrance. At least it's not quite as depressing.

There's a bronze sculpture outside the large courtroom; it depicts a girl who is naked and covering her face with both hands as if she's blocking her own view of something or trying to hide tears. Sometimes I get as close to the sculpture as I can, then reach out and stroke the girl's foot, the smooth surface, following the shape of her cold toes with my fingers. It almost feels like touching a religious relic, the way Catholics do with images of Mary. I don't believe in God, but in my first few years at the court I considered it like a holy vow, a reminder that I was working for justice. I honestly believed that was what I was doing, that I was part of the system that made it possible for us humans to live together, even though we have a tendency to harm one another. I don't know when I stopped seeing the bronze sculpture as a reminder of this belief and instead began to view it as a symbol of injustice, for all of those we were unable to help, for all of those who are vulnerable and exposed to the evils of the world, without so much as a nightgown for protection. I don't know whether it was the tenth time I sat in on a trial that acquitted an alleged rapist; the fifth time I saw the same single mother charged with petty drug crimes; or the hundredth time I heard racist cops loudly commenting on open investigations in our cafeteria.

When I leave my job, there won't be much fuss. I haven't ever claimed to be irreplaceable, I never expected they would beg me to stay once I reached the age of retirement. But I also don't think they considered me a bad employee, not really. I am the perfect bureaucrat, someone who evades notice, someone who no one ever sees, simply on account of the fact that I do what I'm supposed to. Not even my begrudging boss could say I don't complete my pointless tasks, even if she's long wanted to replace me with someone younger, someone who *takes more initiative.*

That's what she calls it: *taking initiative.* But really, it's just that she wants you to do things for her that aren't actually part of the job. I make our department's coffee much more frequently than necessary, considering that I don't even drink coffee, but that doesn't count because I don't bring her coffee to her office on a little tray. She loves the clerks and other employees who do that sort of thing. The clerk girl who stuck her head in at least once a week to ask if she "would like a cup" was given a much better evaluation than her legal know-how merited. My boss also loves clerks who stay late in the evenings, who write the first drafts of articles she wants to publish under her own name, and who spend hours at the copy machine xeroxing old court decisions that she's "going to dive into at home" even though everyone knows she never actually reads them.

The clerks are usually quick to catch on to what's expected of them, or at least the smart ones are, but they also know that she and her demands are a transitory issue. A clerkship never lasts for more than two years, tops. Then they disappear, and most of them are hired at one of the big law firms. But I stayed. I don't have a law degree, didn't want to study at university, so I can't take on more advanced tasks.

At first, I stayed because I liked the job and it provided security. By the time I wondered if perhaps I should do something else, it was too late. A woman approaching sixty can't change careers, no matter how competent she is. She must trust that her employer won't get rid of her; she's entirely dependent on the goodwill of others.

For years my job has felt totally pointless. Nothing I do matters. There's all this talk about AI, and how creative endeavors will be taken over by computer programs. But that's not true of my job. I don't do anything that could be considered creative. My job is literally just shuffling papers. From one spot to another. Emailing them here or there, occasionally collating them in binders; sometimes I have to prepare my own documents, always on a screen, always forms that don't take any brainpower to fill in. I seldom even need to write any words, just click on the proper response. If I make a mistake, nothing happens. Partly because no one notices, partly because the system itself will discover the error and make sure the next unimportant person in the hierarchy receives a notification to correct it.

B. was the one who helped me realize it's possible to evolve without changing jobs. I don't think that was her aim, but it was the end result. When she needed help, and I was able to offer it, I realized, for the first time in ages, that I wasn't powerless after all. It was an initiative that I didn't undertake for the benefit of my boss; it was for the greater good, for something much more important than my boss's coffee addiction. I was able to take initiative and help someone who truly needed it; I was able to go beyond what my position demanded and see the effects of what I had done, even down to the tiniest details. It was perhaps the first time this had ever happened at my job. Or at least that was what I thought, what I was convinced was true. At first, it felt more important than anything else I'd ever done at work. Later on, of course, that was no longer the case. Later, it was nothing but difficult and dangerous and awful. But now I'm getting ahead of myself.

The police tell me very little about how the investigation is going. It's hard to get any clear information out of my attorney either, what with his nervous fiddling with documents, his darting gaze and evasive answers to my questions about the investigation. I don't know if he's avoiding telling me the truth because he's under a nondisclosure order, or if he thinks I'm too stupid to handle it. Sometimes it looks like he thinks I'm too stupid. But most of the time, he looks rather like he pities me. I suspect that's because he thinks I'm a fool. Because that much is clear: They think I'm an old lady who was tricked into doing what I did by a younger woman. They're wrong about that, of course.

Interview. Case number 0230-K2203-24.

Interrogating officer: Kristoffer Karlsson.

Interviewee: Fatima Y.

Relation to suspect: Colleague.

Fatima is asked to describe Sara and the contact they have had at their place of work.

IO: What can you tell me about her?

I: She's pleasant. Very kind, thoughtful. Like a mother, sort of. Always asking how you feel and actually expecting an answer, you know?

IO: You got to know her through work?

I: Mmhmm. Yes.

IO: Do you consider her a friend?

I: I mean. She's, like, old, and I'm...but I mean, I like her. But, like, we've never hung out otherwise. Outside of work, I mean.

IO: Can you describe your work duties?

I: I'm a case manager for civil suits, so I only work with civil suits. Not like...

IO: You don't have a rotating schedule like Sara? You don't work in other areas?

I: No. I mean. I've only been here...like, not very long.

IO: The staff were informed of what had happened when Sara was apprehended at work. What were your thoughts at the time?

I: I was so shocked. I cried. And then I went home. It was just too much. It was such a crazy day. Everyone was so confused and everything, so, like, I felt like I couldn't keep working because I was so shocked and confused and, like, sad.

IO: What were you told when they informed you about Sara?

I: What the prosecutor released in the statement to the press. That was what we were told. All the questions we had, there was no one who could answer them.

IO: Were you surprised? If you were to describe her, what did you think about what she did, or what she was alleged to have done?

I: Was I surprised? I mean. I was shocked. Totally shocked. One hundred percent.

IO: Have you talked about it? You and your colleagues, and so forth.

I: Yes, for sure. We're still talking about it. We're wondering what happened, you know? Did we miss something? Is she not the person we knew?

IO: You were friends with her at work, you say, but do you know about her relationships outside of work, anything about her private life?

I: No...I mean, I know she's married, and she's got kids. But aren't they basically like my age? I don't know. I really don't. She was the one who asked questions, mostly.

IO: Thinking back to recent days, have you noticed any change in her? In her mood or anything, maybe she seemed stressed?

I: No—not around me, anyway.

IO: It seems to me that you might notice when a colleague starts to act a different way.

I: No. I didn't notice anything out of the ordinary.

IO: She's never shared anything about her private life?

I: Right, exactly. She's never said a thing...I don't know, maybe it's like you don't really want to ask, when someone is older and stuff. I guess I didn't want to seem nosy.

IO: How about the duties she has at work? Or used to have.

I: I mean, all I know is that she's worked here longer than anyone else. She works on everything, she's like a part of...that was why it was all so crazy. She works on all sorts of cases, and she was...I mean, she dealt with covert coercive measures, wiretapping and that kind of thing. But I don't know exactly what she did in that unit, because obviously they're not allowed to talk about it. Even though I'm a case manager too, the case managers who work on rulings on coercive measures aren't allowed to tell us what they do. I have no idea what she did there. All I know is that she worked in that unit.

IO: I understand there's a rotating schedule, so a person is there certain days but not others...

I: Right, exactly. Those case managers take turns. Someone draws up a schedule, and then they take turns.

IO: How do you become one of these special case managers? Do you have to express interest? How does it work?

I: It's usually the managers who decide, who ask. But Sara...I mean, she's been one for like a hundred years, hasn't she? I don't know. Definitely for a very long time.

IO: You were never interested in working on that kind of thing?

I: No, I didn't want to work with such sensitive information and all that. And now I really don't want to. It's just all so crazy, so horrible.

IO: Is there anything else you can recall regarding Sara?

I: No. I mean, I don't know how this happened or what happened or what made her do this, you know? I have no idea. I keep coming up with all sorts of explanations. Did someone trick her, was she manipulated, did she fall in love, was there a bribe, I don't know. I really don't. And that's why I'm so shocked too. I saw her as a completely, totally normal, ordinary colleague, like a mom or maybe a grandma? Was she? Is she a grandma? I have no idea.

IO: All right, I understand. I think that answers my questions.

End of interview.

They've filed charges. That means we've gained more insight into the investigation, my attorney and I. I haven't heard from Stefan and the kids since last time they were here, but I assume they've at least been able to read my statement. They would have been in touch if they believed me, if they understood the truth behind it all. But I suppose they think I'm lying.

I asked my attorney to contact B. to give her a letter I wrote, but he refused. He said I could give it to her once the trial is over, but that he can't have any contact with her before then. There's not much about her in the investigation materials, or less than you'd think anyway. But I haven't had time to read it all yet. I can only imagine what the police must be saying to her. I expect they're lying as much to her as they did to me. She must be so scared.

B. isn't exactly a spring chicken either; she has to be over forty. She's in good shape, but there are signs of age under her chin and around her eyes. I remember when the skin under my chin started to go slack, all those hours I spent in front of the mirror, tugging at my skin, feeling betrayed by my body. Aging makes women shapeless; all our contours disappear. It's not fair. Developing a turkey neck is horrifically ugly. It will happen to B. soon; it comes for all of us eventually. I suppose aging is fair in that sense, at least.

B. hasn't been at the district court as long as I have—only three years—and now she has left the position. She didn't work there every day; she had been hired by the outside security company the court used, so she had to help out at other contracted locations on occasion, sometimes for days at a time, maybe even a week or two. But that was where we got to know each other. That was how it started.

Those of us who work at the courthouse aren't actually required to go through the full security procedure, the staff entrance just has one person who sits behind glass and checks our ID badges, but when I arrived through the main entrance I would place my purse on the conveyor belt simply so I wouldn't have to show my badge. I'm not quite sure why, but it felt like I was trying to put on airs if I used my badge. Like I expected special treatment. I prefer to be anonymous, a face in the crowd. Two years ago, a new system was introduced where every visitor had to sign in in a special log, and I didn't have time for that so

I started flashing my badge. But when B. was there, she would usually just smile and wave me through. Despite my mixed feelings, I liked that, how she recognized me. Because she didn't make a big deal of it.

"Hi, Sara," she would say softly. "All good with you?"

The first time, I was surprised. That she had remembered me. It wasn't until the third time it happened that I made sure to look at her badge so I could greet her back. I wanted to know her name.

The police have been asking the strangest questions about our relationship, why we became friends. It mostly seems like they think I developed a crush on her, which is just preposterous. I've never had a crush on a woman. Not that there's anything wrong with that, but I wasn't flirting with her. Nothing like that. She was just friendly, and I was friendly back, which is ordinary good manners at a place of work. If everyone was like B., my job would be much more pleasant.

The first time we ate lunch together was last spring, and it happened by sheer coincidence. Our staff cafeteria was closed for renovations, so I went to the one on the second floor to eat the leftovers I'd brought from home. B. was sitting at a table alone, and when she waved at me, I joined her. It was nice, I don't remember what we talked about that first time, but I know we laughed together. I told her about something Ingrid had done that annoyed me, but when she started laughing I realized it was pretty hilarious so I started laughing too.

The cafeteria renovations took over three months, and we usually took our break at the same time, which was one hour later than most people so it was often just the two of us. It was no wonder when we started delving more into our private lives after a while. She was easy to talk to. I could tell when she was concerned; I asked and she answered, without being pushy or overly sentimental. I think she liked my advice, my kids are over a decade older than hers, they're still in high school and middle school, but I remember very vividly how tough it could be, how confusing it was to figure out when to be stern with your kids and when to be understanding and show them that you were always there for them.

While my kids and I never had problems as serious as the ones B. had with hers, that didn't mean I couldn't feel for her—quite the opposite. She faced very different challenges, a life few of us can understand. But it's our duty, our obligation as fellow humans, to try to put ourselves in other people's shoes.

She told me she was having extra problems with one of her kids. She feared he might be about to fall in with a really bad crowd. And he was only fourteen. But still, he would reach the age of legal responsibility soon, and she didn't have much time to keep his life from being ruined. B. had tried talking to the police, she said, she knows quite a few cops, likely through her job, but they weren't very helpful, and she didn't want to contact social services because she didn't trust them. I understood where she was coming from—it's a flip of the coin whether you end up with a good social worker or a bad one. Some of them think that all parents wish harm on their kids and that all problem children should be moved out of their home environments to be placed with foster families, so I understood why B. was afraid of what might happen if she shared too much with a social worker. Besides, she couldn't share her real suspicions with the police or social services, because if she mentioned that person to the police she risked reaping much worse consequences than a home visit from child protective services. We've had any number of cases like that, and I've seen up close what happens to people who talk to the police about what they've seen and what they know. And you can read in the newspaper about the ones who don't even end up with us. The ones whose houses are blown sky-high or who get shot outside a movie theater or a shopping center in broad daylight but never get any help because the police fail to find the perpetrators and hold them to account.

B's problem was a distant relative. A third cousin who was a gang leader from Björkvalla. Ludovic Balacla, she called him "Lubbe," and I laughed at that, but when she didn't chuckle back I knew it was serious. She was frightened, genuinely frightened. He was trying to recruit her son, she said. B. was terrified of what would happen if Lubbe managed to get his claws into her boy, but she was perhaps even more afraid of what would happen to the whole family if she told the police, or anyone else, what she knew about this nasty third cousin.

But she had to do something. That much was clear. I hadn't seen her scared like this before, but now I could see the desperation in her eyes. It was contagious. It frightened me too, in a way I recognized even though I've never been in her situation. It had been years since I felt that special fear that comes along with having teenagers. I was so scared when the kids were that age. All the time, day in and day out. And they didn't even have anyone like Lubbe trying to make them deal drugs or blow up houses. My kids weren't at-risk that way; there wasn't even room for that kind of disaster in my imagination, and my imagination had *plenty* of room. Even so, I was scared. Terrified, twenty-four seven. There's almost nothing scarier than being the mother of a teenager. From one day to the next, your child vanishes and is replaced by someone who tells lies and hates you, and you know that with every passing day your sweet child is farther and farther away, and you become well aware, although you don't want to admit it, that you will never again be able to control them, protect them, or tell them what to do, yet you know you *must* protect them because if you don't your child will die or disappear or turn into a stranger.

My son stopped looking at me for longer than a fraction of a second when he turned fourteen. It was like he couldn't stand me anymore. My daughter still has that teenage, hate-filled glare. No mother should have to face that. The police insinuate that I'm in love with B., but they are so clueless. They never asked about my kids; I've tried to explain, but they don't listen.

Maybe I can't provide a good explanation for why I decided to help B., but I think it has to do with how I understood her on a deep level. I know how it feels to lose your child, to watch your child disappear. All mothers of adult children know, but few of them dare to admit it.

And B. had a concrete problem. Concrete problems can be solved, you just have to do something.

But what? Each time we met, B. was more desperate and more heartbroken, and eventually she asked me that very question.

"Tell me, Sara, tell me what I'm supposed to do! Because I can't live like this, I'm drowning."

So we came up with a plan. It took perhaps a week before we even realized it was a plan, but it all started when I was taking notes during oral preparations for a civil case between a sporting goods store and one of their suppliers, who claimed the store hadn't paid in full. It was an absolutely pointless meeting, the two parties couldn't agree, but as I sat there listening to their whining it struck me: B. had to make Lubbe an offer, a really solid offer, to settle the matter.

"I'll give you this, and in return you promise never to recruit my son." Something along those lines. Anything can be bought or sold. Even gangs sign contracts. They can hardly turn to the courts to enforce them, but they still enter into contracts; I've seen as much in the cases we've had. It's a language that even hardened criminals understand. And if you have something really excellent to sell, you can demand almost anything in return.

But B. didn't understand what I meant at first.

"What can I possibly offer him?" she asked. She sounded almost angry, or at least annoyed.

So I asked for this third cousin's name and personal identification number. B. didn't know the first four digits, but she found out. And I had a remarkable stroke of luck. There was a ruling concerning him that he ought to be very interested in. So I relayed what I'd found. The police had requested and been granted a warrant to bug two of his phones just a few weeks earlier. She could "sell" him that ruling. He would gain information, and in return he would cut off contact with her son. Because he definitely didn't want to say anything untoward on those two phones.

She was happy, I could tell. So I downloaded a copy of the ruling that very afternoon. It was no big deal. And then we met outside of work, at a café, and B. took my phone and did something with Bluetooth and transferred the ruling to her phone. It all went very smoothly.

Interview with Vivianne Krauss (VK), Sara O.'s immediate supervisor at Stockholm District Court.

Case number 0230-K2203-24.

Below is a summary of the interview. The interview has been archived and recorded in its entirety in audio format.

VK states that she is Sara's immediate superior. She is one of nine managers at the district court. When VK began her position, Sara had already been employed for many years in the unit VK took over managing.

VK considered Sara to be competent and experienced, if a bit easily distracted. VK considered this to be perfectly normal, considering Sara's age and the fact that she would soon retire. A few years after VK started working at the district court, she had a conversation with Sara about her expectations for her last few years. VK felt that Sara took this as criticism rather than an attempt to find ways to increase her motivation for her work duties.

VK did not, however, feel that Sara was hostile toward her work or workplace. She believed that Sara was happy there and that she was extremely aware of the sensitive nature of her work duties. She certainly did not lack confidence in Sara. Her suspicions that something was amiss arose later. Even so, VK feels shocked and betrayed. Although she contacted the internal investigators even before it came to her attention that this investigation had been opened, she didn't think the situation was as dire as it is. She is still hoping for an explanation. Sara is a very private person. She seldom discussed her private life. VK has no knowledge of Sara's life outside the workplace. Both VK and the team appreciated her. Sara was a good worker, and there were never any issues with absences.

When asked about the routines when someone is granted access to files concerning covert coercive measures, VK stated that names are provided to the senior district court judges and the division head judges. If these judges have no objections to the suggested employees, the employees are added to the roster. When asked whether Sara had additional special duties, VK stated that she had full access to all cases brought to the district court. As a STELLA administrator, she also had system access to perform other administrative actions, for example deleting documents or making minor corrections to rulings.

On her own initiative, VK brought up the issue of how Sara could have removed classified materials pertaining to a certain individual from other district courts, in the manner covered by this investigation. She explained that a clerk with Sara's level of access can request documents from another district court and that all it takes is for the person to contact the district court in question and request those documents. Typically, this type of request is done by email. Then the documents are handed over to the requestor, even confidential ones. In the case of confidential documents, the requestor might be asked the reason for requesting them, but typically this is not the case when the requestor is someone with Sara's level of access. Typically, a person with Sara's level of access would not ask another district court to check whether coercive measures have been initiated against a specified individual, but in practice there is nothing to bar such a request from being made. Scrutiny would naturally be different if the request was being made for the benefit of a private citizen, but there is no reason for a person with Sara's level of access to request documents unless it is for the benefit of the district court. *Private citizens or journalists must always request documents from the district court that holds the materials, and a confidentiality review is always performed before these documents are released (addendum following readback of interview).*

VK also explained that in practice there are other situations in which a person with Sara's level of access might search for material concerning a particular individual, even if such a search were of limited scope. The district court is responsible for providing on-call staffing alongside other district courts. This means that staff (a court clerk, a case manager, and a judge) can be assigned to work weekend shifts at another district court, work that may involve receiving assignments from public defenders, processing requests for remand, and booking appointments for detention hearings, as well as expediting warrants, including those involving covert measures. These cases may include documents from other district courts, although seldom ones concerning covert coercive measures. During these on-call hours a staff member might handle other district courts' cases. However, it is not possible to perform a digital search that can call up every warrant for covert coercive measures concerning a given individual because such decisions are largely handled in hard copy. They are not registered digitally. An appointment is made for the hearing, and consequently everything is deleted from the computer system, and the documents are stored in a folder in a lockbox. Furthermore, after what has come to light regarding Sara, the routine has been restructured. Case managers still book hearing appointments, but they are not privy to the topic of said hearing, and they forward the email, as well as the password to open the email, to the presiding judge. Subsequently, the judge is the one to open the email and place the documents in the folder. *The lockbox and folder have been moved to another room, and any access must be logged (addendum following readback of interview).*

Break 11:34. Resumed 13:20.

During the break, VK went to get her laptop. She looked up the dates of Sara's on-call shifts. She was on call on April 25, June 10, and August 16 this year. Weekend on-call workers are paid overtime. While they are voluntary, it is typically not difficult to staff these shifts. Sara worked six extra on-call shifts during the summer. It's uncommon for someone to volunteer for this many shifts during a period when most people want to take time off.

Read back over the telephone on November 20 at 11:00 with no objections beyond those noted above.

At first, everything went well. Those initial documents I gave to B. had exactly the effect we'd hoped for. I had no reason to distrust her. She seemed happy and extremely relieved. We went out for dinner together. She wanted to pay, but I refused. I earn more than she does. Even so, she wouldn't let me pay her share. When I got the check anyway, she Swished me the money, more than she needed to, but I let her do it so she wouldn't feel like she owed me anything.

"You saved my life," she said. And she repeated it more than once. *You saved my life.*

We had become friends, despite the age difference. We had so much in common. I understood her; she understood me. We laughed at the same things. We meant a lot to each other. None of what happened later on can change that.

And it's not just that I helped her; she helped me as well. Because I'm all alone. That may sound strange, given that I'm married, with two kids and a cat. But dammit, I'm still so alone. On my way to work I get the bus, and then the train, and sometimes it's so crammed I can feel other warm, human bodies moving against mine, sometimes I lean into someone when the driver takes a curve too fast.

"Pardon me," I say. "It was an accident." But I do it on purpose, to remind myself that other people exist, even if they don't see me anymore.

I would hardly tell the police all of this. I don't want them to feel sorry for me. There's no reason to feel sorry for me. It's just a feeling I have, and maybe I'm making too much of it. My children would certainly think so, if I were to tell them how I feel. And it's no use talking to Stefan, he wouldn't understand. We stopped sharing anything of importance with one another years ago. I don't know if this was before or after we stopped touching each other, but it was around the same time. He's not young anymore, and by the time he finally retired he'd been eager to do so for years. Of course I don't begrudge him his quiet life, sleeping in each morning and staying up late at night. There's no need for him to ask me how my day was; I never ask him. I don't want him to dote on me just because I still work; he's no good at cooking or any of that. And just because it says in the evening papers that people over sixty are having sex like bunnies these days, that doesn't mean it's true. I'm definitely not walking around hoping Stefan will start taking Viagra or that we'll start going to sex camps like in some American film where the woman looks like Diane Keaton or Helen Mirren. It's nice that he has his interests, has friends to go cycling or cross-country skiing with. He seems satisfied with his life. And maybe things will improve once I retire too. Maybe we can ski together again if I get that operation on my knee. I did used to enjoy skiing, at least when it wasn't too cold and the hills weren't too steep. And the kids have lives of their own, I know I should be proud of that, and maybe we'll see each other more often again once Oskar's baby arrives. All new parents need some respite. But I don't want to ask, and they share so little about all that. We don't have that kind of relationship. I'm not complaining, I'm just stating the truth. I've entered that invisible age that everyone talks about.

One day I was walking around the grocery store with my nearly empty cart—Stefan and I don't need to buy that much food anymore, but I want my cart, I'm used to having a cart. I spotted my boss by the seafood counter, I said hello, she looked at me in bewilderment for a few seconds and then laughed.

"I didn't see you there under that hat," she said. But the truth is, she didn't see me at all. We've worked together for six years, but not even my boss sees me anymore.

With B., it was different. She saw me. She leaned on me, and I leaned on her. Neither of us needed to apologize. We were grateful to have each other. I know that's true. And I don't blame B. for what happened later. No matter what the police say she did, I know the truth: We were both naive. Neither of us understood what would happen, how it would end, and that was stupid, of course, but it wasn't our fault. We shouldn't have to shoulder the blame. Everyone makes mistakes, and we were only doing what we had to, to keep things from getting even worse.

I just wish I could say so to B. I wish I could tell her I don't blame her, that I'm not angry with her. Of course, I have plenty of questions about what went on between her son and Lubbe. Why she said what she did instead of telling me the truth. She might not believe it, but I'm sure I would have understood even if she told me the truth. Because I'm certain B. was doing what she had to do, and no one can convince me otherwise. She would never betray me, not on purpose; she simply wouldn't do that.

Witness interview. Case number 0230-K2203-24.

Interrogating officer: Inger Lidman.

Interviewee: B.

Relationship to suspect: Former colleague.

Interrogating officer telephones B. at appointed time. B. had previously been advised of this call by a written summons explaining the nature of the call and a text message advising as to the time of the call.

IO: I told you why I'm calling, why I sent the letter.

I: Yes, you said it was about that court case manager.

IO: Right, exactly. Sara O. Tell me about the contact you've had with her.

I: Unfortunately, I can't comment.

IO: She's a friend of yours, isn't that right?

I: No comment.

IO: You were not friends? Is that how I should interpret what you're saying? I can tell you that we have been given to understand that the two of you were in close contact.

I: Well, I have no comment.

IO: Is there anything you can tell me about her?

I: No, I have no comment about that.

IO: Sara has a lot to say about you in her interviews.

I: I can't help that.

IO: She says you have received threats from Ludovic B., and the two of you did what you did because you were afraid of him.

I: I'm not afraid of Lubbe.

IO: You are aware that we can help you if you are, right?

I: No comment.

IO: She says you asked her to help you because you were afraid your son would be drawn into criminal activity.

I: I don't have a son.

IO: Why does Sara think you do?

I: No comment.

IO: As I explained to you earlier, you are not considered a suspect.

I: No, but I am choosing to remain silent anyway. I have no comment regarding your questions.

IO: Not even about going to her house? Or going out to eat together? Going to a café? Exchanging a large number of text messages? And...

I: No, I have no comment regarding your questions.

IO: Wouldn't it be easier if you came to the station, if we chatted in person and you could see for yourself the information we have gathered?

I: No, I have no comment at all regarding your questions. I invoke my right to remain silent.

IO: Well, okay, but that's more for if you are a suspect. Right now it seems to me that you're only—

I: It doesn't matter. I have been summoned as a witness. You have summoned me as a witness, correct? This is a police interrogation and I am invoking my right to remain silent, so I will not answer any questions, so...you can ask all the questions you like, but you're not going to get any answers.

IO: No, but even so we appreciate your agreeing to talk to us.

I: Sure.

IO: We would also like to talk to you about your relationship with Ludovic B.

I: I'm not going to talk about him.

IO: Do you live together?

I: No comment.

IO: We would like you to explain why you forwarded the information Sara gave you on to him.

I: I'm afraid I need to go now.

IO: You have no explanation? According to Sara, he threatened you both. Or was it just you?

I: No comment. How many times do I have to say it?

IO: We can help you if you feel you are being threatened.

I: (laughter) You don't need to help me. I don't need help. I'm going to hang up now.

IO: We would very much like to talk with you some more.

I: If you call, I'll answer. But I don't have anything else to say.

IO: Well, thanks for letting me know.

Call disconnected.

I didn't tell B. she wasn't allowed to say where the information had come from. But I took for granted that she wouldn't. Yet she told that Lubbe guy that I was the one who had dug up the information. And that was when things started to go awry.

B. drew up a contract with Lubbe, just as I'd suggested. But a week after he received the initial case documents, B. approached me as I was having lunch in my cafeteria, she came up there even though we didn't usually meet there, not since the renovations were finished. But she had a note. It was handwritten. Lubbe was demanding more information in order to keep his end of the bargain, she said. He had looked me up and learned that I had access to more information. He wanted it. This information revolved around another name, and B. said I had to "check it out." She seemed stressed, yet cool-headed. Not the way she usually was, more disengaged.

I refused. I calmly explained that we must not discuss this sort of thing in the courthouse and that she shouldn't let herself be intimidated. I asked how her son was doing. That seemed to make her angry. I shouldn't be talking about her son, this was much bigger than that, this wasn't about her son anymore. I didn't quite understand what she meant, but I could tell she was agitated and unable to think logically. Speaking as placidly as possible, I instructed her to explain to Lubbe that I refused, that such a general search couldn't be done by name, that it wasn't like on TV where everything was digitized and can be printed out in seconds. I also told her to relay that I had taken a big risk in handing over the information I'd already provided, and that this strategy would never work in the long run. I didn't go into detail about what is and is not possible, but I think she realized I was getting uncomfortable and also a little upset.

We didn't argue. But she stood up to leave. She was clearly frustrated. I told her to call me that evening; we would do better to speak in a calm environment. We hadn't said anything anyone could overhear, but it was still not something I wanted to discuss in the staff cafeteria of the district court. But she didn't contact me that evening, and when I tried to call her, she didn't pick up. I sent a text, but she didn't respond to that either.

The next day, B. wasn't at work. But that didn't strike me as odd. I know I even thought it was probably a good thing if we didn't see each other for a while. She was surely in need of some time to digest what had happened, to talk to Lubbe or maybe someone else in her family who could help her convince him to leave her alone. And I didn't know what I would say, how I would handle all of this. Two weeks later, I called her again. She didn't pick up the phone, but this time, at least, she texted me back. She had been assigned to work at Kronoberg for a month, she wrote, and she would be in touch "when things settled down." I thought that sounded like a good plan, good for both of us.

The first time Lubbe came to see me was a Wednesday. I know because Stefan plays floorball with his friends every Wednesday, and he wasn't home. I knew it was Lubbe even though he didn't introduce himself and I didn't ask. He's not the type of guy you ask questions. He was waiting at the bus stop when I stepped off the bus.

"Pardon me, Sara?" he said as I passed by. His voice sounded soft and friendly, and he kept his distance, raising his hands a bit as if to indicate that I shouldn't be frightened. That he wouldn't hurt me. And I wasn't frightened, not until later. At first, I suppose I was mostly shocked. But his voice was gentle and he never acted violent. Men like him don't need to.

B. had gotten a new job, he explained. She'd had to quit the security firm entirely and had moved away. No, she wasn't at Kronoberg. Where had I gotten that idea? He didn't want to say what she was doing now. She had given him my name and told him to get in touch with me directly, because she and I couldn't have any more contact, she couldn't risk it, for the sake of her children and so on. That's when I knew he was lying. Why would she say that? What we had, she and I, was special, she wouldn't dump me on him. But I suppose she was scared, just like me.

"I'm sure you don't want her children to come to any harm," he said. He was very well-spoken. Not at all like gangsters in the movies, or like the way real gang leaders usually talk on the surveillance tapes that are sometimes played in court. No minority slang or broken Swedish. He sounded more like a lawyer. Maybe he was making an effort because he was talking to me. Speak the customer's language and all that. He handed me a note, much like the one B. had shown me, but this time there were two names on it instead of just one. He told me to say hello to Stefan and the kids. "Hope your daughter is enjoying her new job," he added. Just like in a movie. Death threats disguised as friendly comments, reminders that they know everything, that they can do anything they please at any time, and that you're at their mercy.

I didn't ask any questions about B. I didn't ask how she was doing, I didn't beg him to treat her and her family well. I didn't want to talk about her with him. But I did what I was told. As best I could.

First I went through the binders we had at the courthouse that contained information on upcoming decisions.

I found two that pertained to Lubbe and two more that pertained to the people on his list. I also emailed two other district courts and asked them to check if they had any covert coercive measures in effect against Lubbe. They didn't. I also performed the searches available to me. But most of the hits I got weren't related to classified information. I downloaded them anyway. And when I found any classified appendices I accessed them.

I used my phone to take photos of everything I found. Then I sent them from my private email to the email address Lubbe had given me. I cc'd B. I don't know why, maybe because I thought it might help her. But the email bounced back. She must have gotten a new account.

I suppose I realized even then that it was only a matter of time before I was caught. But I didn't feel guilty; I still don't. Partly because I didn't have a choice, partly because it's not like I was giving him state secrets or anything. Even the electronic surveillance warrants typically don't mean much in the real world. They seldom lead to anything actionable. People like Lubbe don't say the important stuff in the chats or phone calls the police might be listening in on. They do it all in encrypted chats, the kind that have to be hacked. And if what I gave B. could save a young boy from being dragged into a life of crime, then it was my duty to help B.

But Lubbe still wasn't satisfied. He didn't return to my bus stop; he started texting me instead, and he asked me to check other district courts he suspected might be about to issue rulings against him and his friends. I did exactly as I was told. I signed up for weekend on-call shifts all summer, to make it easier to access sources I needed to search in order to help him. I had thrown myself over a cliff, and now I was falling into the abyss. But what choice did I have? I became sloppy, increasingly careless. Maybe I knew it was impossible to hide what I was doing; maybe I just wanted to get it all over with.

Witness interview. Case number 0230-K2203-24.
Interrogating officer: Christer Henriksson.
Interviewee: Ludovic Balacla.

IO: You have asked me to begin this recording by stating that you are being questioned as a witness, not because you are a suspect in any crime.

I: Thank you.

IO: But I must also inform you that we have information suggesting you have subjected Sara O. to threats. That you have threatened her.

I: If that's what I'm being interviewed about today, I'll have to end here.

IO: No, we don't need to talk about that today, but we will be returning to it another time.

I: I look forward to it.

IO: You look forward to it?

I: Are you going to get to the point, or should I leave?

IO: What is your relationship to Sara O.?

I: None at all.

IO: Why did she provide you with classified information?

I: You'll have to ask her.

IO: You're suggesting she came up with the idea all on her own?

I: No comment.

IO: Can you tell me about your relationship with B.?

I: No comment.

IO: She claims that you are a couple, while Sara seems to believe you are related.

I: I wouldn't trust Sara on that count.

IO: So B. is your girlfriend? Do you live together?

I: [In English] No comments.

IO: Were you planning to answer any of these questions?

I: No comment.

IO: Then I suggest we end this interview.

Today I was given a date for the trial. It will begin in six weeks. I have to stay in jail until then. The proceedings will take a week, two full days and three half days. My attorney has also advised me that I should expect to be convicted. He will claim necessity, since I've said I was acting under threat, but that was only in the end—I can't claim necessity for the information I provided to B. I understand his reasoning, but I can only continue to believe that I did that out of necessity too. We were trying to save B.'s son. It was an emergency situation.

The police and my attorney say that B. doesn't have a son, only a daughter. And this daughter is not fourteen; she's only nine. He has also told me that Lubbe isn't her relative, but her boyfriend. I don't quite know how I should take this information. At first I thought the police officer was lying, telling me things just to see how I would react, but my attorney assured me it's true, and I don't know why he would lie about something like that.

I've asked my attorney why the police aren't investigating Lubbe's crimes. It's against the law to make a threat on someone's life. He could go to prison for that. But my attorney says the preliminary investigation was closed because I have no proof that he threatened me. B. doesn't want to cooperate, so it's my word against his. All the emails and texts Lubbe sent me, everything the police can read, is friendly, not threatening at all. I also asked the police why I would have given him information if I wasn't afraid of him. But once again, they just gazed at me with pity in their eyes. They still seem to think I'm in love with B., and that's why I gave her and Lubbe everything they asked for. We've had a lot of conversations about money too. Like whether I was paid for the information I gave them. They found four Swish transactions from B. to me, and I've tried to tell them those were from the times we ate dinner together and I paid the whole bill and B. Swished me her share, but I don't know if they believe me. They also don't seem to care that we're talking pittances. So it turns out that when it's my word against that of B. and a criminal gang leader, the police choose to believe the gang leader.

I also asked my attorney why I'm the only one facing charges. If what B. told me isn't true, then she lied to me to get her hands on classified information. If what she told the police to protect Lubbe isn't true, she's obstructing a police investigation. Besides, she's the one who gave the initial documents to Lubbe, and she's the one who put me in touch with him. But my attorney says it's not against the law to receive classified documents, only to distribute them. Not to mention that she hasn't threatened me, not with violence or in any other way, and that's true. B. didn't force me to do anything. But I refused to believe she conned me. There must be another explanation.

Because I saw how relieved she was when I gave her that first document; she couldn't have faked it. Her fear was real, her relief was real, her desperation can't have been an act. Everything we did, we did because we were afraid of Lubbe.

Interview with prime suspect Sara O.

Case number 0230-K2203-24.

Basis of interview/charges of which suspect has been informed: Aggravated computer fraud, accomplished. Aggravated breach of duty of confidentiality, accomplished.

Interrogating officer: Christer Henriksson.

Assisting interrogating officer: Inger Lidman.

Defense attorney: Adam Seiger.

IO: You know why we need to talk to you again.

SUS: I know why you think you need to. But I have confessed to distributing the information, so I don't quite understand why we're here.

IO: We'd like to talk to you about the reason you decided to do what you did.

SUS: I have already explained that as well.

IO: You wanted to help B.?

SUS: Yes.

IO: So her son wouldn't be forced into a life of crime?

SUS: Yes.

IO: We've spoken with B.

SUS: Mmhmm.

IO: And like we've told you, she doesn't quite share your interpretation of what happened.

SUS: You have to realize that her . . . that this Lubbe, as she calls him, he's a dangerous man.

IO: She told you he was a relative?

SUS: Yes. A third cousin, I think she said. But that wasn't the important thing, the problem was that he was trying to recruit her son.

IO: She doesn't have a son.

SUS: So you've said.

IO: You can see a copy of her national registry records, if that would help. She does not have a son. And Lubbe is not her third cousin. They aren't related. But they do live together, at least some of the time.

SUS: He is a dangerous man.

IO: Yes. That was why he was a target of coercive measures. That was why the police wanted to surveil him, so they could put him away.

SUS: [inaudible]

IO: You're an intelligent woman. You realize that your actions amount to obstruction of justice, and that this makes you an accomplice to all of the serious crimes he's involved in.

SUS: You're saying I'm involved in gang crime? That's ridiculous. I've worked at the district court for—

IO: What you did makes you an accomplice, yes. Did you think it was exciting?

SUS: [inaudible]

IO: What I don't understand is how a person like you can decide to betray everything you've worked for . . . your whole life . . . or maybe this isn't the first time? Have you done this sort of thing before?

SUS: You can't say that. You can't sit here and accuse me of whatever you like.

IO: Sure I can. This is a criminal investigation—of course we can look into your past actions.

Attorney: Am I to understand that you have expanded this investigation to include criminal acts beyond those we have been informed of?

Assisting IO: No. We have not . . . we will limit ourselves to this topic. Sara, can you tell us why you decided to help B.? She said her son risked being drawn into a life of serious crime. But you didn't look into whether she really had a son, or whether Lubbe was really her cousin?

SUS: Third cousin. No. Have you checked to see if there are any other children in B.'s life who . . .

IO: We have spoken with B. She says that she and Ludovic B. have been a couple for a few years. She also said that it was your idea to give him the information. Not hers.

SUS: I wanted to help her with her son.

IO: Did you think it was exciting?

SUS: What do you mean by that?

IO: You liked B., didn't you?

SUS: Yes. We're good friends.

IO: You say that a lot, that you're good friends. But B. doesn't seem to agree.

SUS: She's scared. She's afraid of the consequences.

IO: You believe she's afraid because her son will be roped into a life of crime?

SUS: No, but she is afraid of Lubbe, I know she is.

IO: She claims that's not true. We conducted another interview with her during which she said she thinks you wanted to demonstrate to her and Lubbe that you were important, that you could play an important role in their life and that was why you gave her the information. She says she thinks you are very lonely and you wanted to become close friends with her, and that you were prepared to do anything to make that happen. But she thought you became too pushy, and she found it quite alarming, so she broke off contact with you.

SUS: [inaudible]

IO: You have to speak into the microphone, Sara. What did you say? You think I'm lying? I can show you a transcript of that interview.

SUS: She'll say anything to avoid the risk that Lubbe might hurt her.

IO: Would you say that you're gullible, Sara?

SUS: No. But B. . . . how did she explain why she wanted the information? Why did she have to get hold of that information? Have you asked her about that?

IO: She says it was your idea.

SUS: But why? Why would I want to give her that information?

IO: Well... according to B....

SUS: No, I did not give it to her to seem special. Or to buy her friendship. It was to help her son.

IO: You've said in previous interviews that the two of you became very close. In what way were you close? Has she been to your home? Have you been to her home? Has she met your husband?

SUS: I'm sure she was forced to say that. There's no other explanation. She is not a bad person.

IO: Did you understand that what you were doing was illegal?

SUS: Yes.

IO: And yet... you have to help me out here, Sara. You have to help me understand. You say B. needed help, but why didn't you suggest she go to the police? Or to social services?

SUS: I did.

IO: You did?

SUS: Yes, but... I've also seen what happens. How many people need help and how few of them actually receive any. And what I gave her to give to Lubbe, it wasn't... it's so rare that the police actually get anything useful out of that kind of surveillance anyway... they're more careful than that.

IO: Yes, after you informed them they were under surveillance, the subjects didn't say anything of note, that is true.

SUS: But...

IO: But you weren't satisfied with that?

SUS: I told you... he threatened me.

IO: Did you tell anyone about these threats?

SUS: No. You know I didn't.

IO: Not even B.?

SUS: She wouldn't answer my calls or texts.

IO: Not your husband, your children, your boss...

SUS: What could they have done?

IO: Helped you? Helped you file a police report. There are special security measures that can be put in place for people who handle sensitive information. Your boss could have helped you.

SUS: Do you honestly believe that?

IO: I believe in the system, yes. I believe that we must depend on the police and let law enforcement do its job, yes. I also believe that people like you are a big part of the reason why it's difficult, and sometimes impossible, for them to do it—their job, that is. I believe that as long as there are people doing what you did, we will never get gang violence, organized crime, under control.

SUS: So now I'm in the mafia? Is that what you're telling my family? That I'm a member of a gang?

IO: Your husband believes you're depressed. He told us you've had previous episodes...

SUS: Episodes? [inaudible] You're lying. He never said that. He wouldn't have said that. What kind of episodes is he talking about?

IO: Maybe he didn't use that word. But your husband and children have reported that you've appeared to have bouts of depression, and that you have pulled away over the past year, that it's been hard to reach you.

SUS: They said that? That I pulled away? That's the silliest thing I ever heard.

IO: Your daughter wanted us to have you evaluated...

SUS: I am not depressed. This is nonsense. I did what I did because I was threatened. I didn't do it to make a friend. I did it to help a friend, and because I was threatened. I knew...I knew it was wrong, but I didn't see any other way out. I don't know...it's not exactly a cheerful situation, that's for sure, I guess I've been...maybe I haven't been in great shape recently. But I'm not crazy.

IO: No one thinks you're crazy.

SUS: Or would that be a good thing? If I were crazy? That would give you a simple explanation. That would mean you all didn't do anything wrong. Because you never do anything wrong, and we don't live in a country where only some children get help when they need it, where only some women can live in safety, without their lives being threatened by men who live outside society's rules. If I'm crazy, we don't have to admit that there's something wrong with the judicial system when even someone like me, an old lady who pushes papers at district court, is forced to take justice into her own hands to help the women Sweden doesn't give a shit about.

IO: Pushes papers? Is that what you think of your job?

SUS: That's not what I think about my job, that IS my job.

IO: You feel your job is pointless? That what you do is banal? Have you always thought so? Was this an exciting adventure? Did it make you feel like you were part of something...

SUS: [inaudible]

IO: Is that how you feel? Like what you do has no purpose?

SUS: Can we take a break? I want to take a break.

Attorney: My client needs a break.

IO: Of course. You'll get your break. But just answer me this first, Sara, if you'd be so kind. I think it's important. Was that what happened? You felt that what you were doing for B. was important? While your job isn't?

SUS: That's not something I felt. It was true. I haven't done anything important for someone in years, not at work, not at home, not anywhere else. You can pretend that's not the case, but I know it is. With B., it was different. Concrete. It turned out to be wrong, I understand that, but at first it was the right thing to do. What I did made a difference. For the better. And even if you say she doesn't have any kids that age, and that Lubbe is actually her partner or boyfriend or whatever, there's no way for you to know why she asked me...why she wanted me to do it. And maybe what she told me was even true. Maybe she wanted to protect someone else's son, make a deal with this man to save a child. Just like me. If she lived with him, maybe she saw what was about to happen. We wanted to save a child, B. and me. Or else maybe B. fears for her own life. Maybe she made it all up to protect herself. You know how dangerous he is. You also know how hard it is to get at him. You don't even want to help me now, not even when I tell you he threatened me, because you say there's no proof. My testimony is not sufficient proof. So how can you claim it's more likely that I was so bored with my life that I started stealing classified information so I could flirt with organized crime? How can you think that is more likely than my being forced to do it?

IO: Did B. threaten you?

SUS: Absolutely not. Aren't you listening?

IO: Did you give her classified information even though you knew it was illegal?

SUS: Yes.

IO: We can take a break if you like. Shall we resume in an hour?

Attorney: Twenty minutes will do.

IO: All right then.

B. lied to me. I understand that. I still don't know why. Had she been planning to dupe me all along, or was it something Lubbe forced her to do? Maybe I will never know. But whatever her reasons, I allowed myself to be duped. *Are you gullible?* It was that officer called Christer who asked me that. I've never considered myself to be naive, but I was wrong. I let myself be tricked. Like that lady who only wanted to be loved, so she sent 250,000 kronor to a person claiming to be Kevin Costner. Or some other celebrity, I forget. I basically got catfished. I'm a pathetic old woman whose own children don't even visit her. That's my life now. It is what it is.

It's quiet in jail. No fights. No loud arguments. I don't talk to anyone, barely even the guard who walks me to the exercise yard and back every day. If I'm sentenced to prison, I'll have to move to another facility, presumably a minimum-security one. They don't think I'm much of a danger, except possibly to myself. A psychiatrist came to examine me. He wanted to medicate me, but I declined. My attorney says he'll do everything in his power to keep me from being locked up, and the time I'm here will be considered time served, but he seems to think I'll have to spend at least a few more months incarcerated after trial. The big question is where I will live once I'm out. Stefan hasn't brought it up, but I have a hard time imagining he'll want me to move home again. I don't know where I could afford to live if I had to find a place of my own. But I should be able to demand half of what our home is worth and purchase a small apartment. Not anywhere near the city, that would be too expensive. Maybe I should move farther away. Get a fresh start. I don't need to live near Oskar and Ingrid. They still haven't been in touch, and if they don't want to see me, I'm certainly not going to beg for their mercy and forgiveness. I didn't do anything to them.

I will survive this no matter what happens. Being locked up won't kill you; moving won't kill you. Not even being lonely will kill you, as I well know. It's not terrible here in jail. It's not pleasant, but it's okay. All the guards are friendly, and the other inmates mostly just seem to want to be left alone. Except for the woman in the neighboring cell. She talks about her knitting needles every time I see her. Objects that could be used to harm oneself or someone else are not allowed in jail. So she's not allowed to have knitting needles or yarn. She just wants something to do, she says, to knit mittens or a sweater. She's about my age but already has four grandchildren. I wonder if Oskar and Erika have everything they need for the baby yet? In my opinion, you shouldn't buy that stuff until the baby arrives, once you know how everything will turn out, but these days you have to order a stroller six months ahead of time to be sure of getting the one you want. That's what Erika told me last time I saw her, when they told us about the baby, before all of this happened. I didn't point out how expensive the stroller was; I just said congratulations. I don't want to be one of those grandmas who goes on and on about how everything was better in the past. She's very pregnant, must be about to give birth any day now. I wonder if they'll call to tell me what it is, I don't know if they're expecting a boy or a girl.

In my cell—or my room, as the guards call it—you could hear a pin drop. Each evening at six, after they serve dinner, they lock my door and it's so thick you can't hear anyone else ring for the guards, can't hear anyone else crying or screaming or starting a fight. It's so quiet in here that I have trouble sleeping.

My hearing has always been perfect, and that hasn't changed. When I had a physical check-up at work last spring, I was told I had the hearing of a twenty-five-year-old. That came as no surprise to me. Stefan has trouble hearing, like most men his age. And sooner or later, everyone who lives long enough will lose the ability to hear the singing of the crickets, grasshoppers, and katydids. Women have better hearing than men, it's not just me, but after menopause the differences typically even out. It has to do with estrogen—aging is brutal, it catches up with you and everything goes silent, with nothing to replace it but emptiness, an eternal auditory black hole. Some people don't notice when sounds begin to fade. People typically don't miss those insects and their racket, the constant whine of a summer's night, like the harried buzz of city people, in every ditch and patch of tall grass. Because you never see them, only hear them. Until they fall silent and vanish completely. I will miss them, the crickets. But by the time summer arrives, I should be home again. And then I'll ask B. if she can still hear them. I bet she can.

THE REPORTING ACT

DEPARTMENT OF JUSTICE 2022:12

The girl sat in the corner by the row of sheds where the playground toys were stored; she was leaning against the wall, her head bowed, her neck at an unnatural angle, her knees pointing sharply away from her body. Her brown hair fell over her face, and she was veiled in shadows and darkness. The streetlights were out; the municipality had decided to cut back on electricity as part of the cost-saving measures being implemented across the country. But the girl's general outline was visible. Even so, he was practically on top of her before he noticed her there.

She must be freezing, was his first thought, because she wasn't wearing the type of clothing a girl should be on the night before Christmas Eve, out in the powdery snow and merciless cold. It looked as if she had undressed—her shoes were kicked off nearby and her coat was scrunched around her waist. His second thought came an instant later: *She's dead.* And that thought washed over him just as his third, and most inappropriate, thought struck him: *Fuck! I don't have time for this.*

That was a terrible thing to think, obviously he knew that. If a girl is lying dead in the middle of the most beautiful park in the capital city, you take your time dealing with it. You call the police, make a report, consider the grave implications, perhaps battle some tears. But the fact remained: He had a thousand other things to do. He'd worked nearly seventy hours over the last week, not because he loved his job and never wanted to go home, but because it was the only way to make ends meet. Half above board, half under the table, all of it paying the bills.

Perhaps they ought to move somewhere cheaper, maybe outside the city, but then his wife wouldn't be able to keep an eye on her dad, who lived a stone's throw from their apartment. His daughter would have to change schools, and he would no longer be within walking distance of work, they might have to get a car, and he hated to drive. It's worth the constant work, he'd assured his wife. You'll get a raise soon, he'd added, without really believing it. But at some point, that time should come. All the praise heaped upon her and her colleagues during the pandemic, all the people suddenly fearing death and hanging out their windows at night to applaud and bang pots and pans with wooden spoons—surely all of this gratitude would one day be converted into a tangible reward, one that would appear in her paycheck, right? It was high time both of them got some relief from the grind, high time they, too, got to live a tolerable life.

Right now, his wife and daughter were waiting for him to come home at last, so they could all decorate the tree together. His wife had bought Christmas presents for their daughter; they'd agreed not to exchange gifts with each other. And tomorrow he could sleep in, they would celebrate Christmas just the three of them, and he wouldn't say the wrong thing, wouldn't end up tired and irritated. Wouldn't lose his temper. If he had the energy, he would run out and buy something for his wife after all, he knew he should, he had to. He would. He would take his time. She deserved it. But for this—this girl—he had neither time nor energy.

He stood there for a moment as his eyes adjusted to the darkness and the moon peeked out. The girl's bare arms and hands gleamed in the faint light; it looked as if frost had settled on her hair, and was that a bruise on her wrist? What had happened to her? People start to feel hot when they're freezing to death; was that why she had kicked off her shoes and wriggled out of her coat?

Fuck, he swore again, and now he was fighting tears. He fished his phone from his pocket. No point in dragging this out. *I have to help, what if someone saw me running away? What if they thought I had done something to her?* He took off his glove and poked at the phone with his thumb. But the screen was black. No amount of tapping would help. The battery was drained. Dead. Like her.

He looked up, scanning the area in vain for someone to call out to. He crouched down. Maybe the girl had a phone he could use. You could always call the emergency number, even while the screen was locked. His gaze ran over her as he mustered the courage to touch her, rummage through her pockets.

That was when he realized. The coat was what he recognized first. He'd met this girl before. He didn't know her name, but she had come into the kitchen where he was working earlier this week, had stepped all the way into the steam from the dishwasher and caught her breath before asking for something to eat. "I'm hungry," she'd said. As if that was his fault, his responsibility. From his place at the cutting board, where he was chopping vegetables, he told her to leave—not in a mean way, but firmly. "Go home, you can't be in here." Then the teenager who picked up shifts working the cold prep snapped at him, "You can't say that." And she gave the girl a container of hot food. No one protested, even though it was wrong. The restaurant took thirty-nine kronor out of the day's pay to cover a staff lunch, but this girl wouldn't have to pay at all.

"She's going to be deported," the teenager from cold prep declared, her voice trembling, after the girl left. "She's in hiding." *But how can she sleep outside, in this weather?*

He had asked how she knew so much about a girl who had stepped into the restaurant out of nowhere and demanded to be cared for. The teenager hardly deigned to look at him. *You don't know what you're talking about*, her gaze said. He was used to it. It was the same look he got from his wife and daughter then they discussed what needed to happen in Sweden. They didn't agree with him and couldn't even bring themselves to discuss the matter. "I'm a volunteer," the teenager spat. As if that should suffice to convince him that she actually *knew* this girl and knew more than he did about what it meant to struggle. That upper-class kid with her blood-red scooter, the one her parents bought her so she could ride it to the job she got because *it's so smart to get work experience.* He wanted to tell her what it was like to live in Sweden with no money, with no contacts, with no time for having values or getting burned out, with no time for volunteer work. *You should be ashamed of yourself,* he wanted to say, but he didn't. He had a job to do.

He didn't believe for a second that this girl was a refugee. *This is a regular old teenager who ran away from home after someone caught her doing drugs*, he muttered, but only to himself. Soon she would get sick of playing runaway and slink back home to her parents, where she would slam doors and complain about being grounded and not having enough data on her phone. Children don't get deported to countries where no one can care for them. Because there are authorities and courts to hear every case, he thought. Sweden is a democracy. Only the evening papers, full of bleeding-heart tales about people their readers have never met, promote that kind of propaganda. It wasn't his fault that Sweden was full of people who fell for it, and that his own wife and daughter were two of them. *Women*, he figured, that kind of sentimentality is just in their nature, they couldn't control their desire to take care of everything and everyone even when it involves a half-baked idea that will only make things worse. There had to be clear rules about what one could and couldn't do, or else society would fall to pieces. At least, it would if sentimental women like his wife, who refused to face reality, were in charge.

But now this girl was here, right in front of him, demanding his help once more. He looked around the park again. Not a soul in sight. Not even the rats seemed to be out. On the night before Christmas Eve, people stayed home to gather their strength before arguing with relatives and eating rich food. Was he really going to have to touch her? He could smell her—something acrid, was that filth? Or death? He didn't want to touch a dead body. He'd done that twice, and he didn't want to do it again.

The first time, he was only eleven. His mother hadn't wanted him to be the one to find her; Dad was supposed to come home first, not him. Everything he saw that time was a mistake, and he had devoted his life to pretending it never happened. The second time, the corpse belonged to his father, and that was only ten years ago. The police found him after the neighbors called in. It was a heart attack, and they had taken him to the morgue, had washed him and made him presentable before it was time for the viewing. The staff referred to this as "saying goodbye." His father had lain there, so swollen he was unrecognizable, under a white sheet in a stark room in a freestanding annex of Karolinska Hospital. Someone had lit a candle next to the bed. He had blown it out before he left. *I am an orphan now*, he thought.

Today, in the park, he took a breath as he readied himself to pinch the girl's thin coat as gingerly as he could, to keep from leaving fingerprints. It wasn't hard to guess where her phone must be; he could tell it was in her right-hand pocket. He would lift the fabric slowly, a millimeter at a time, and fish out the phone with his other hand. But before he could start, something happened. It happened so fast, he didn't even have time to be startled.

The girl woke up.

He could hear his wife's and daughter's voices as he entered the front hall. Their chatter made a faint hum, backed by the music from a Christmas playlist. But they didn't come out to greet him, so they didn't see her until the two of them walked into the living room.

He started by shoving her into the easy chair, pulling it closer to the radiator, and draping his coat over her. He'd put her shoes on her in the park, but now he took them off, wrapped his scarf around her feet, and lifted them up so they were closer to her body.

"This is Stella," he said. "She needs to stay with us for a bit."

His wife had turned away from the tree; she was still holding a shiny gold glass ornament. She looked him straight in the eye. His daughter was sitting on the floor, her mouth half open, as if she had been about to say something and then forgot what it was. He had no idea how to explain what he'd done, so instead he handed over the thin envelope the girl had given him, which contained the notice from the authorities ordering her to surrender herself to them immediately. The notice that confirmed that she was going to be deported.

During his military service, he'd learned about the warning signs of hypothermia. Sound judgment is the first thing to go. With a body temperature of 91 degrees, you stop shivering and become unresponsive. If your temperature falls even more, your heart slows and blood pressure becomes difficult to register. *Almost dead. Soon. But not quite yet.* Maybe it was his memories of the strange survival exercises in the military, the war games and the officers' loud, sharp voices, that made him spring into action. *March! Halt! Execute! Ready front!* The first thing he did was put her hat on. Once he got her shoes and coat on, he pulled her to her feet. *She doesn't have any parents*, he thought as he read the deportation order. *We're orphans, her and me.* And then they began to walk, as if they had come to an agreement, even though she hadn't asked and he hadn't answered. In the elevator on the way up to the apartment, he took her hands. Tried to warm them in his own.

Now he heard her weak voice from the easy chair.

"You can't . . . ," she began. "You can't help me. It's against the law."

His wife looked up from the document she had removed from the envelope and had just finished reading. His daughter's eyes flicked between him and the girl and her mother. They didn't have to explain to her what the letter said and what consequences it would have, what the law said her mother must do now. The phone calls she was required to make—she must immediately inform the police so they could see to it that the deportation order was carried out. His daughter knew this already; it had been explained at school. "Being undocumented is not a stable life," the headmaster said after the law took effect and two of the school's students disappeared. "They will have a better life in the country where they are meant to be, and we must ensure stability and uninterrupted schooling for all our children."

"Mom . . . ," their daughter whispered. "You can't help her."

"And yet we have to," he heard himself say.

He saw his wife nodding as if this were the most sensible thing he'd ever said, and just what she expected to hear. And his daughter exhaled, put down the ornament she had been about to hang on the tree, and smiled weakly.

"I'll run a bath," his wife said. "That's a good way to warm up."

ACKNOWLEDGMENTS

"Let he who is without sin among you cast the first stone," Jesus says in John 8:7. "In dubio pro reo" is a basic principle of justice that directs us to let someone go free rather than convict them if there is the least doubt about their guilt. But we do the opposite. We are quick to judge, no matter how much or little we know about the circumstances. And if there's anything I want to accomplish in my storytelling, perhaps it's to show that our justice system and our dry legal texts describe the reality we all exist in, that law and justice is about people who are trying to live their lives, just like you and me.

Fiction tends to depict crime with dramatic flair. We are drawn into narratives of serious crimes and complicated motives because we want to know how they happened, who is guilty, and why everything turned out so badly. The tale demands that the guilty party be punished and the victim get revenge. In reality, a crime is rarely so tidily resolved. Many crimes are never even discovered, and far from all perpetrators are held accountable. Because we all make mistakes and cause harm to others. We all do things we regret, things we're ashamed of, things that are hard to forgive, because that's what it is to be human.

An especially warm thank you to Astri von Arbin Ahlander, Åsa Selling, and Katarina Ehnmark Lundquist, my most important readers and companions in the literary world.

Thanks to attorney Peter Althin for being willing—once again—to read what I write and to discuss the shortcomings and winding paths of the justice system with me. Thanks to my dear friends Mari Eberstein and Måns Hirschfeldt for reading and commenting.

And finally: Christophe, Elsa, Nora, Bea. Thank you (and I'm sorry).

Malin Persson Giolito

ABOUT THE AUTHOR

Malin Persson Giolito was born in Stockholm and grew up in Djursholm, Sweden. She holds a degree in law from Uppsala University and has worked for the biggest law firm in the Nordic region, and as an official for the European Commission in Brussels, Belgium. Her previous novels include *Quicksand* (Other Press, 2017), which was adapted into a Netflix series in 2019, *Beyond All Reasonable Doubt* (Other Press, 2019), and *Deliver Me* (Other Press, 2023). Persson Giolito lives with her husband and three daughters in Brussels.

ABOUT THE TRANSLATOR

Rachel Willson-Broyles holds a bachelor's degree in Scandinavian Studies from Gustavus Adolphus College in St. Peter, Minnesota. She started translating while a graduate student at the University of Wisconsin-Madison, where she received a PhD in Scandinavian Studies in 2013. Her translations include Malin Persson Giolito's *Quicksand* and *Beyond All Reasonable Doubt* and Ann-Helén Laestadius's *Stolen*. Willson-Broyles lives in St. Paul, Minnesota.

Praise for ***Crescendo*** by Anthea Kreston

"An indomitable spirit." —**Yo-Yo Ma**

"A singular voice in music, and now in words. *Crescendo* is a searingly honest look at the classical music world from within and manages to be as funny and uplifting as it is devastating. The same vulnerability and power that makes Kreston such a compelling instrumentalist is equally commanding in her prose. This memoir is a necessary and insightful look at what makes being an artist, a woman, a mother, and all three at the same time so incredibly challenging, but worthwhile." —**Ling Ling Huang**, author of *Immaculate Conception* and *Natural Beauty*

"Anthea Kreston is a world-renowned violinist and an intense, endearing mess. She opens her life to us so vividly that we are actually with her, whirling through concerts, crises, and the seeming impossibility of working parenthood, loving life and finding it hard to breathe all at the same time. A lively and refreshing read." —**Anne-Marie Slaughter**, CEO of New America, author of *Unfinished Business*

"Kreston—who demystifies the process of classical music through her popular blog—details the real lives of performers, behind the scenes. This tale sparkles through hilarious exchanges, always taken with a light heart by the author." —**Blair Tindall**, Author, *Mozart in the Jungle: Sex, Drugs, and Classical Music*

"Anthea Kreston writes with passion and an insider's authority about life in a world-class string quartet. In prose that sometimes jumps off the page, she gives us detailed descriptions of her family life, her colleagues, her individual working process, the interactions of four distinct personalities and the music that binds them onstage and off in a never-ending quest for transcendence." —**Eugene Drucker**, Emerson String Quartet, author of *The Savior*

"I had only known Anthea as a superstar violinist with a dreamy career traveling the world with one of the most celebrated string quartets until I read *Crescendo* and felt like we were best friends, two cocktails in, catching up after years apart. She trusts us readers with the hardest and most meaningful parts of her life in stories that make me want to be a better musician, friend, and lover. What a badass!" —**Hunter Noack**, pianist and founder of In a Landscape: Classical Music in the Wild

"Anthea Kreston tells an inside story that has never been recounted before. The life of an international string quartet is a closed book, a high-tension confrontation between four exceptional musicians. In Kreston's narrative, everything is out in the open and the players are fighting for their existence. She's an extraordinary storyteller with a remarkable tale to tell." —**Norman Lebrecht**, founder of Slipped Disc, and author of *Who Killed Classical Music*

"Anthea Kreston's *Crescendo* gives some fine and rare insight into the inner workings of a string quartet. I found it to be a real page-turner! She is a fine writer and I highly recommend it." —**Peter van de Graaff**, Radio Host, Beethoven Satellite Network